CW00616177

CHIPPED

Neville Steed

ARROW BOOKS

Arrow Books Limited
20 Vauxhall Bridge Road, London SW1V 2SA

An imprint of the Random Century Group

London Melbourne Sydney Auckland
Johannesburg and agencies throughout
the world

First published in 1988 by George Weidenfeld & Nicolson

Mysterious Press edition 1990
Arrow edition 1991

Phototypeset by Input Typesetting Ltd, London
Printed and bound in Great Britain by
Cox & Wyman Ltd, Reading

ISBN 0 09 964240 9

To Scooter,
with love

1

I had not been prepared for it. Even the whooshing sound failed to trigger my, by now, wine dampened reflexes, so mesmerized was I by what I was attempting to do with the lighted taper in my hand. In sober retrospect, I guess I must have heard someone shout 'Look out!' or 'Duck!' or similar 'I'm glad it's not me' injunctions, because I did actually duck. If I hadn't, I wouldn't have ended up with a seared right ear. Just a singed back to my anorak. Marks and Sparks can supply new anoraks. Need I say more?

However, all this did have its good side (and I don't mean my left ear). My stoic shout of pain attracted the attention of a dreamy kind of girl I had noticed earlier, in the frequent flashes of the fireworks. Well, more than noticed, actually. Noted down to talk to later, when we would all repair indoors to warm ourselves against Philippa's roaring fire and drink hot toddies.

'Wow! You poor man. Are you badly hurt?'

I loved it. Her voice was like an Irish coffee, creamy on the surface but with quite a strength underneath. I turned to her and forced an intrepid smile.

'How did you know I was poor?'

She rightly ignored my post-rocket attack attempt at humour and prised my trembling fingers from around my ear.

'Have you got a handkerchief?' she asked. I fumbled for one and handed it to her.

'I may need it back in a second. I shall cry any minute.'

She laughed. Instantly she was my friend for life.

After licking an edge of the hanky, she began gently to wipe my ear-lobe. I flinched.

'Sorry, but I have to get all the soot off to see what remedy is best.'

The pain was not starting to get to me, but somehow I felt comforted that it was she, rather than anyone from the ring of gawpers that was now around us, who was administering the aural aid. And it had nothing to do with her almost gipsyish sex appeal. She had a touch of the mother earth about her and I suspected her kind of remedies would make Prince Charles proud of her and conventional doctors jealous.

While I awaited her verdict I said, 'I'm going to sue Express Dairies.'

She stopped her inspection, her big brown eyes full of question marks.

'Express Dairies? What have they . . . ?'

'Everything,' I interrupted. 'Their milk bottles won't stand upright long enough for rockets to shoot sky-wards, rather than Marklin-wards.'

She resumed her medical examination.

'That your name? Marklin?'

I nodded and was relieved my ear did not fall off.

'Well, Mr Markin, what you need is some ice on that ear of yours.'

I was somewhat disappointed in her choice of remedy. I was expecting something more akin to 'ear of bat, leg of toad, sprig of nettle'.

Just then, I felt a hand on my left arm.

'Peter, I'm terribly sorry.' I glanced around. It was my Guy Fawkes hostess, the smashing Philippa. Lady Philippa Stewart-Hargreaves, if you want to know the whole mouthful – owner of the garden nursery in whose grounds we were standing, and cousin to my distant love, Arabella, who was currently slaving over a hot typewriter in California, on behalf of the *San Francisco Examiner*.

'Gregory's only just told me what happened,' she

2

went on, then glanced across at my ministering angel. 'How does it look, Merinda?'

So that was her name. I might have known it wouldn't be as simple as Jane or Mary or Gladys. Virginia would have been my guess – organic, like the creeper.

'We should get some ice on it. It's rather red,' she recommended, and Philippa took my arm. 'Come on in right away. Someone else can light the Catherine wheels.'

I had almost forgotten that's what I'd been about to do, to help out some guy Philippa was employing to mount the firework display. I looked around for the taper. It was on the grass next to me, and just about to set light to the shoelace of my sneaker. I stamped on it viciously, and allowed myself to be led indoors – to the fridge.

Half an hour later found me both better and worse. My ear was the former: no longer stinging, but still a bit warm and red against my rather singed locks. My spirit was somewhat the latter. I had discovered that my decorous gipsy had a six-foot-six boyfriend named John-John, with whom she lived in a caravan that was currently parked just off the road to Corfe. And the reason they were at Philippa's Bonfire Night party was simple. John-John was helping restore the old stone barn that lay at the northern end of the nursery's fifteen-acre plot. Philippa had told me some weeks before that she had obtained planning permission to convert it into a craft centre, but I had not realized that work had already started. Apparently, John-John had been trained as a stonemason before he began his nomadic life with Merinda in the caravan. Certainly, even his big hairy sweater could not hide his hairy muscles that rippled underneath it. He looked capable of lifting Nelson onto his column without a crane. But his manner was as

3

gentle as Merinda's – which was just as well for the world.

He asked me what I did. When I told him all about it, his rather solemn features were transformed by the broadest of smiles.

'So we're kind of kindred spirits, you and I,' he said, in a voice that had more depth than the Pacific. 'You opted out of the advertising world to follow your love of old toys.'

He looked round at Merinda. 'We chose the freedom of nature and finding work where we can, rather than the claustrophobia of living and working in the kind of northern back-streets where we both were born.'

'I sort of envy your choice,' I said half truthfully. 'You can go where you like, when you like . . .'

'. . . when the authorities don't move us on,' he rightly interrupted.

'True. But I'm rooted to the spot, dealing in old toys. I have to have a shop, a permanent address for my mail-order customers, otherwise I don't make a bean.' I grinned. 'But it's a darn sight better than what I was doing before – rooted to products I didn't really care about, clients I didn't really like, advertising campaigns I didn't really believe in.'

'But can't you lose yourself in antique toys?' Merinda asked. 'I mean, in their charm, in their innocence?'

'I guess so,' I replied. 'I have to admit, me and my money do get lost in them, sometimes.' I was going through a tight November. It's funny, the big selling times for children's toys are often the slowest selling periods for collectors' pieces. Maybe it's because collectors are often dads and mums too, with other things on their minds and bank balances than indulging in their own childhood nostalgia just before Christmas.

I turned to Merinda. 'And what do you do? Carve stone too? Sculpt, maybe?'

She blushed and, for a moment, with the long peasant dress, looked like some Thomas Hardy heroine. Tess,

4

maybe – which I guess was only fitting as we were in his Wessex.

'No, I have no talent like that.' She hesitated and John-John stepped in.

'She paints. She's a very good painter. Lady Philippa says she will exhibit some of her work when the craft centre is open.'

'Did I hear my name taken in vain?' My hostess advanced on my now almost empty glass with a steaming jug of mulled wine.

'I was just hearing that Merinda paints and you're going to hang some of her work.'

She topped up my glass. 'I think you would like her stuff, Peter. I certainly do. It reminds me a bit of Monet. The evocation of the countryside, I mean. But then again, there's something surrealistic about some of the paintings. Merinda adds curious little touches to ordinary scenes that make them extraordinary. Like in one painting of the Cob at Lyme Regis, way in the background you can just spot a seagull with two heads.'

She caught my expression. 'Sounds awful the way I describe it. It's so discreet in the picture and yet it lends mystery to the whole scene. I love her style.'

I looked around to Merinda but she had gone. So had John-John. And I couldn't see them anywhere else in the room. It was like they had evaporated into the night.

Philippa laughed. 'Don't worry, Peter. They are both terribly shy about their work. I daren't really praise either of them in their presence.'

I was about to comment, when a big, blond head with smuts on it popped up beside Philippa.

'Any more of that tremendous toddy going?' it asked in a breezy boyish manner and proffered a glass. 'I'm effing frozen. I've just come down from crawling all over the thatch of your barn trying to find a ruddy rocket that landed there. Didn't want the straw to catch, otherwise you might have to forget your whole craft

5

centre project. By the way, I hope I haven't ruined your thatch, climbing up on it.'

She filled up his glass. 'Don't worry, Gregory. It leaks already in several places. The thatcher's coming next week to re-do the whole roof.'

She held out her hand to me. 'Oh, I'm sorry, Peter. Let me introduce you. This is Gregory Mann, an old family friend of ours. His parents live up in Shropshire, near Arabella's and mine. Now he lives in Bournemouth.'

I shook hands. 'Peter Marklin.'

Mann held onto my hand. 'Hey, wait a minute. You must be the Peter Arabella is nuts about. I've heard my parents talk about you. And Philippa.'

'You don't need to see me again, you know,' I smiled. He relinquished my hand.

'Oh, every report was favourable, don't worry. I bet my girlfriend's parents don't speak about me that way. Only wish they would.'

He drained his glass as if he had been in the heat of the Sahara rather than the cold of a Dorset November, and extended it again to Philippa.

As she poured, she said, 'Gregory practises professionally what you, Peter, have sometimes done as an amateur.'

I looked at him. Underneath the smuts was a face that more or less matched his voice and manner. Boyish, alive, reasonably refined and regular in features. Nothing very out of the way, now that 'designer stubble' has the British Establishment seal of approval, except perhaps for the eyes. They were the darkest of dark brown and would have made good lasers if they had ever lingered anywhere long enough. Their dancing disconcerted me.

'Oh and what's that?' I feigned ignorance, hoping against hope that he wasn't what I was now suspecting. But it was not to be my night.

'I'm a Bournemouth Pinkerton, for my sins.' He grinned. 'You don't need to see me again, you know.'

Philippa put her hand on his arm. 'Now, don't run yourself down, Gregory. You're a very good and very discreet private eye or gumshoe, or whatever you people call yourselves.' She whispered to me, 'It was mostly his evidence that helped me in my divorce.'

It was the first time I had heard Philippa ever directly refer to her divorce, which had occurred a year or two before I had met her cousin Arabella. Her husband had apparently been a commodity broker in the city, dealing heavily in sugar and coffee and other people's wives. The nursery gardens in sleepy old Owermoigne that Philippa had started immediately after her decree nisi must have been the perfect balm to heal the wound.

'And you, Peter?' His laser eyes flicked over to me. 'You've done a bit of amateur sleuthing?'

I shrugged. 'Once or twice. Just ferreting around a little to help friends, really. Nothing worth mentioning.'

I wonder I wasn't struck dead, but I had no desire to go into the two cases with which I had been involved up to and including my precious neck. I frowned at Philippa to encourage her to drop the subject and she reacted like a dream.

'Where's Sally? I haven't seen her for a bit.'

'I think she's still outside,' he replied. 'Helping to pick up the spent fireworks and collect the glasses.'

'Oh, Sally shouldn't do that . . .' she began, but was quickly interrupted.

'What shouldn't I do?'

A distinct aroma of Opium by Saint Laurent wafted over my left shoulder, reminding me of Arabella. I looked around at the newcomer and was pleasantly surprised. She was seventy per cent Charlotte Rampling and thirty per cent Jacqueline Bisset, and both in the right places. Gregory Mann had taste.

'Do my job, Sally,' Philippa countered. 'I can clear up in the morning.'

'Done now,' Sally beamed. 'What you've got in that jug looks pretty good.' She looked around for a glass. I gave her one from a tray on a side table near me.

'Thanks . . . er. Sorry, I don't know your name.'

'Peter Marklin,' Philippa chipped in, as she filled Sally's glass. 'He's a great friend of my cousin, Arabella. She's in San Francisco for a year, so I'm doing my best to prevent him feeling too lonely whilst she's away.'

'Live near?' seventy/thirty asked jauntily.

I nodded. 'Studland.'

She clasped my arm. Wow, this was quite a bouncy lady. 'Oh, I love Studland. Gregory and I use the beach there often in the spring and summer. It's much prettier and far less crowded than ours.'

'Where's yours?' I asked.

'Sandbanks. We just take the ferry over. Only takes a few minutes.'

I hesitated to ask her which part of the beach at Studland she used. The Swanage side is conventional enough, but the Bournemouth end is all Health and Efficiency, but without the volley-ball. But I should have known she would volunteer the information. What's the opposite of shy?

'We use the nudist bit. I like an all over tan and Gregory likes ogling my competition, don't you, Gregory?'

'Don't take any notice of Sally,' he smiled. 'She's quite a voyeur herself. Saves her buying *Playgirl*.'

Philippa laughed and left us to re-toddy the rest of her guests. Sally moved across and put her arm around Gregory's waist. Somehow, the gesture seemed more proprietorial than loving and I noticed he seemed consciously to ignore her action.

For want of anything better to say, I asked, 'Known each other long?'

'Long enough,' he replied. 'About three years.'

8

'Nearly four,' she corrected him. 'It's three years since I came to work with you.'

'You a private eye too?' I ventured.

She laughed. 'No way. He gets all the fun. I sit in the office to answer phones, make appointments and type invoices. General dogsbody, me.'

I smiled to myself. That all dogs should have a body like hers.

'Still, I'm hoping it will be different soon,' she went on and looked up at Gregory. 'When we're married and move into the cottage.'

I raised my glass. 'Congratulations. When's the happy day?'

Gregory cleared his throat. 'When the cottage is fit to move into. It needs a lot of work. It didn't have a bathroom until last week. The kitchen is going in tomorrow. And the roof is being re-done directly old Tom Sweet has finished rethatching Philippa's barn.'

'We live over the office at the moment,' Sally observed, rather apologetically. 'We're next to the newsagents, in the row of shops at Sandbanks.'

'Yes, I sort of know them,' I said doubtfully. 'What's your business called?'

'Ask-Force,' he grinned. 'Sorry about the name, but I wanted something people would remember – you know, come and ask us and we'll ask around, etcetera.'

'We're all black glass and ring the doorbell for entry,' Sally added. 'The name is in tiny gilt lettering on the door. People sometimes think we must be a turf accountant – or worse.'

Now I remembered the place better. I too had imagined it to be a betting shop.

'Business brisk around Bournemouth?' I asked, eyeing his clothes that were as designerish as his stubble.

'Not bad, not bad,' he smiled. 'Lot of money in Bournemouth. And where there's money, there's trouble. Not that all my clients are private individuals.

9

Some are corporations, worried about insurance claims or who is whipping what from their factories, or whatever. No one day is really like the next.'

'It is for me,' Sally yawned dramatically. 'The day you get yourself a secretary . . .' She suddenly stopped and turned to me. 'You ever been married, Peter?'

That's the trouble with being a perennial thirty-nine. People assume you must have been spliced at some time in your romantic career.

'I was once.'

'What happened?' She sounded genuinely interested.

'Deborah went on liking all the things I grew out of. We parted amicably. Our divorce was less fuss than our marriage, actually.' I glanced at Gregory. 'No need of private eyes.'

'Your friend Philippa mentioned – what is her name – Annabel?'

'Arabella.'

'You two serious?'

Whilst my cheeks must have gone as red as my ear, Gregory came to my aid. 'Now, come on, Sally. That's enough of your leading questions. I must apologize, Peter. Sally could never make a private eye. Her investigative technique is anything but subtle.'

'Oh, I'm not offended, don't worry, Sally. In answer to your direct question, here's a direct answer. We're serious enough to have agreed to take a year apart, so that we can work out just how important we are in each other's lives. That's why Arabella accepted the offer of the reporting job on the *San Francisco Examiner*. You see, she's quite a few years younger than I am, and I wanted her to be really sure it's me she wants and not some young, bearded Californian he-man, for instance.'

'And you, Peter,' Sally teased, using every ounce of her weighty sex appeal, 'what is it that you're going to find out in your year apart?'

10

'I'll only know that at the year's end, won't I?' I parried. 'There are still eight months to go.'

'Found out anything yet?'

'Yes,' I mumbled, gingerly fingering my ear. 'I shall never marry anyone from the Brock family.'

Gregory couldn't stop himself laughing. 'Yes, I saw that milk bottle fall over. I shouted to watch out, but I'm afraid there was so much other noise.' He pulled himself together. 'I'm sorry. I shouldn't laugh. How is the ear now, by the way?'

I couldn't resist it. I leaned further towards him, cupping the afore-mentioned.

'Pardon?' I said.

2

I had just taken the first hub-cap out of the box I'd picked up from the local chromers, when I heard the wheezing and coughing that were Gus Tribble's equivalent to the dawn chorus.

I quickly pushed the cap onto the offside front wheel of my 1966 Daimler v8 which I kept down at Gus's in an outbuilding, there being no room at my place for more than my Beetle. Whilst Arabella had been away, I had at long last got down to restoring the car from the dilapidated state in which I'd bought it, to a degree of former glory – the degree depending entirely on my equally dilapidated purse. In fact, right then I was rather proud of myself. I had to admit that even in its blotchy, aerosol-applied primer state, the old Daimler now looked a pretty solid proposition, only awaiting a professional spray job for the final coats to bring it up to scratch. (Maybe that's the wrong phrase to use for shiny cellulose.) And I'd already arranged to have that done by a guy I'd met through my toy connections – Jimmy Richardson who lived on the Wareham side of the beautiful village of Corfe.

The grunts and groans were now almost upon me. I hoped against hope that Gus might have a hot cup of tea or coffee in his hands for it was mighty cold that morning and I hadn't quite recovered from the excess of mulled wine I'd had the night before. But no, he had considered his endearing presence on its own was quite enough to warm my soul.

'Morning, Gus.'

His old leather wallet of a face, tanned to a turn by

12

his years of fishing round the Dorset coast and over matured by years of drinking on the Dorset mainland, bleered across at me. When he had achieved focus, he muttered, 'Oh, it's only you. Thank the Lord.'

'Well, who did you think it would be on a Sunday morning, Gus? The vicar?'

I think my sarcasm was justified, not only because the vicar would be the last person to call on Gus, but mainly because it's hard for anyone to call on him at all. First of all, his so-called garden is so overgrown it makes reaching his front door a hit and miss affair. And secondly he's often out in his dreaded upright model Ford Popular. And when he *is* in he's often, as they say, 'not at home', for he has a tendency only to come to the door when he wants visitors to call, as distinct from when they want to call on him.

I think in his past there were a few maiden aunts he hated, relatives he could do without and always the fear that a hand on the knocker might herald some reason for Gus shelling out money – either for a bill he hasn't got round to paying or for tax he has no intention of paying or – his latest aversion – for sponsored walks, swims or cycle rides. (He doesn't really comprehend that the money does not go to the child but to a charity. I've tried to explain, but he always cuts in that no one's ever paid him to ruddy walk, swim or ride a bike and he doesn't know what the present generation is coming to.) Now, do you understand about the vicar?

'No, don't be daft. Heard a noise. Woke me up, it did. Came across in case it might be a burglar, trying to make off with your old car.'

I put my hands on my hips. 'Gus, this is the third time in a month you've thought I was a burglar.' I grinned. 'Mind you, this is the first time you've come down with your pyjama jacket still on.'

Gus looked down at himself. 'Oh yes. Got into me trousers. Thought I'd already changed me top. Anyway, it's as well to keep your eyes and ears peeled these days. Can't be too careful with all these ruddy burglaries going on round 'ere.'

'Gus, all right, so there's been a spate of robberies recently. They go in cycles: gangs do a district and then they move on. You know that.'

'Maybe, old son, but . . .'

'There's no "buts", Gus. Nobody is going to mark your cottage down for a big heist exactly, now are they? I don't want to be rude, but . . .' I stopped abruptly. I didn't want to be rude. But between you and me, Gus's whole place looked next door to being derelict. The only people it might attract would be archaeologists or property developers.

Gus emitted a couple more grunts, then asked the time. I looked at my watch.

'Quarter to eleven.'

'Oh,' he said. He did not need to say more.

I went back to my box of rechromed hub-caps. 'Well, hang on, Gus, until I've put these other three on.'

'No hurry,' he lied. 'I'll just go back in and put me shirt on.'

The grunts receded and I was once more alone. I was just about to breathe a sigh of relief, when I realized Gus had actually left a kind of vacuum behind him. I cursed, quickly banged on the other three hub-caps and trudged out across the tangled weeds towards the cottage. That's the trouble with Gus. You dread his coming, but sort of miss him when he's gone.

'Taking the car tomorrow,' I said, pulling on the ring of my second Heineken. Gus was on his third. 'Be out of your hair for a bit.'

'Hope that mate of yours doesn't ruin it,' he mumbled. Gus isn't given to praising people over much.

'He won't. You ought to see some of the restoration work he's done on old toys. You would never know they weren't original.'

14

'Well, they're only ruddy toys, aren't they? Anybody can repaint an old toy.'

'That's just where you're wrong Gus. Anybody can't. You have to be both talented and quite meticulous to restore, say, a tinplate toy made before even you were born. The detailed work necessary is a thousand times more complicated than anything he'll have to do on my old Daimler. After all, that's how Jimmy Richardson makes his living – with old toys, not with real cars. All the big collectors take their too-far-gone finds to him. So my car should be a doddle.'

Gus shrugged and reached for another beer from a pile of cans next to his chair. I'll swear Gus keeps almost everything he might need in any twelve hour period within stretching distance of his chair – from alcohol to aspirins, from a grubby first-aid kit to a grubbier tool box, from matches to baskets full of logs and old newspapers. Sometimes he looks set for a siege.

'Dunno why you lot are so obsessed with having everything bright and new and sparkling. What's wrong with a thing looking its age, dents and all? You can't go through life without getting a few chips, you know.'

He pointed a huge and well-worn forefinger at me. 'To go and look around your shop, you'd never think toys were meant to be played with. There they all are, prim and proper in their showcases, like ruddy virgins that have never had a finger on 'em. Doesn't seem right, grown-ups paying fancy prices for them, just to move 'em to their own show-cases or stuff 'em in their attics, when they all should be giving some children somewhere a load of fun.'

I put down my beer. 'I doubt if a present-day child would reckon a 1905 De Dion Runabout by Bing much of a turn-on. Or a tinplate boat that rusts almost immediately you put it in the water. Or a Dinky toy car with no windows or doors to open, and no seats to boot. Hardly space-invader stuff, are they? Kids are much more sophisticated now . . .'

I stopped. One, because, curses, I realized Gus had deliberately got me going again. When will I ever learn? Two, because even if his point had been serious, it didn't warrant an answer. And three, I could see from Gus's eyes that I'd lost him. Or rather, as I immediately discovered, he had lost me.

'Talking of boats going in the water,' he began, 'heard the latest?'

There was no point in saying anything but no.

'Heard it on the wireless. Old Redstart is up to his shenanigans again.'

He looked at me lingeringly, as if that incomprehensible statement had illuminated the universe.

'Well, go on,' I said. 'That can't be it, can it?'

Gus looked disappointed. 'Can't you guess, old son?'

'Look, Gus, I've never heard of Redstart, so I can't be expected to know his old shenanigans, let alone his new ones.'

Gus raised his bushy eyebrows. 'Cor. I thought everybody round here knew about Patrick Redstart. Dear, oh dear. Where've you been?'

'All right, so I'm an ignoramus. Who is this Redstart, when he's at home?'

'He's not at home very often. Always off somewhere in one of his boats.'

So that's why I hadn't heard of him and Gus had. I'm not up in the yachtin', boatin' fraternity, for one simple reason: boats will keep bobbing up and down in breezy weather. And when I'm on board, whatever I've eaten recently tends to do the same. Sick transit Marklin.

'So Redstart owns some boats. What has happened that's got him on the radio?'

Gus took an interminable draught of his beer before replying. If he was a newsreader, there wouldn't be time for any other programmes.

'Kerpow!' he said, throwing up his arms dramatically.

'Kerpow?' I repeated, though more quietly.

'Kerpow.' His eyebrows did a rhumba. 'Blew up.'

'He did? Or his boat? Or both?'

'No, me old love, he's right as rain. You've got to hand it to him.'

Another ruddy great silence.

'So this Redstart's boat blows up. He survives. Boats do blow up occasionally. I seem to remember our little experience of a couple of years back. Where are these shenanigans of yours?'

'You don't know Redstart's reputation. Dodgy. Runs around four or five boats out of Poole – three fast cabin cruisers with engines far too big for just cruising, a poncey great floating brothel of a thing with a couple of two hundred horse engines, and a yacht, twenty-two footer.'

'What does he do with them all?'

'They're chartered most of the season. Lord knows why. He charges more than anyone has a right to.'

'And off season?'

'The big ones are usually laid up, but he keeps the three cabin cruisers in the water. And they're used too.'

'What on earth for? He can't use all three at once, himself. And who is going to hire them in the winter?'

Gus put on a knowing face. 'There's always someone who wants to go from A to B, isn't there?' He leaned towards me. 'Or wants *something*.'

I thought for a minute. 'Presumably it was one of these small jobs that blew up?'

He nodded. 'Sank to the bottom, it did.'

'But Redstart survived by taking to the dinghy that was being towed behind?'

Another nod.

A second minute's thought.

'Water too deep to be economic to recover the boat?'

Gus gave a thumbs up.

17

'Insurance job?' I smiled.

He smiled back. 'There's something else. The wireless said he was picked up by a Customs boat that just happened to be in the area. Happened, my eye.'

'You think . . .' I began, 'You think . . . he, er, scuttled his boat, maybe, because he knew the Customs were after him?'

Gus did a papal blessing act. 'Who knows? Who knows? But a bit of a coincidence, wasn't it, Customs boat all ready and waiting to pick him up?'

'Couldn't they send divers down to search the wreckage?'

'They could, old love, but I doubt if they will. When a small boat like that blows up, it disintegrates good and proper. So does the stuff it might have been carrying. And if it was white powder, it would be half-way to Sweden by now on the south-westerlys. They'll begin wondering why people are hanging about in the Stockholm streets sniffing the bloody air.'

He slapped his thigh, laughing, and a distinct puff of dust rose from his trousers.

'So what you're saying, Gus, is that Redstart has a reputation for smuggling. That it?'

He slurped some more Heineken. 'Let's just say no one can quite figure how he can run a flashy great Jaguar, a bloody great house and a string of fancy women and live the life of Reilly he does, on the kind of money those boats bring in.'

'Perhaps he was born with a silver spoon in his mouth. Or has other business interests you and your fishing friends don't know about.'

Gus threw his rheumy eyes to the ceiling. 'Silver spoon, my eye. His dad used to run the Sea Trout Inn in Weymouth. Ran off, he did, with the barmaid leaving his old mum penniless. And the only other business he dabbles in is old junk. He calls the stuff antiques, but you ought to see the rubbish he sells. You know that little shop in Corfe that sometimes has furniture

18

on the pavement? Well, that's his. Got another in Lyme Regis, I'm told, but I've never seen it.'

'Lot of money to be made in antiques,' I commented, now anxious to get off the subject of this Redstart, whose antics were starting to bore me, and onto the little matter I wished to raise with Gus.

'Told you. It's all junk, that stuff of his. Not anything worth a monkey's.' He looked across at me, when I didn't reply. 'Boring you, am I?'

'No, no, Gus. It's just that I should really get back to the Daimler. I haven't finished stripping the chrome off yet, and it's going in in the morning, as I've told you, for its spray job.'

'But when I came out to you just now, you were putting chrome on, not off.'

I laughed. 'Ah, that's because I wanted to see how the rechromed hub-caps looked on. I'm taking them off again now. Together with the grille, bonnet strips, fog-lights and all the bits and pieces. The bumpers are already off. If I don't do it, I'll have to pay Jimmy to strip them and it's costing me enough already.'

Gus put down his can of beer.

'He wouldn't like to spray my old Popular at the same time, would he?'

'You mean within the same price, don't you?'

He grinned. 'Well, whilst he's got his spray-gun out . . .'

I looked hard at Gus. 'Have you really looked at your old car recently?'

'Course I have. Drove it into Dorchester only yesterday, didn't I? Runs like a bird.'

I knew the kind of bird to which he should have been referring: a dodo.

'I meant its bodywork, Gus.'

'What's wrong with its bodywork?'

'Well, you can strain vegetables through it. If Jimmy started spraying that, three-quarters of the cellulose would end up inside the car.'

19

He looked very taken aback. 'Well, old son, if you feel that way about my Popular, then you won't want a ride back in it from the sprayer's tomorrow, will you? Still, you can always get a taxi.'

Sod him. Gus had been way ahead of me and had raised the little matter I was about to raise with him. In the end, it took the promise of a six-pack to get my lift reinstated – the first time ever I've paid to go in Gus's car. Normally it should be quite the reverse, not so much because of the vehicle as the way that it's driven. There should be a long section in the Highway Code entitled 'How to miss Gus Tribble', followed by some notes on first aid.

When I got back from Gus's, Bing looked at me with a certain amount of steel in the blue of his eyes. He tends to do this whenever I spend some hours away from home. Then he gave a miaow that would make even other Siamese cats seem quietly spoken by comparison.

I fed him quickly to encourage azure to replace the steel, but I knew I wouldn't really be forgiven until I settled down in front of the telly or with a good book and let him curl up on my lap. But before that could happen, I had some packing up to do for the orders that had come through the post over the last few days. And for that matter, I had to have a meal too.

I bunged a frozen pizza in the microwave and went on into the adjoining shop. I live alongside and over my Toy Emporium – that's its name – in a quaint old building that used to belong to my aunt. It's the last in a row of shops that flank the narrow road that leads from Studland across the dunes to Sandbanks ferry. Just down the road on the right is the sea lane that leads to Gus's cottage.

As I was about to get the stack of letters from under my counter, I noticed something lying on the mat by the shop door. I went across and picked it up, thinking it would be just another query from some collector who was after a toy he'd seen through the window. But this was no offer to buy. There were two Polaroid photographs wrapped in a note and held together by an elastic band. The letter was brief and to the point: was I interested in buying the two old toys shown in the photographs? If so, would I ring the Bournemouth number given. Apparently, they had turned up at a car-boot sale.

The pictures were fuzzy and the colour values were next to non-existent, but nothing could disguise the desirability of the items shown.

The first was a unique toy I knew very well. It was a tinplate circus car, clockwork, made in Japan as late as the sixties. Its great novelty lay in the one thing missing in the pictures, the small ball that it kept suspended in mid-air by means of a jet of air, even when the car was moving. And it looked in almost mint condition. Which is more than I could say for the toy in the second picture, although it was this that really made my mouth water. Battered as it was, it was clearly identifiable as one of those finds that, in good condition, could fetch up to ten thousand pounds at, say, a Christie's auction – another tinplate car, but this time by Carette of Germany, dating from around 1908. It seemed to be complete with all four passengers, and even its real glass windscreen was still in one piece.

The Polaroid trembled in my hand. Opportunities like this just don't tumble through my letter-box and I cursed having missed the caller. Ignoring my mail orders and my now steaming pizza, I rushed to the phone. An hour and a half later, Bing's eyes had turned to the coldest blue outside the Poles, as he watched me let myself in, clutching a biggish parcel wrapped in old *Daily Mirrors*. As I unwrapped it, the white ball fell out. (Yes, the circus car had proved to be complete.) Normally Bing would have rushed to play, but now he studiously ignored it. I'm afraid, by the time I had

21

stopped drooling over the rear-entrance Tonneau by Carette (that's its catalogue name), and had worked out what best to do with it – which was to take it along with my Daimler to Jimmy Richardson on the morrow – and then marvelled at the little ball defying gravity above the circus car, Bing had repaired to the land of Nod.

3

It was one of those bright crisp mornings that make you forgive November. The Daimler burbled beautifully all the way to the Wareham side of Corfe, where Richardson lived in an old cottage that long ago used to have thatch, but now sported grey stone tiles in true Corfe tradition. In my mirror, Gus's Popular bobbed and weaved about like a demented boxer (the similarity terminates short of the blue smoke), and I had to throttle back to keep him and his exhaust emissions in my sights.

I pulled into Richardson's yard and he was there to greet me. Built like Oliver Hardy, he extended a thick arm and pointed out where I should park. I inserted the Daimler neatly between his ancient but immaculate Volvo (the nice one that looks like a forties American Ford), and an old Flying Standard 12, that was still in grey primer.

He stared at me as I took out a box from the rear seat.

'What have you got there, Peter?' he piped in a voice too light for his body. 'You're holding it like it contains the Crown Jewels.'

I was about to let him know it was tantamount to the Crown Jewels, when he had to be as nimble as a matador to miss Gus's Popular as it charged into the yard, then shuddered to a stop. He turned to me. 'Who's this? Anything to do with you?'

'Yes,' I stammered. 'He's a friend of mine. Gus Tribble. He's giving me a lift back.'

'Are you well insured?' he whispered, then laughed

23

with every ripple of his body. I was always amazed that such a huge flabby man could display such manual dexterity and finesse as to be, perhaps, the finest antique toy restorer in the country.

I introduced him to Gus and saw him, like all introduced to Gus, flinch at the handshake. I'll swear they modelled the vice on Gus's grip. Then, whilst Gus wandered off to peer at the old Standard, I opened the lid of my box, and lifted out the delicate and rather spindly Carette car. I could see from his eyes that he was as spellbound as I had been. He took the toy from me and carefully inspected it.

'Where did you get it?' he said, at last, still not taking his eyes off the car.

'Car-boot sale,' I semi-lied.

'Some boot,' he smiled. Then added, 'So you didn't pay a king's ransom for it?'

I shook my head. I was almost too ashamed to disclose how little the previous evening's purchases had cost me – fifteen oncers for the ball-blower and forty-five for the Carette. It wasn't that I wouldn't have gone higher, much higher, it's just that the seller started off the whole shebang by stating categorically that it was fifteen pounds and forty-five pounds, take it or leave it. I took it.

'Which do you want me to do first,' he grinned, 'This or your Daimler?' He ran a finger over the toy's battered and chipped cream and black paintwork. 'It's a pity it's just too far gone to leave it as it is.'

'Which will take longer to do?' I asked, knowing the answer.

He held up the Carette.

'How much?'

'What am I charging for your Daimler? I've forgotten.'

'Four fifty.'

He looked at the toy and fingered the crumpled wings, and the torn and twisted roof.

'More man hours in this. But I'll let you off easy. Same again.'

'Nine hundred for both, then?'

'Cash.'

'Cash.'

I shook hands on it instantly. I've known Jimmy Richardson charge over a grand for some of his toy restoration, but true collectors don't blanche, for over and above the authenticity and intrinsic beauty of his work, they know that a thousand spent with him can often add thousands to the value of their finds – unlike poor or amateur restorations which subtract enormously from the value of any vintage toy.

'Get anything else with the Carette?' he asked, knowing full well that discoveries often come in twos or threes.

'Nothing of significance,' I said, more or less truthfully. 'Just a fun toy from the sixties.'

'No doubt I'll see it in your shop window sometime,' he remarked, not really believing me. As it turned out, he never did because I didn't end up putting it there. But I run ahead of myself.

I went back to the shop but only had two customers all day. One, a bald headed man in a tatty Morlands coat, peered at, prodded and picked up almost every item I had on display, then left with an 'I'll be back'. Not if I saw him first. The old toy business is up to the counter in gawpers and touchers. We call them the G and T brigade. The second customer, who looked too tall for his health, appraised everything with a schoolmasterly 'herumm' and ended up buying a Minic Greenline coach, mint boxed, marked eighty pounds and a Bayko Building Set No. 4 (You know the one, with metal rods and bakelite bricks and windows. Make smashing miniature houses. You can be your own architect or follow one of the very thirties suburban plans.), marked thirty-five pounds. I let him have both for a hundred and five as he came up with cash.

It was dark by the time I took Bing for a walk on his lead down to the deserted beach. The air was already sharp, though there was no wind. The waves kissing the shore looked stunning in the moonlight. But I didn't linger long; the scene was just too romantic and it needed two not to waste it, the other being female and given to holding hands. A bit like Arabella, who was way across another ocean. I took a deep breath and came home.

When the telephone rang, I smiled to myself, wondering if it might be the boot sale buyer who'd just found out the true value of the Carette. But to my even greater surprise, it was Philippa in somewhat of a state. She's one of the sanest, calmest people I know and for her to sound agitated is a major event.

'Peter, I'm sorry to bother you, but I wonder if you could do me a favour?'

'What is it, Philippa? Is anything wrong?'

'Not with me, no.'

It was then I thought I could hear someone crying in the background.

'Then what?'

'It's Sally. Sally Newton. You remember her, don't you? At the fireworks. Friend of Gregory's, the private eye.'

Yes, I remembered her. I could still smell her Opium.

'What's happened? Is she in trouble?'

She went off the line for a moment and I could just hear her trying to comfort whoever was crying.

'Look, Peter, I hate to ask you to come out on a cold November night, but I wonder if you could pop over. I'll explain everything then.'

'Now?' I asked.

'Well, this evening sometime, if you could. Have you eaten?'

I liked the sound of the last bit. Philippa's cooking is

the bluest of Cordons, whilst my own attempts are totally colourless.

'No, I haven't. If you'd like, I can be right over.'

Five minutes later, I was Beetling my way towards the Dorchester road.

By the time that I arrived at the nursery in Owermoigne, Sally Newton (it was she who had been crying) seemed to be fairly composed and only the slight redness around her eyes gave the game away. Even so, she was a million miles from the bouncy self of Guy Fawkes night. Philippa thrust a Scotch and soda in my hand, almost as I walked in the door, and led us all into the Scandinavian-style drawing-room, that was more Uppsala than you'd think Dorset would dare.

'Are you desperately hungry, or shall we get down to why I asked you over first? Then have a meal.'

The look in Sally's eyes removed the option. Besides, I was curious.

I relaxed into an oatmeal chair. 'No, tell me what's the problem. Until I know, I won't have an appetite, anyway.'

Philippa sat down next to me and crossed her long and lovely legs. (They're tanned all the year round, and if she hadn't had a cousin, who knows . . . ?)

'Well, I think it's better if, Sally, you tell Peter what has happened. Just as you told me.'

I looked across at Sally who looked anything but relaxed amidst her oatmeal cushions. She leaned forward. 'It's awfully good of you to bother to come out on my account,' she began.

'Forget it,' I interrupted. 'Just tell me what's worrying you.'

She sighed. 'You see, it's Greg. I don't know what's happened to him.' She put her head in her hands.

I looked at Philippa.

'He's disappeared, Peter, and, quite naturally, Sally is going out of her mind with worry.'

'Disappeared?' I repeated, like a prize idiot.

27

'Yes,' Philippa continued. 'He went off on his Honda on Sunday morning and hasn't been seen since.'

'*On* his Honda? You mean a motor bike, not a Honda car?'

'That's right,' Sally answered in a voice betraying her emotion. 'Greg has a car, an old Triumph Stag, that he adores, but he's always had a thing about bikes. He bought this big Honda last year. Just uses it for spins at weekends. Helps him let his hair down, I suppose.'

'Any reason you didn't go with him?' I asked.

'I never do. He knows I don't like riding pillion, especially on a big heavy thing like that Honda. I always lean the wrong way . . .'

'So he just went out for a spin?'

She nodded. 'I didn't get really worried until he wasn't back for lunch. We were going out to a pub in Wareham. We had booked a table. We often go out to lunch on a Sunday.'

'He didn't mention where he was going? Or what direction he was taking?'

'No, he never does. And I never ask. He just goes . . . for a ride. He likes it this time of year because there's almost nothing on the road compared to summer.'

'Did he take anything with him? I mean, like an anorak or a bag or parcel or anything?' I was really floundering. And then I suddenly realized what I was floundering at. I glanced at Philippa and I knew she could read what was passing through my tiny mind. She reached for my hand.

'I'm sorry to get you involved, Peter. I know how you feel about being employed as a kind of Dorset Paul Temple, but I didn't know what else to do. Sally's at her wits' end with worry and the police . . .'

'What about the police?' I interrupted, hopeful I might find an 'out' by restricting the problem to the boys in blue. That is, if there actually was a problem. For it had occurred to me that old Gregory might

28

deliberately have skipped to avoid the nuptials that he saw glinting in his beloved's eyeballs.

'Sally naturally informed the police on Sunday evening, when Gregory still wasn't back. They took down loads of particulars but, apparently, showed little concern.'

Sally wiped her eyes and took up the story once again.

'They said that it was more than likely that there was a good reason why he had not returned and that I shouldn't worry unduly for a day or two. And to keep them informed, of course.'

'Did you get a cup of tea?' I asked. She looked puzzled, as well she might. 'Forget it,' I added quickly. 'So the police won't take any action yet?'

'It doesn't seem like it. A constable called at our office this morning to say that there had still been no reported accidents or signs of Greg's bike being abandoned anywhere.'

I thought for a moment. The police, alas, were not giving me an automatic 'out'.

'Has Gregory ever done anything like this before? Gone off for a bit, I mean.'

'No, never. Other than weekend jaunts on his bike. I usually know where he's going. I keep his appointments diary in the office, anyway.'

'Did he have anything down for yesterday?'

She shook her head. 'No. He always tries to keep weekends free.'

'Did he have appointments for today?'

'Yes. Nothing this morning, but he had to see somebody in Poole this afternoon. I had to ring and apologise. Mr Redstart wasn't at all amused.'

My ears picked up. 'Redstart, did you say?'

'Yes. Mr Redstart was annoyed at having to see Greg in the first place. I had great difficulty in making the arrangement last week. When I rang to say Greg wouldn't be able to make it after all, he really blew up.'

29

'Like his boat,' I muttered.

Sally frowned, then double-took. 'Oh, I see what you mean. Well, I don't suppose the loss of his boat helped his mood.'

'Do you know what Gregory was seeing Redstart about?'

She wrinkled her forehead. 'I suppose the same as last time – insurance queries. Greg is acting on behalf of Seaspray Insurance – they're mainly marine insurers. Apparently, they think Mr Redstart may be a bit dodgy with some of his claims.'

'They will think that even more after Saturday's explosion, won't they?'

'I think that boat was only bought this year. After Seaspray had started to have a query or two.'

'So that would have been insured with someone else?'

'I guess so. Seaspray certainly haven't been on to us about it today. Anyway, you don't think Redstart has anything to do with Greg vanishing, do you?'

'I don't think anything yet.' I downed a long draught of my Scotch, as if its glow might illuminate my mind. 'I tell you what. I'd like to come to your offices in the morning and run through his files with you. Who knows, there might be a clue somewhere there.'

Certainly, I didn't have a clue from where I was sitting, and it was all I could think of to say. So much for the brain-feeding powers of Scotch. Maybe, if Philippa was serving fish for dinner . . . ? Anyway, I hoped the fact that someone had shown willing to help Sally would at least give her a night's sleep.

Philippa now took up the baton. 'Greg wouldn't have gone to visit any of his relatives, would he? I know it's a long shot.'

'No. He wouldn't have gone off like that without any luggage. Anyway, I've rung all his relatives I have telephone numbers for. He hasn't been near any of them or made any contact. The dreadful thing is that none

30

of them seem very worried – even his mother.' Tears started to reappear in her eyes. 'I think they just imagine he's left me and hasn't the courage to tell me. You see, he jilted a previous girlfriend apparently only three days before the wedding. They had to give all the presents back.'

She put her head in her hands and started to sob like I had heard over the phone. I looked at Philippa and she nodded.

'I think maybe we should leave it there until the morning, Sally. All I wanted to do tonight was to get Peter over here so that you could outline your worries to him. It enables him to have a bit of a think before he sees you again tomorrow.'

Sally looked up at me through now damp fingers.

'I'm sorry, Peter, for being such a wet week. It's not like me one bit. But I'm so worried about him. I can't say how grateful . . .'

'Don't even think about it. Anyway, who knows, by tomorrow Greg may have turned up.'

My attempt to buoy her spirits unfortunately only succeeded in swamping them. With a wail, she ran out of the room and we heard her footfalls on the polished boards of the Uppsala staircase.

'I won't follow her,' Philippa said quietly. 'She's better left alone for a little while, I think. I've got her to stay the night and, if necessary, I'll drive her to Sandbanks to meet you in the morning.'

I sighed mightily. 'The course of true love . . .' I stopped. I couldn't quite remember the other bit and I reckoned Philippa's opinion sufficiently not to come over as a hundred-and-one per cent fool.

'So you think he might have run out on her?'

'How can I know anything? I've only met them both once for a few minutes. Even then I had one us ear.'

She leaned across and stroked the tip of my convalescing patient. 'I should have asked you before. How is it now? It looks almost better.'

31

'It is what it looks, I'm glad to say. Its only trouble now is that it doesn't like what it hears tonight. Tell me, how well do you know Gregory Mann?'

'Not all that well. We've seen each other on and off since childhood, but after I got married to Mr Horrid there was a bit of a hiatus. That was when he got engaged to that girl he jilted.'

'What kind of fellow is he?'

'A bit impetuous, but pretty regular really. Game for anything, he claims, but I suspect underneath he's more conservative than he would admit. Mind you, he has started up quite a few career paths before the Bournemouth gumshoe bit.'

'Such as?'

'After leaving the London Synagogue of Economics, as he used to call it, he became articled to an accountant. That lasted five minutes. Then he joined a firm of estate agents in Church Stretton.'

'Ten minutes?' I ventured.

She nodded. 'Then he spent a year abroad with British American Tobacco, I think it was. Came back covered in nicotine and tried his hand at journalism up north. He didn't like the hours, so he . . . what did he do then? . . . ah yes, he took up flying.'

'Didn't like the heights?'

She laughed. 'Something like that. Anyway, he had one or two other jobs, then went to America. Dallas, Texas, to be exact, where I gather he shacked up with a girl who was secretary to a private investigation company. That's where he got the idea from originally. A year or two later. I heard he was back in England, trying his hand at that game up north. He soon found there wasn't really enough money up there and the jobs, he told me, were a bit rough for him. So he came down to Bournemouth. That's it. That's really all I know.'

So this Gregory had danced around jobs the way his

eyes danced around a room. Maybe, he had just waltzed away from Sally. It would follow.

'Where do you think he's gone?' I asked Philippa.

She shrugged. 'I really don't know. I can't believe he's just upped and left without a word to anyone, and without taking a stick or stone with him. I guess he might have done that ten years ago but I wouldn't have thought now. He's matured quite a bit. Anyway, he's got quite a successful business now, I gather.'

'So you don't think it could be debts he's running away from?'

'I doubt it.' She drew in her breath. 'I just pray it won't all turn out to be like that case I read about in the paper the other day.'

'What case?'

'Where a poor man's motor bike skidded off the road, went across a field and fell into a ditch. And the fellow just lay there for three days, too hurt to crawl to get help. They only just found him in time.'

I looked at her. 'So that's what you think may have happened?'

She shook her head. 'Well, it would explain everything, wouldn't it? And that Honda is a hell of a size and a hell of a handful.'

She suddenly looked at her watch. 'My God, I've forgotten all about the trout in the oven.'

She was gone in a flash, leaving me with my thoughts. None of them now were about food, more's the pity. I was concerned about the huge change in Sally, from the confident party-goer of Guy Fawkes night. Her eyes had exchanged allure for alarm and despondency. I wondered if she knew more than she was telling about her Mann's disappearance.

And I was concerned about myself. It was happening all over again. I could feel the hook in my throat. But what could I do? Say no to the elegant lady wielding the rod? 'You've landed the wrong fish, ma'am. Go try your line in another pond.' After all, the Sally Newtons

33

of this world meant nothing to me. Or did they? Anyway, I owed something to the fisher-lady, besides her being Arabella's cousin: she had more or less saved my life – and Gus's – once, a fact that's pretty hard to ignore.

I got up and went into the kitchen, but my appetite seemed to have fled. Much more of this and I wouldn't just be a Sam Spade, but top of the list for a new 'Thin Man' series.

Gregory Mann didn't roar back overnight, so next morning saw me behind the black glass of the Ask Force office in Sandbanks. The sandman seemed to have soothed Sally somewhat, for a degree of her old buoyancy had returned to her manner and I no longer felt I had to stand by with the biggest handkerchief in the world. In fact, apart from the hurt in her eyes, she looked great. Disturbingly so, for a guy who had lived more or less a monk's life (the 'less' bit is because monks don't drink as much Heineken as me and Gus) since Arabella's flight to the Golden State.

Sally made me a cup of instant coffee instantly, then showed me a small stack of files she had obviously pulled together for my benefit. Beside them was a big, black leather diary, with the initials G. M. embossed in gold at the base of the cover. Gregory obviously liked everything he touched to be generously built.

'There are more files in there.' She pointed to a matt red filing cabinet. 'They go back quite a few years, some of them before my time, when Greg was up north. I thought you might like to start just with the ones covering our present cases.'

'That will be fine,' I smiled and sat down behind what was clearly her desk. Gregory's was obviously the one across the room, near the window, for it was twice the size and all voluptuous curves in two shades of walnut. It looked like he could have bought it from

Warner Bros in the forties, had he been born at the time.

Sally looked nervously down at me. 'Would you, er, like me to stay . . . or what – whilst you read them? Or, you know, I could take you through them, if you like.'

I liked, so she took me through them. Saved time and saved her from being alone with her worries. Her chair was bang next to mine, and although she wasn't wearing Opium she looked very glamorous despite her baggy fisherman's sweater.

Gregory Mann was certainly a professional and Sally Newton was obviously an efficient secretary. The files were exemplary in that they were all clear, comprehensive and to the point. All correspondence was duplicated, all dates sequential, all interviews and meetings minuted, and all expenses noted. Actual bills, Sally informed me, were kept in accountancy files, which she offered to show me later, but I declined. Bills, even other people's, always gave me a headache.

After three cups of coffee, two custard creams and two and a half hours, I'd got a pretty fair picture of Gregory Mann's recent and current business. He was quite a busy chap. I put aside those files that covered, albeit quite lucratively, minor and sometimes downright frivolous assignments – for example, a lost pedigree Dobermann Pinscher (he found it); a missing dinghy from a yacht (turned out the millionaire owner had forgotten he'd lent it to a friend of his son. His loss of memory cost him a cool five hundred pounds); a woman who wanted her eighty-two-year-old husband watched in case he was frequenting a massage parlour that had just opened locally – which left me with just three main current files. One of them, of course, was the Seaspray Insurance Company's investigations into Gus's *bête noire*, Patrick Redstart.

From what I could gather from the file, Gregory Mann had been following Redstart's movements for

35

some little time – that is, on dry land. He seemed never to have tracked him once he'd left Poole harbour, which it appeared Redstart was in the habit of doing fairly frequently.

Mann had recorded only one actual interview with him, a fortnight previously, during which he had vigorously denied making any false statement or inaccurate insurance claims at any time in his life. The interview had come to an abrupt end with the arrival of a Miss Abigail Gordon, whom Mann had described earlier as a close friend of Redstart and whose home was above his antique shop at Lyme Regis. The most recent note in the file was dated the previous Thursday: 'Next interview fixed Monday 7 November, 3 p.m. at the boat'. I checked in the smart appointments diary. It was duly noted against that afternoon in Mann's handwriting.

The second file was a strange and disturbing one. The assignment had originated with a visit from a lady who lived in Bristol. She was a widow who had just one child, a young girl of sixteen called Priscilla Teddington, who was a boarder at a school I had vaguely heard about, Ferndales, which operated amongst sumptuous grounds just north of Wool.

Now I had better explain why I should have heard of this school. No, I'm not a voyeur at hockey games. It's just that Ferndales has a touch of a 'tut-tut' reputation for its so-called 'progressive' ways. You know, it's co-ed, for a start. Now that wouldn't be a big deal if it wasn't for the school's philosophy of letting the child find his or her true self through freedom and opportunity. So what did that really mean – besides a few pregnant schoolgirls? (That's how Ferndale's reputation had spread locally, despite the cover-ups. There's always a gardener who'll talk.) From the school's prospectus that Mann had so conscientiously included in the file it would appear that lessons were voluntary, not obligatory. So was sport. Every creative leaning was to be encouraged (they didn't mention procreative), and there seemed to be more art teachers than I've seen outside the Royal Academy. Oh, and swimming naked in a person-made lake in the grounds got a passing mention – 'to help rid the body and soul of all the fetters . . . blah, blah, blah.' I put down the prospectus at that point.

Well, back to Mum's worries about young Priscilla and why she had called in a private investigator. From the notes on her first meeting with Mann, it would appear that Mrs Teddington was becoming a mite concerned about stories her daughter had told her of certain 'goings-on' at the school, notably, between the headmaster, a Mr Jonathan Smythe, who from his picture in the prospectus looked like a ball of hair with eyes, and the matron, a Miss Mary Withers, whose likeness to David Bowie was as startling as it was disconcerting.

Priscilla, apparently, had been somewhat of a rebel and a total-what of a liar all her life, which perhaps explains her incarceration in boarding school. So poor Mrs Teddington was at her wits' end what to believe or what action to take. That is, until she thought of going to a local private eye.

Armed with a more than generous starter of a thousand pounds, Mann had started his investigations with a few of the staff he had discovered lived outside the school premises. These included a gardener, who confirmed a couple of pregnancies, a piano teacher (spinster), who had shown Mann the door directly the subject of s-e-x had been, albeit delicately, raised, and a cleaning lady, who seemed to be so taken with the ball of hair with eyes that she wouldn't hear a word against him.

Subsequently, Mann had arranged a meeting with the headmaster, pretending he had a daughter who would soon be of an age to come to the school, but the interview produced nothing but the usual clichés that headmasters come out with directly they smell the heady scent of additional fees. Mann had asked to be introduced to the matron, expressing interest as to who would be looking after his gel's physical welfare, and a brief meeting ensued. Mann's handwritten comments indicated he was impressed with Miss Withers' obvious efficiency, but found her sex ambiguous, to say the least. The file ended with no indication of any further steps Mann contemplated to earn his first fee.

I asked Sally about it.

'No, this Ferndales case has Greg a bit flummoxed. He realises he can't pull the fake daughter act again or ask to see Priscilla herself. I suggested he might let me go to the school under some pretext – you know, as a reporter for some obscure magazine or that I was in the middle of writing some great tome on twentieth-century educative methods, but he wouldn't hear of it. He said he would think of something.'

I pointed back at the file. 'There are no notes in here as to what Priscilla's stories were all about. Just that they involved the headmaster and the matron some-how. Do you know any more than that?'

She blushed. 'No, not really. Greg had a feeling, as you might imagine, that they were sexual. The stories, I mean. But Mrs Teddington wouldn't actually say. He did ask her. She just said something like, "You find out what you can your end, then we will compare your findings with what my daughter has said. If they match, I'll tell you. If they don't, your work will be completed." '

I thought for a moment. 'This Mrs Teddington, it's a crazy notion, but Greg wouldn't suddenly have taken it into his head to bike all the way up to Bristol to see her, would he?'

Sally shook her head. 'I don't think so for a minute. Anyway, she phoned last Thursday to say her old mother was ill in Scotland and she would have to go and look after her for a while, and to keep all findings until she was back. Greg gave a huge sigh of relief at the news.'

The third current file was a very different kettle of fish – or rather, of animals. It was an assignment from that pharmaceutical company that has a large research establishment near Bournemouth – the Fellowes Laboratories, part of the famous Fellowes Foundation. Their brief was very simple. Who was stealing the animals they kept for their research purposes?

The MD of the Labs, a Mr Smallbrother, said, in the notes of Mann's first meeting with him, he had 'no desire to bring in the police at this stage, as it would undoubtedly involve publicity that we at the Foundation have no wish to attract. There is enough unjustified outcry against the use of live animals in research, as it is, without triggering more . . .' And so on. By the end of the interview, Mann had secured a five-thousand-pound assignment, half of it paid in advance.

The investigation was currently in its fifth week, with Mann seemingly pretty convinced he had discovered the instigator of the theft (or, perhaps, the release) of the animals, if not the actual perpetrator of the break-ins. His name was Robert Stringle and he was the founder of an animal rights movement I'd vaguely heard of called ARAG, Animal Rights Action Group. From Mann's notes, Stringle certainly seemed a likely suspect, being an ex-scientist himself, responsible over the years for the painful deaths of many animals for which now, retired and sixty-five, he wished to attone – presumably before he met his own and the animals' Maker.

Mann had questioned him twice at his house on the outskirts of Swanage, but had got nowhere. He had been given swift denials followed by a propaganda broadside and a selection of leaflets on animal rights, all of which were appended to the dossier. The file ended with a letter from Mr Stringle, dated a week before, stating that if Mann did not stop his 'persecution', then he, Stringle, would invoke the law to prevent further harassment.

Checking with Sally, I discovered that Mann intended to await news of the next break-in at Fellowes before taking further action. And Sally had made an arrangement with the laboratories' MD that Ask Force would be informed the very instant another incident occurred. For Mann wanted to catch Stringle before he had time to secrete or spirit the animals away.

So there we were. It certainly didn't seem likely our missing person had gone to see Stringle, or anyone else, on that Sunday morning, with the possible exception of Redstart. As I sat there I had a feeling Philippa might well be right and that poor Gregory Mann was lying in a field somewhere, the victim of two wheels not being as stable as four. Or, of course, he could just be ducking out on another lovely lady who heard marriage bells. But surely Sally Newton couldn't be so terrible that it was worth walking out on a business as lucrative as Ask Force. So, maybe he was suffering from amnesia somewhere, but how and why I couldn't figure. All I did know was that there was not much more I could do at Sandbanks, except hold Sally's red-tipped hand.

Just then the phone rang and whilst Sally was answering it, I took another look at Gregory's gargantuan diary. I went back a few pages, but all that seemed to be in it were the appointments I already knew about from the files, and a few little doodles that Greg and Sally had scribbled while they were thinking. I returned to the recent entries and noted, yet again, the blank for the Monday morning, and the appointment for three o'clock in the afternoon with Redstart at the boat. For the Saturday and Sunday there was nothing. No appointments, that is. There was another doodle on the Sunday page, what looked like a sort of art deco style '4'. You know the kind of lettering art directors were fond of in the thirties, 'thicks' made up of a lot of thin lines and 'thins' being just a single thin line. It didn't seem significant and when Sally came off the phone, I asked her about it, just in case.

'Oh, I saw that too. Doesn't mean anything. Greg is always doodling away, especially if he's on the phone.'

I pointed to Mann's voluptuous curved desk. 'Is Greg into art deco?'

'A little. He's thinking of changing our logo into a thirties type of script. Someone gave him *The Savoy Cocktail Book* for Christmas and he fell in love with the style of lettering.' She looked down at the '4' on the page. 'I guess he's doodling the kind of style he's after.'

'But why a four, do you think?'

She thought for a second. 'I suppose because our new cottage is number four. Number four Shepherd's Lane.'

'Tell me about the cottage. It's nearly ready to move into, as I remember?'

'Yes,' she said, with a sigh.

'Hey, he wouldn't have gone there, would he?'

She resumed her seat next to me. 'That was the first thing I thought of on Sunday. I've been there and searched every inch of the house and grounds. There's no sign of his having been there, not even motor cycle tyre marks. Anyway, that phone call was from the guy who is doing the kitchen to say it's finished and where should he leave the key.'

So much for that brainwave. Before I could react again, the desk was covered in fisherman's sweater, as Sally collapsed forward onto it with a little cry.

'Oh God, Peter, what shall I do?' she sobbed. I put my hand on her shoulder. 'He'll turn up soon, Sally, I'm sure,' I lied, but what else could I say?

'But supposing he doesn't? You read about people who disappear for years, sometimes and then turn up . . . when it's all too late.'

'Give it a few more days.'

She looked up from the desk. 'In a few more days, the thatcher may want to get on with that cottage roof. If Greg isn't back by then, what should I do? Let him carry on, or what? I can't afford to pay for everything myself whilst . . .'

She stopped abruptly, then turned to me, with tears welling in her eyes.

'I'm sorry, Peter, but when you've been living with someone you love and are very close to, then suddenly that someone is gone . . .'

I put my arm around her shoulder and hugged her to me. 'I know . . . I know. . . .' I said quietly.

And for all the world, we must have looked like the Babes in the Wood. Certainly, I prayed that Gregory had chosen to leave an even trail of bread behind him so that we would have some idea where he had Honda-ed.

4

Soon after, I got back to my Beetle. And now, just to cheer me up, the sky was crying too. Its tears, as always, had found some stitching holes in the convertible top where the thread had broken. Sod's law, they were right over the driver's seat. But, in my preoccupation with Sally's problems, I sat down first and wiped the seat second. Not that it then needed much wiping. My trousers made a great sponge.

Clanking back on the Sandbanks/Studland ferry, I reviewed my progress. It didn't take long. I came to the conclusion that all I'd been doing was filling a void in poor Sally's life and giving her the feeling that somebody was doing something about her Gregory's vamoose. But I comforted myself that such a service, on its own, was worthwhile, and in a day or two, anyway, the police would be bound to swing into action and take the onus off my shoulders, should the gumshoe not be back by then.

As I drove off the ramp of the ferry, the rain now blurring road into sand-dunes and pit-pattering my head with cold reminders of the advanced age of my rag top, I felt, nevertheless, a little better. That is, until I remembered what had been bugging me right from the start, at Philippa's the previous evening. It was Sally herself. For some reason, I thought I detected she was holding something back. It wasn't anything she said. It was kind of what she didn't say. And the trouble was I obviously didn't know what she didn't say. It was only a gut impression. And there was little I could do about it right then, anyway.

Sally's mental balance was currently a little too precarious to accommodate direct questions along the line of 'Are you sure you've told us everything?' or 'We can't help you unless you come clean.' Anyway, I could be so wrong. I still didn't really know Sally from Eve. Maybe her manner is always a bit enigmatic. Only dear Greg would know for sure. And I could hardly ask him.

In fact, I concluded that it was a good bit too early to ask anybody anything, for if I rushed off prematurely to interrogate every name in his files, I might be jeopardizing his whole business. Private eyes who disappear and have amateur sleuths like me looking for them don't win many brownie points with their clients. And I didn't relish the thought of old laser eyes' reaction, should he return out of the blue, to a 'To Let' notice plastered over his black windows.

By the time I parked my Beetle under the confusion of timber that pretended to be a garage behind my shop, I was in no mood for either Bing's complaints or opening up the Toy Emporium to the millions of customers who wouldn't turn up. However, I had to earn a crust, so I swung my 'Closed' sign to 'Open' and sat behind the counter waiting for the invasion.

Naturally, at low times like these, the first ding of the doorbell doesn't herald a customer. Or even, for that matter, anything recognizable as a human being. It heralded a world first – a tarpaulin that moved under its own power.

I noted the trail of water it left behind all the way up to the counter. They would have to get that cured on the production model.

'Came earlier. You were out.'

It spoke too. A kind of tarpaulin's Teddy Ruckspin. I humoured it.

'Oh, great leaking tarpaulin, doest I need thy permission to travel abroad?'

44

The dripping fabric fell away to reveal a face. Well, a sort of face.

'What?' it said intelligently.

'Gus, would you beach that ruddy sou'wester thing outside the door. I don't have an ark amongst my toys unfortunately, nor have I yet arranged them two by two.'

He grinned. I was amazed he got the point.

'I'll look out for one, old mate,' he said. Perhaps he hadn't got the point – or had he?

'Gus, would you mind putting that . . . thing in the porch. Anyway, how on earth did you get that wet? Your car's not that full of holes, is it?'

He mumbled all the way to the door by a different route from whence he'd come, leaving water trail number two. Then having doffed his thing, returned with a 'didn't come by car. Walked, didn't I? Damp's got in me electrics.'

'Your electrics, Gus?' I laughed. 'I thought you ran on gas.'

'Me car's, you prize berk. Coming back from Poole. Coughed and died, it did, on the perishing dune road. I saw you, you rotten sod, flashing past in that yellow horror of yours without so much as a nod. Call yourself a mate.'

I tried to cast my mind back, but everything had then been a blur of windscreen wipers, worry and clouds of spray. I wouldn't have known what I was passing, even if I'd been able to see it.

'I'm sorry, Gus. With all that rain and my roof leaking, I must have missed you.'

He sat down on a stool I keep for customers and sniffed. 'Well,' he began, then I could see his brain take another tack. 'What were you doing in Poole, anyway? You must have gone early to be back by now.'

'I did go early,' I grinned. 'You're right.' Two could tease.

He sniffed again. 'Someone ring about some old toy, then?'

'No,' I said.

'Erm . . . sell something, did you?'

'No.'

Moment's silence, if you don't count grunts.

'Can't think of anything else you would be doing in Poole, seeing as how you don't reckon boats.'

'Wasn't in Poole.'

'Bournemouth?'

'No,' I cheated.

'Well, where then? Can't have been far away because . . .'

'. . . I wouldn't have been back by now,' I mimicked.

He threw his overweight eyebrows up to the ceiling.

I laughed. 'All right, Gus, I'll end your agony. I was in Sandbanks.'

'Sandbanks is part of Bournemouth.'

'I know.'

'So?'

'I was trying to help a friend.'

'You don't know anybody in Sandbanks.' His eyes lit up. 'You haven't met some new fancy piece or other, have you?'

'Not in the way you mean, Gus, no. And the friend I'm helping is Philippa. You know, over at Owermoigne.'

'How can you help her in Sandbanks, then?'

So I told him the whole shebang. It cost me five of a six-pack before I had finished. And not one single customer interrupted my saga to help pay for them.

Gus picked a wayward baked bean out of a back tooth. Mr Heinz had just kindly provided us with one of his 57 varieties of repast.

'Well, 'Ercool, what you got in mind?'

Ignoring his mal-pronounced Poirot-ism, I shook my

46

head. 'To be honest, I haven't the faintest idea, right now.'

'Lucky you're not being paid for it then,' he grinned.

'Yeah,' I said, and drained the last of my last Heineken. 'Any ideas?'

Gus idly picked at the remains of his sweater, like a grooming lemur in Peru or wherever. I almost fell asleep before he replied.

'Well, first thing that strikes me is where's his ruddy motorbike?'

I frowned.

'I mean, with persons who go missing, they usually find their means of transport pretty quickly, don't they? You're always hearing of "Car found abandoned at somewhere or other still with its ignition keys", or "Van found in car park", or "Bike discovered on tow path", that kind of thing. Yet, with this Gregory, nothing's been traced at all. And it's a fancy bike too, you say.'

'Maybe it's so fancy, someone found it somewhere and nicked it instead of reporting it to the police.'

'Yeah. S'pose so.' He shook his empty can. I shook my head.

'Still doesn't explain what's happened to him, though, does it?'

'Nope. Maybe he's running away from something none of us know about except him. Wants to disappear like that MP fellow years ago. You know.'

'Maybe. But he's not pretending dead, like that MP and leaving his clothes on the beach. And we do live by the sea.'

'Too obvious, now that chap's done it, p'raps.'

Bing strolled into the room, took one look at us both, sitting there amongst our empty Heineken cans and chose the wisest course: he went out again. But his entry did remind me that there were more things in life than worrying about a missing person, whom I had only met for a flash and who had laughed about my rocketed right ear, to boot. I rose from my chair.

'Look, Gus, there's no real action I can take right this minute, as far as I can see. I'm going to give it another twenty-four hours. Maybe by then Gregory will have returned to the fold, or been discovered by the police or something. Someone may have reported seeing him or have found his bike. Who knows? As I've said, I can't go ferreting around his clients just yet otherwise he may end up without any clients when he returns.'

Gus unfolded himself reluctantly. 'You sound as if you think he's all right, I mean, not dead or anything.'

'I don't think anything. I'm just praying he'll be back quickly so I don't have to get out my magnifying glass and deer-stalker hat.'

'Be like that 'Ercool Parrot, you mean?' Gus asked with a smile.

'Something like that, Gus.'

He shuffled over to the window of my shop, just avoiding knocking over a neat stack of mint boxed Corgi toys from the fifties and sixties. I'll swear he does it on purpose to keep my adrenalin going.

'Stopped raining,' he muttered. 'Think I'll walk back down the road to get me car going. Should have dried a bit by now.' He laid such emphasis on the word 'walk' that I had no option. I got out the Beetle and gave him a lift. But I made him leave the tarpaulin in the porch. Air-cooled cars aren't crazy about having water-cooled interiors.

But the next morning there was still no sign of our missing person. I opened up shop. Even though I turned over some two hundred pounds on a mint boxed Dinky Mayo Composite (that unique piggy-back combination of the late thirties: big Shorts flying boat underneath; smaller seaplane on its back. Idea? To enable the smaller plane to have enough fuel and range to carry mail across the atlantic. Project cut short by the war

48

and imperfection of in-flight refuelling) and a slightly chipped Sikorsky s42 flying boat, no box, the sales did little to lift my sense of guilt at my lack of both ideas and action on the Gregory case. And it wasn't just because I so liked Philippa and owed her a big one, either. I was discovering that I sort of wanted to help Sally Newton, for Sally Newton's sake too. (No, it wasn't only for her Rampling/Bisset physical character-istics – least, I hoped it wasn't.)

After lunch, I couldn't bear it any longer. I got out the Beetle and headed Owermoigne way. I didn't quite know what purpose it would serve talking to Philippa, but at least it was better than twiddling guilty thumbs.

When I arrived at the nursery, I couldn't park where I normally did, by the barn, as the drive outside was littered with dead, grey thatch and neat bundles of bright new straw. The thatcher had obviously started on the roof, though I couldn't see him.

The sight of work proceeding on the barn reminded me of my gipsy nurse on Bonfire night: Merinda of the dark eyes and the talent for painting, whose work would eventually be offered on the walls of the craft centre that the barn would become. I looked around for John-John, but of him there was no sign.

I was startled by Philippa's voice beside me. I hadn't heard her come out.

'Hi, Peter. How nice to see you.' She kissed me lightly on the lips. 'Unexpected visits are always the best.'

She pointed up at the barn. 'It's going to look nice, isn't it? Costing me a bomb, but it should be worth it. I've already let some space for when the craft centre is open.'

She shepherded me towards the house. As we neared the back door, a man came out. When he saw us he hesitated.

'Oh, ma'am, I didn't know you were having visitors, otherwise . . .'

Philippa cut him short. 'Don't worry, Tom, this is a friend, not a visitor. Great friend.' She turned to me. 'Meet Dorset's ace thatcher, Peter. Tom Sweet.'

We shook hands. His was brown and almost twice the size of mine. The skin felt tough as hide, no doubt from years of working with straw and withies.

'Pleased to meet you.' His voice was as Dorset as you can get: rich and burry, and rounded as a chestnut.

'Getting on with it, then?' I said limply. (I'm always at a loss as to what to say on these occasions.)

'Will do. If we can get a bit of a dry spell.' He turned his huge frame to Philippa. 'Anyway, thanks for the tea, ma'am. Now I'd better get back to it. Mustn't waste time while the rain holds off.' He turned back into the kitchen. 'Molly, you come on out, girl. Her ladyship has a visitor.'

Philippa touched his arm. 'No, Tom, let her stay. She's playing happily. She won't be in our way.'

He pushed his flat cap to the back of his head, his forehead now displaying the tell-tale line between tan and paleness.

'Are you sure, ma'am? She's very used to amusing herself while I work.'

'I'm certain,' Philippa smiled reassuringly. 'Don't worry.'

He frowned, whilst he weighed up what he could do. And for all the world, he looked like an old Victorian photograph of a village artisan, sombre and sober, tall and Godfearing, features so chiselled and weathered by the elements that they seemed archetypal rather than individual, and with eyes so deep-set under craggy brows that the camera would only be able to record their darkness. The perfect Purbeck man. Thomas Hardy would have been proud.

'I don't think I should,' he said slowly.

'You should,' Philippa said quickly. 'Now off you go and don't give it a moment's more thought.'

He looked down at his hands, then nodded almost

imperceptibly and strode off towards the barn. I went inside with Philippa, curious to see this Molly of his. For he looked somewhat old to have a child who still was at a playing stage of life.

'Molly, this is Peter,' Philippa said. 'Peeeterrr,' she repeated in slow time.

'Peeeterrr,' came a croaky imitation from someone I had not been expecting at all. (But I should have, really. It was term time, after all, when most young children should still be at school at that hour of the afternoon.) She was about five feet four or five tall. Age? Difficult to judge. Her large face and head were those of a trusting and too innocent child, but her body was so over-weight, it could have been that of a thirty-five- or forty-year-old washerwoman straight out of Dickens. I guessed she was actually fifteen to seventeen, and Philippa told me later I wasn't far wrong. She was sixteen. And tragically, as you have probably already guessed, retarded.

I propelled a toy dog on wheels towards her – one of many toys on the floor that Philippa had apparently got down from the attic especially for Molly, relics of her own childhood in Shropshire.

'Doggy,' she cooed and pushed it backwards towards me. By the time we had done the to and fro game for a bit, I could see from Molly's narrow but nevertheless beautiful eyes, that I had ceased being a stranger to be wary of and was now an acceptable friend.

'Daddy's thatching,' I said, pointing out the window. She shook her large head wisely. 'No. Not window.' She pointed upwards. 'Roof. Daddy thatch roof.'

I had to admit she was literally right. Daddy wasn't thatching windows. He was upwards, not sideways.

'She would like your toy shop,' Philippa grinned. 'Peeterr's house . . . is . . . full of . . . toys. Peeterr coll . . . ects . . . toys.'

'Toys,' she repeated, and I wiped a slight dribble

from the side of her mouth with my handkerchief. I opened up an old *Girl* annual in front of Molly.

'Is mummy working?' I whispered to Philippa out of the corner of my mouth.

'Mummy's long gone,' she said quietly.

'Gone away or gone . . . ?' I pointed upwards.

She pointed upwards back (if you see what I mean).

So that's why the thatcher took his daughter around with him. Philippa helped me up off my knees.

'Peeterr and I are just going into the kitchen to have some tea. You know where that is. Kitchen?' Philippa continued to speak slowly.

Molly smiled. 'Kitchen,' and pointed in the right direction.

'That's right. You come in if you want anything. Understand, Molly?'

Molly nodded and went back to the book, idly flopping the pages to watch the colours strobe by.

I started almost to tiptoe out of the room, as if I was in some kind of hospital and Philippa immediately admonished me with her eyes.

'Come on, Peter. Have a cup of tea and tell me why you've driven over to see me instead of picking up the telephone. Is it about Gregory? Have you found out something?'

'Yes to both,' I said, with a sigh. 'It is about Gregory. And I have found out something.'

Her lovely eyes glistened. 'Come on, tell me what.'

'That I don't know what the hell I'm doing.'

The tea had gone and the afternoon with it. The thatcher had tipped his cap, picked up Molly and disappeared in his Ford pick-up with a 'See you tomorrow'. And now I was two Scotches into the evening, still with Philippa. I was in no mood yet to go back on my ownio to my Toy Emporium and to Bing's totally justified cat-calls, for, to be honest, attractive women's company always reminded me how much I missed another attractive lady's company – with this Gregory business to further lower my spirits.

Philippa raised her glass of white wine.

'Here's to the death of guilt.'

I raised my Scotch. 'One more of these should help spring the trap,' I smiled.

'I was hoping my scintillating divorcée's company would have hung, drawn and quartered it by now. Let alone all my persuasive chat about "not feeling guilty about something that shouldn't, by rights, be your problem", and "you're doing all you can at this early stage", and so on. I mean it all, you know. It's not just blah.'

'I know,' I smiled. 'I wouldn't have come around here for comfort, if you had been a blah lady.'

She looked hard at me. 'Are you sure your feelings are just about what you see as your inadequacy over Gregory's disappearance?'

'What do you mean?' I blushed, somewhat alarmed that Philippa had cottoned on so quickly to what I was only just starting to suspect myself.

She sipped her wine. 'Well, I don't, of course, know all the ins and outs of your and Arabella's arrangements to try a year apart, but . . . er . . .'

The 'but . . . er' melted in her mouth, so, reluctantly, I came to her rescue.

'You think I might be feeling guilty for encouraging her to go?'

She shrugged. 'Maybe. I don't know. Then again, you might be feeling a bit guilty for, I don't know quite how to put it, let's say, finding other women attractive in the meantime.'

I took umbrage. 'What do you mean? Of course, men find lots of women attractive and vice versa, whether they are already married or have a partner or whatever. Anyway, I've been living the life of a monk, a non-teetotal monk, I have to admit, since Arabella went away.'

She reached for my hand. 'I know. Least, I'm sure you have.'

'Then why did you . . . ?'

'The way you looked at Merinda the other night. Not just when she was tending your ear – before. I noticed you looking at her quite a bit over the evening.'

This time I really blushed. 'She's a very striking girl. You can't help noticing her.'

She relinquished my hand. 'All I'm saying is you shouldn't feel guilty about anything at all. Gregory's case or Arabella going away for a bit or looking at other ladies. There would be something wrong with you if you didn't do the last now and again.'

She was right. There *would* be something wrong with me, if I didn't. After all, I was young-ish. I'd only been thirty-nine twice. And I was vaguely healthy, give or take a creak. So I did look at other ladies now and again. Trouble was, recently it had been now and again and again. Even ex-party-goer Sally was starting to get to me.

I drained the last of my Scotch. 'Astonishing,' I smiled broadly. 'I do believe my guilt has just flown out the window.' Philippa really should be a National Health option for everyone. 'Just as well,' I grinned. 'I don't want to be asked to blow up a balloon on the drive home.'

'You won't. There's some quite good blotting-paper in the oven at the moment.' She looked at her watch. 'It will be ready in about twenty minutes.'

What a lady. I'd hardly noticed her put it in the cooker.

'Philippa,' I began, then cleared my throat. It was to be a tricky question, that I had never asked before. 'Why haven't you married again?'

She took a deep breath. 'I'm not against it, if that's what you're thinking. Bit afraid of it, I guess. I don't want to be a two-time loser.' She smiled across at me. 'A bit like you, I suppose. Being cautious. Funny thing, you asking now, because Gregory Mann is one of those I've turned down.'

'Gregory?' I repeated in surprise. 'He proposed to you?'

'Some time ago now. When he first came down to Bournemouth – before he met Sally. You know I used him to get some evidence for my divorce. And one thing led to another.'

'Was it too early, or did you just not go for Gregory?'

'Both, I think. He's not really my type. What did you think of him?'

'Not my type either,' I laughed. 'No, what I mean to say is that something bugged me about him. He seemed to be a little too good to be true, in a way. And then, there were his eyes.'

'His eyes bug you too?'

I nodded.

'I don't go for eyes that have St Vitus' Dance – '

But the rest of my statement was cut short by the phone. Philippa excused herself and went into the hall to answer it. It was about quarter of an hour before she was back.

'Well, they've got up off their backsides at last,' was her first enigmatic comment.

'Who?'

'The police. That was Sally. They've just left her.'

I breathed a sigh of relief. 'So they are taking Gregory's disappearance seriously now?'

'Yes, it would seem so. Sally's in a bit of a state. They gave her quite a grilling, apparently.'

'Gave *her* a grilling?'

'She says she thinks they believe she may have had something to do with his vanishing. You know, Peter, the first person to suspect in any missing person case is often the nearest and dearest.'

I stood up. I can't think as straight sitting.

'That's impossible. What idiots. Sally doesn't know

anything about his going, I'll swear to that.' I was surprised at my own vehemence.

'I haven't told you the unfortunate bit yet.'

'What, there's more?'

''Fraid so. The police got Sally to admit she'd had quite a quarrel with Greg on the Saturday night.'

'And had she?'

'So she says.'

'Do you know what it was about?'

'Some woman or other Sally suspected Greg might be seeing on the side. She wouldn't say any more.'

I rested back against the wall. 'That's all we need, Sally withholding information from us, which she's quite willing to give to the police. It's funny, I sort of suspected she wasn't telling me everything, but I was too scared of hurting her to probe. Did you know anything about all this?'

Now Philippa looked quite hurt. 'No, honestly, Peter, it's all news to me. I'm not really surprised, though. I don't think Greg is ready yet to settle down – with anyone.'

'But they've bought a cottage.'

'Correction. *He* has bought a cottage. Who knows whether he really intended it to be a marital home or a bachelor base.' She looked at her watch again. 'Anyway, I'd better see how the meal is getting on.'

'Hang on. How did you leave it with Sally?'

'Oh,' she said and I could tell from her eyes that she wished I'd asked that question *after* being softened up with her Cordon Bleu blotting paper.

'I said, er, I expected you might want to pop over and see her tomorrow.' She smiled awkwardly and vanished into the kitchen.

I sat down again. By the time I had chewed over the significance of the last few minutes, and where it landed me, my appetite had again taken flight. If nothing else, finding Gregory was now becoming vital in the fight against malnutrition.

5

Despite her red rims, I had to be stern

'Look, Sally, if I'm to help you, you have to tell me everything. And I mean everything.'

She collapsed, rather than sat, down onto her desk chair. 'I'm sorry, Peter. I meant to tell you, but I was – embarrassed, I suppose. And I was afraid you might get the wrong impression.'

'So now the police have got the wrong impression.'

Suddenly, I couldn't go on being Mr Nasty. I came around behind her chair and put my hand on her shoulder.

'It's all right, Sally. Now tell me what the police said.'

She looked up at me and, curses, her worries had not worn her attraction one bit.

'They were here ages.'

I stopped her immediately. 'Who were here? What were their names?' I asked, just in case I knew any of them.

'I don't remember all their names. There was one man in uniform and two in plain clothes. I can only recall one name. He did all the main questioning. Whetstone. That was his surname. Can't – '

'Digby,' I interrupted. 'That's his other name. Digby Whetstone.'

'Do you know him?' She sounded somewhat surprised.

'I came across him when I was looking into something else. Big, fat sort of chap.'

'That's him. Anyway, he did most of the talking,

whilst the others sorted through the files and took fin-ger-prints. That kind of thing.'

'How did he come round to being aggressive with you?'

'I don't know, I really don't. Maybe he thought I was being a bit hesitant, or something. You see, I was a bit scared. They didn't say they were coming and suddenly, to be confronted by these policemen – '

'I know, I know. So you told him all you've told me, plus the bit you didn't – the bit about the quarrel.'

'That's right. That's all, I swear.'

'How did he get you to talk about the row?'

'He asked me outright, had Greg and I had a quarrel? And I felt so awful, I just had to confess to somebody.'

I thought she was about to cry, so I sat down beside her at the desk. She went on, 'I'm sure I would have told you, had you asked.'

'I didn't like to, but the question did cross my mind.' I smiled reassuringly. 'Now tell me exactly what the quarrel was about.'

'Abigail Gordon.'

I frowned. 'Do you mean Redstart's girlfriend?'

She nodded.

I waited a moment, then asked, 'Was Gregory seeing her?'

She put her head in her hands. 'I don't know. I'm not sure. . . .'

'Then how . . . ?'

'A girlfriend of mine says she saw Gregory with her in a pub in Wareham.'

'Maybe she was mistaken,' I tried.

'No, she wasn't. I clung to that straw but she's adamant that it was Abigail. She was at school with her.'

'And you tackled Gregory with it after the Guy Fawkes party?'

'Yes. We had both had a bit to drink, as you know, and I suppose the booze gave me Dutch courage. So when we got home, I asked him whether he had been seeing Abigail.'

'What did he say?'

'He denied it absolutely. Said my friend must have been mistaken. I'm afraid, then, I lost my temper and called him all the names under the sun. Accused him of acting like he did with his previous girlfriend, and that he'd probably chicken out of the wedding, like he did with hers.'

'Then what?'

She sighed. 'Nothing, that's what. I thought he was going to hit me, but all he did was turn on his heel and go upstairs to bed.'

'And did you make it up later?'

'No. When I eventually went upstairs, I found he had locked himself in the spare bedroom. I didn't seem him again until breakfast.'

'Did you make it up then?'

'Sort of. Maybe. Neither of us mentioned the row at all. He seemed to be fairly normal towards me. Then after breakfast, he gave me a kiss and said he was off for his usual Sunday spin on his bike and would be back way before it was time for lunch . . . and I haven't seen him since.'

'Did Digby Whetstone say what his next moves would be? I mean, how was it all left?'

'In the air, really. He thanked me for my time and said he would be contacting me again.'

I pointed to the filing cabinet. 'Did they take any files away with them?'

'Yes. They said they would be returned today. I guess they must be copying them or something.'

I smiled weakly. 'Well, at least the police have got up off their jacks.'

'I know.' She turned and grasped my arm. 'But, Peter, you don't think Whetstone suspects me of anything, do you? After I told him about the quarrel, he didn't look as if he believed anything I said. But you all *have* to believe me.' She was now almost shouting. 'I didn't have anything to do with Greg's going. I don't know anything about it, anything. Oh God, I only wish I did. You believe me surely, Peter?'

I held her hand in mine. 'It's all right. Now calm down. Digby Whetstone is a funny man. He was probably just enjoying the rare opportunity of power over a pretty woman. Anyway, what do you imagine he might think you're guilty of?'

'Murder,' she breathed. 'Murder.'

I left soon afterwards. I don't know whether I had cheered up Sally or not, but somehow the clouds that were lowering over my life, whilst still there, seemed a trifle lighter. As I analysed my way home I came to the conclusion it was because now, at last, I was committed to helping Sally. Before I had really been treading water, waiting for the police to surface. But curiously, now that they had, and I knew they were being led (or misled) by one Digby Whetstone, I felt a little effort on my part, even if it turned out to be merely duplication, might not come amiss. Anyway, now that the police would no doubt be knocking at the doors of Gregory's clients I would not be personally guilty of ruining his Ask Force business by knocking on a few myself. All I had to work out was which doors and in what order. But I didn't have to be an 'Ercool Parrot' to designate the first who would have their knocker lifted.

Lyme Regis is on one hell of a steep hill that climbs up from the cob, made famous nowadays by Meryl Streep in Fowles's *The French Lieutenant's Woman*. Both sides of said hill are lined with shops, which presumably have either the fittest customers in the world or the most out-of-breath. I pretended to be going to grab a pint in the pub at the bottom of the hill, and parked my Beetle in its minute parking area. Then I puffed my way up

60

the seemingly vertical High Street, looking for the coyly named antique-cum-junk shop that Gregory Mann had noted in his files – The Wood Worm.

I almost mistook it for an old bookshop, for in front of its window, on the pavement but under the awning, was a display of old Penguins (dating from when they had simple and sensible orange or green jackets to denote their categories) and other well thumbed paperbacks. By peering behind them, I could just discern in the darkness of the shop, a Lloyd Loom chair, a rather too stripped-pine dresser and a stuffed owl under a glass dome. I went in.

At first there seemed to be no one about, just a jungle of battered and fading items of furniture of no particular period, and bric-a-brac of no particular value. And the whole place had a jungle smell of rising damp and deathly decay. Anthony Perkins and Alfred Hitchcock would have loved it all. I didn't. I missed Janet Leigh.

It wasn't until my elbow must have jiggled a Victorian ewer standing in its cracked basin that a door I hadn't seen in the corner of the shop opened. It wasn't Janet Leigh though, but the next worst thing. Even in the gloom, I could read its message.

'Hello. Can I help you?' She was about my height, which is so-so for a man, but looks impressive on a woman. Dark hair framed a tanned face, one feature of which blinded you to the attraction of the others – her mouth. It was not so much that it was large and full lipped, it was the way she used it. She made Shirley Bassey look as if she'd just come from the dentist.

'Oh, I'm sorry.' I reset the jug in the centre of its bowl.

'Are you looking for some nice jugs?' she asked, and I saw the mischievous gleam in her eyes. 'We have others.'

I didn't rise to it. 'No, actually I'm not. I'm not here really as a customer at all.'

'Don't tell me you're from the VAT? I thought VAT men always wore suits.'

I chuckled. 'No, I'm not. And I think they always do.'

She stood with a hand on one hip, so that I could see her figure. I'd already seen it.

'You wouldn't, by any chance, be Miss Abigail Gordon?'

She looked at me a little harder.

'Do I know you?'

'No.'

'Then how . . . ?'

'I was given your name.'

She suddenly looked less than sure of herself.

'By whom?'

She was scared and I wished I knew why.

'By Gregory,' I tried. She did a slow blink, so I missed her eyes.

'Gregory whom?' she rejoined. 'I know at least three people called Gregory.'

'Unusual,' I smiled.

'I've got lots of friends,' she smiled back. I bet she had.

'Mann. Gregory Mann.'

She blinked in slow motion again, blast it.

'Ah, *that* Gregory. So what did he give you my name for?'

'He didn't really,' I said, trying to work out how good an actress she was. 'I just heard you and he knew each other quite well.'

She now put both hands on her hips. 'You had better ask *him* that. And anyway, Mr . . .'

'Marklin. Peter Marklin.'

'. . . Mr Peter Marklin, what the hell has all this got to do with you? You come in here – '

I wondered if her aggression was just a handy front to hide her embarrassment behind.

'I came in here,' I interrupted, 'to discover if you know where Gregory is now.'

'What do you mean?' Her puzzlement act was pretty good. It would be hard to tell from the genuine article. 'You must know where he lives.'

'I do. My concern now is to know *if* he lives.'

'*If* he lives,' she repeated quietly, her mouth no longer doing the Shirley Basseys. I wasn't puncturing her act, so I came clean.

'Gregory Mann has disappeared. He hasn't been seen since Sunday morning. Haven't the police been round to see you yet?'

'Disappeared? Police?' she said breathlessly. Move over Meryl Streep or was I doing Abigail a disservice? 'What do you mean?'

So I told her. The Reader's Digest version, short and boringly to the point, leaving out anything that might incriminate anybody. When I'd finished, she was sitting on one of her chairs looking, like it, somewhat the worse for wear. She didn't react for quite some time.

'Why have you come to me?' She looked up. 'And why have *you* come, anyway? You say the police are now involved, so why not leave it to them?'

'I'm helping an old friend of mine.'

'Who's that? Sally Newton?' Her mouth swivelled again, as she said the name.

'No. Someone you've never heard of. Knows Gregory from when he was a child.'

'Still a child,' she muttered, then stopped as she saw me looking at her. From then on, she shut up. She wouldn't answer any more questions of any kind, although I had a bundle ready – like how buddy-buddy were she and Gregory and what did her friend, Patrick Redstart, think about it all. And then I had others to ask on Redstart himself. But it all had to wait. Miss Abigail Gordon had shut up shop – a few minutes later, quite literally.

It was easier walking downhill to my car. And the

cob looked a photographer's dream in the thin November sun. I stood and just looked at it for quite some time before I reached for my ignition keys. One has to get one's uppers where and when one can.

The afternoon I just had to spend in the shop, to keep the wolf from the door. (Sally Newton had offered to pay a small hourly rate for my help, but I had declined. First, because it didn't seem right, but more importantly, because then she would be counting hours of action and not really judging progress. For instance, would just sitting and thinking count for payment? Who knows?)

Anyway, that afternoon. I did just that. Sat and thought. Behind the counter. I only had one interruption and, thank the Lord, a worthwhile one. An elderly gentleman brought in a box of old toys he had found in his attic, whilst packing up his house to move into a nursing home in Branksome Chine. And it was a box of delights. Nearly all tinplate and dating from the twenties, varying from a lovely miniature Model T Ford by Bing (no relative of my cat) to a much larger Rolls-Royce by Jouets de Paris (later to become the famous JEP company) and a sleek Napier Campbell Bluebird II record car by the Kingsbury company of America. They were not mint, by any means, but nor were they so far gone to need the attention of Jimmy Richardson. Despite their chips and dents they were still pretty handsome and I instantly shelled out the asking price for the lot – a hundred pounds. But they were not destined for display in my shop. They went to the attic to await the next Christie's toy auction, where they might fetch anything up to one thousand or fifteen hundred pounds, given a good day.

But back to my sitting and thinking. Basically it was all pretty tangled and tenuous at this stage, so in the end I had to get out a piece of paper and jot down my

main lines of thought to make any sense of them. They
were as follows:

1) Why had Gregory disappeared? Was it voluntary or
involuntary? If the former, was he just hiding from
marriage with Sally or from some debts we know
nothing of or from another person or persons or from
some threat not yet identified?
2) If involuntary, what could be the cause?

a) An accident with his bike? Unlikely now so much
time had passed and no traces of him or his bike had
been found.

b) A kidnapping? Unlikely too, I felt, as kidnappings
usually end in ransom notes. And I didn't think Sally
or Gregory's family had that kind of loot.

c) Abduction, leading not to a ransom note but to a
death sentence? I decided it was a bit difficult to abduct
a man tearing through the countryside on a high-pow-
ered Honda, unless someone had known of his movements in advance and had thus had time to lay a credible
and effective ambush. But I didn't rule it out.

d) He had been injured or killed, intentionally or
accidentally, whilst in pursuit of some enquiry or other,
and his body and bike concealed somewhere. But what
enquiry? He had nothing marked down for that
Sunday, just a doodle. And Sally knew of no assignment that day. Anyway, Gregory had apparently said
he wouldn't be long and they had both planned to go
out to lunch that Sunday.

e) He had been killed in some hit-and-run accident
and the motorist or lorry driver involved had hidden
away Gregory's bike, so as to avoid any police action
against them. A bit unlikely, I thought, but who knows
what people can do in a panic?

Exhausted by my alternatives, I then wrote down a
list of people who might have a reason for wanting
Gregory out of the way. The list was headed, of course,

by Redstart. But I must admit, I was uneasy about his placing as it was almost entirely due to Gus's totally biased description of his reputation. The fact that it was not 'entirely due' was occasioned by my uphill visit to Abigail Gordon. She wasn't exactly the kind of sweet, unspoilt thing nice guys go out with. I'm not saying she was a siren exactly, but she did sound alarms in me about what any close man friend of hers would be like. I'm a great believer in birds of a feather.

So that left me with:

1) Redstart. He could have wanted Gregory out of the way for at least two reasons. Firstly, to stop his investigations. Secondly, to stop his dalliance with sweet Abigail.

2) Then there was Abigail herself. Gregory could have been on his way to see her that Sunday morning. And she had killed him, maybe, for trying to end their relationship, or whatever.

3) and 4) were the hairy head of Ferndales School, Jonathan Smythe, and the animal rights activist, Robert Stringle. Either of them could have a motive for silencing the persistent private eye.

5) My rag-bag of wild and woolly possibilities that had, unfortunately, to include Sally Newton herself. Wild, yes. Woolly, yes. But possible, nevertheless. (For a second I had even thought of including Philippa as she has obviously once been pretty close to Gregory Mann. But then I thought, if I did I would have to include almost everyone who had ever met Gregory in his lifetime and that was both ridiculous and beyond my meagre powers of deduction. Anyway, Philippa couldn't possibly have done it: that would be like suspecting a blood brother – or is it a blood sister? (Or these days, I guess, a blood person?)

In the rag-bag were also, would you believe, the girl Mann had stood up at the altar in the Midlands, any and every one of the seemingly unimportant clients in his files and perhaps, other clients we knew not of from his first gumshoe operation up north. Then Gregory Mann had lived abroad a bit before that. Maybe it was someone he had wronged out there, come back to England to take vengeance. . . .

Oh God, by this time my brain had begun going and I decided that sanity would only prevail if I restricted myself to those investigations that I could successfully attempt in my little area around Purbeck. After all, I was not a one-man Interpol and I didn't have access to those wonderful police computers that were in danger of substituting a policeman's intuition for his fingers on a keyboard. What's more, I also had to find time to earn a crust. (I wasn't like 'Ercool Parrot, who never seemed to have this worry. Was he on some pension, one wonders? Or did his Belgian parents leave him *bien-off*?)

Before I shut up shop for the day, I did make one last list – of those I would try to interview over the next few days and the order in which I would ideally place them.

That evening I sat through the Six O'clock News and looked through the programme listing in the *Independent* to find murders seemed to be the order of the day. The news had covered two in Belfast, three in the Middle East, and ten in a group massacre in Sacramento, California. And the evening's entertainment continued with a repeat of Miss Marple on BBC 1, *Murder She Wrote* on ITA, an investigation into sectarian killings on Channel 4 and a documentary on carnivorous plants on BBC 2. Besides, the evenings were when I missed Arabella most.

So I went around to Gus instead.

Our local was surprisingly full for a chill November evening, and Gus and I thought we would have trouble finding a seat. That is until Gus pulled his 'hitting his head on the beam' act. I've seen him do it at least three times before, and it's always worked. This time was no exception: a young couple I have never seen before immediately rose from a window-seat and offered Gus and, of course, me their nicely warmed places. I really felt guilty, but what could I say? I would have looked heartless if I had claimed that Gus's head-holding wobblings were simply all an act to get a seat. Besides, I'd have lost Gus's goodwill. To assuage my feelings of guilt, I added a round for the young couple, when I bought our two pints.

'You're shameless, Gus,' I hissed.

'More comfortable being shameless, isn't it?' he remarked, patting the soft cushions on which we were perched. 'Anyway, cheers.' He raised his glass and emptied half of it before I'd even picked up mine.

'So you haven't got very far, then?' he sniffed. I had brought him up to date with the Gregory case in the discomfort of his cottage, where I had come upon him washing his socks in Dettol because they'd accidentally fallen in the loo. (Gus has clothes lines in almost every room in the house. His ceilings look like those in department stores years ago. You know, when they had those overhead railways for getting you your change.)

'You can say that again,' I muttered. For once, he didn't. Another slurp of beer and he said, 'I've seen that Abi-whatsit woman, you know.'

'Have you? Where?'

'Hanging about Redstart's yacht. Mouth like a cavern, she had. Must be the same woman. Got in his red Jaguar like she owned it.'

'Perhaps she does.'

Gus guffawed. Only half the pub looked round at us.

'Women like that don't own anything. They're pilot fish and ruddy good at it, too. That's until their looks go, that is. Then they hang about in bars, waiting for their luck to change. Never does.' He turned to me with a knowing expression. 'But, in their prime, they can be as dangerous as ruddy sharks. So you watch out, old son. You ought to leave her to me.'

I blanched at the thought of Gus in the great maw of this man-eater. 'What makes you think you're shark repellent?'

He rolled up the sleeve of his sweater. 'See those little scars there.' He pointed to some small indentations nestling under the hairs on his arm. These I had never noticed before.

I frowned. 'They were made by a shark?'

He shook his head slowly to and fro. 'No, my son, by a woman. But I got away.'

His expression instantly changed from the super serious to the hysterically comic and he nudged me in the ribs. 'Got you going there, didn't I, old mate?' he wheezed.

And, sod it, he'd done it again. But he had given me an idea: I would take him with me when I went to see Redstart. Not because of Abigail, though. But because there might be nautical tricks that Redstart was pulling that I would never recognize, that Gus just might. I knew Gus would jump at the opportunity to go sleuthing. He always had, for under the thick sweater, there beat the heart of a regular thick gumshoe. Still, he had got me out of the odd tight corner in the past, I had to admit.

By the time I had at last persuaded Gus that it was his turn now to buy a round and he was up at the bar, I noticed the attention of a few of the regulars was directed at the door. I glanced across and was glad I did, for, lo and behold, here was the bewitching gipsy maiden who hadn't put eye of toad on my burnt ear on Guy Fawkes night. Towering in attendance was John-John, dwarfing a guitar he had slung across him. Merinda saw me almost immediately and came across, lugging a satchel full of what I took to be canvases.

'Hello,' she said, and quick as a flash, 'How's the ear?'

I rose from my seat and smiled a warm welcome.

'Fine. The plastic surgeons are very pleased with it. Here, come and sit down. It's nice to see you.'

She put down her satchel beside me. I was right. It was full of canvases. Then she leaned forward and whispered, 'I'd better not. Better get my singing over first, I think.'

'Singing?' I asked dumbly, then saw John-John's great fingers limbering up for an assault on his guitar strings.

She nodded. 'I only promise to stop if the customers buy one of my paintings,' she laughed.

I liked this girl. And a moment later, I realized, I liked her singing too. Normally I don't go for the folk song brigade any more than I go for Morris dancers, but Merinda's choice of songs was at least not about mining disasters in the nineteenth century, hunger-strikes and Tolpuddle-type martyrs, nor simple mind-edly rural nor Greensleeves with bells on. John-John, as they say, plucked a mean guitar, and by his granite presence alone would have prevented the occasion from ever being twee and embarrassing. Indeed, I've never seen our local so riveted by anything – save, perhaps, when the landlord was being given a Strip-o-gram for his last birthday.

Gus sat silent save for the slurps, throughout, and applauded with the rest at the end.

'That's the one you told me about, isn't it?' he stated and asked, all in one. 'The one who mended your ear. Saw you talking to her when I was getting the last round.' He emphasized the word 'last' and, of course, his glass was now empty again. Then he went on, 'Didn't you tell me she lived in a caravan over Corfe way?' He pointed to John-John. 'That her boyfriend then? Must be a bloody big caravan.'

'Thank you, Gus,' I muttered and struggled across to the bar with our two glasses. As I passed, I asked the performers, who, by the tinkle of the coins in John-John's cap were faring well, what they would like.

After considerable protestation, they conceded that two lagers would suit them. So I returned to Gus with four glasses, which he interpreted as saving him the next round. I hated to disillusion him.

After the collection, Merinda and John-John sang a few more numbers by request, then joined Gus and me by the window. To my amazement, Gus actually offered up his seat and Merinda accepted it. After the necessary introductions, I asked Merinda if I could look at some of her canvases. She nodded and moved the satchel nearer me.

I won't bore you with detailed descriptions of every painting in the satchel. Suffice it to say, they were quite as remarkable as Philippa had described them and I could see instantly why she wanted to hang them in her craft centre. It wasn't Merinda's deft brushwork or the attractive rural settings of each painting, but her style that was so stunning – her choice of angle, proximity of point of interest and unusual arrangement of elements.

In a way, Merinda was doing with paint what the world's most inspired cameramen and film directors achieve through a lens. They select and arrange with such startling vision that the viewer is forced to evaluate the familiar all over again. Then, as if that weren't enough, in some of her paintings, but not all, she had added a surrealistic element, like the two-headed gull Philippa had already described to me. For instance, in one work depicting the old Sandbanks ferry as seen across the Studland dunes, she had added a detached motor car headlamp alight on the sands. In another, a landscape with hay lying in the right foreground under black polythene weighed down by car tyres to prevent it blowing away, she had left the car wheels on the tyres and some were still complete with hubcaps. Curiously, the effect was never odd, just compelling.

I asked her the price of the landscape, which I found almost as attractive as its creator.

'Forty-five,' she replied, hesitantly.

'Is that all?' I exclaimed.

'Well, you know the paints cost quite a bit now and . . .'

I touched her arm. 'No, I mean it. Forty-five pounds is kind of ridiculous. You could get much more, Merinda, if you . . .'

'Forty-five is enough,' she said quietly, but firmly. 'I don't want more.'

I didn't argue. Merinda had a calm strength about her that it would have been folly, and almost immoral, to fight.

'I suppose cheques aren't any good?' I asked. 'I would like to buy the landscape.'

She looked up at John-John. 'We don't have a bank.'

'Can I give you cash tomorrow?'

She handed me the painting. 'Any time.'

'Tell me exactly where your caravan is and I'll drop it by tomorrow morning.'

She explained and then John-John added, 'When we've shown Merinda's work to a few more people here, why don't you and your friend come back to our van this evening and share some supper with us? Then you'll know exactly where we are.'

I fell for the idea immediately, but I had to check out Gus. 'Sounds great, don't you think, Gus?' I said between as clenched teeth as wouldn't be too obvious.

Gus scratched his head. 'Is it wet?' he said.

'What's that got to do with anything, Gus?' I asked irritably.

'Well, you know . . .'

I didn't know, but Merinda was on his wavelength, clever girl.

'We've got some beers in the van,' she smiled. 'It's not dry.'

'Ah, well then,' said Gus. But we bought a couple of six packs from the bar as well, so that we wouldn't drink them out of caravan and home.

To Gus's relief, we didn't have to journey far afield. In fact, the field in which the caravan rested was only just off the rather charming road that led from Studland to Corfe, cutting off Swanage to its left. The Beetle bounded up the muddy track and I blessed the fact that, with the engine at the rear, I had plenty of traction.

In the headlights, the caravan looked a good deal better than I had been expecting; so used had I become to those rotting hulks one sees in summer solstice convoys on television, that I was pleasantly surprised by its smart, almost Caravan-Club condition – even though its soft and pleasantly rounded shape betrayed its real age.

We were soon inside and sitting at the rectangular table that, I assume, became the floor of the double bed our seats would become at night. Heinekens poured (we insisted on opening our purchases first), I asked John-John how they fared finding sites for the van.

'It's getting harder all the time. All that Stonehenge publicity has got people like us a bad name. Even though we always travel on our own, we are lumped together with the "hippie convoy" lot in everyone's mind.'

'How did you hit on this site?'

'By accident. We wanted to winter in Dorset this year, and we were just touring around and saw this track. We got out and walked up it and found it ended in a little wedge of land, totally overgrown with brambles, nettles and weeds. It didn't look as though the spot had been cared for by anyone for donkey's years. So we stayed. I went to work with a hook and cleared the place up a bit. It looks pretty good now – in the daylight.'

'And you will be here until the spring, anyway?' I asked innocently.

Merinda sighed. 'That was the plan but I can't be certain now. We've had the odd objection.'

'Who from?' Gus asked, rather belligerently, as if he were willing to offer any objector a knuckle sandwich.

'Two or three people. There's a headmaster of some school or other, who has written to the *Western Gazette*, saying caravans have spoilt Dorset enough already without us. And one day someone left a nasty note pinned to our door. Oh, and a council man came round, complaining that we were trespassing on private land, which isn't, apparently, true. John-John looked into it and the track is a public footpath and this little wedge seems to be owned by no one.'

'That explained why it was so neglected,' John-John remarked, then, with a broad smile, added, 'So you could say, Merinda and I have become land developers, couldn't you?'

I looked across at Merinda. In the soft glow of the gas mantle, the unstudied naturalness of her beauty was almost painful. Eat your heart out, Rossetti, that you died before laying eyes on her.

'Where will you go if you have to move on?'

'I don't know,' she said quietly. 'Lady Philippa has offered us a site behind her barn, but we don't like to bother her.'

'And we always prefer to be on our own,' John-John added, 'away from people, however much we love or like them.'

Yet again, I envied them but knew, deep down, I needed others too much to ever live totally free.

I decided to change the subject, for my questions were seeming to put a damper on the evening. I pointed to a painting that was hanging on what I took to be a wardrobe door. 'What is that of?' I asked.

'Oh, round here. Up the road, in fact. There's a lovely old barn. I discovered it when I was looking to see if there were any late mushrooms about.'

I got up to have a closer look at it: a lovely old barn in one corner of a steeply rising field, but as you might imagine, she had added a surrealistic touch – a real dog climbing up the thatch of the roof.

'It's very striking. But I prefer my tyres around the hay,' I smiled and sat down again. But my change of tack worked and from then on the evening really took off, all worries forgotten. At least, that is, for the time being.

Much later, in the wee small hours, as we drove unsteadily away, I turned to Gus and said, in my all aglow mood, 'Aren't they nice, Merinda and John-John? I wonder what their other names are. Maybe they don't have them. Or even need them. Come to think of it, you and I don't really need ours. You're Gus; I'm Peter . . . or maybe you should be Gus-Gus and me Peter-Peter. That's funny, now you sound better than I do . . . So let's put Tribble and Marklin away in some dustbin somewhere. Gus-Gus and Peter. Singular Peter's better.'

I leaned further towards Gus. 'Don't you think so, Gus-Gus?'

He didn't reply. 'Gus, don't you think so?'

It was then I heard the snores. Gus goes to sleep even quicker than a peer in the House of Lords. As I was straightening myself again in my seat, I was suddenly blinded by a blazing light that seemed to be right in front of my bonnet. My instincts, rather than my befuddled mind, responded and I swung the wheel violently to the left. The Beetle crumped up against the bank and came to a tilting halt as I heard a motor bike roar past me and back down the road.

'What the bloody hell . . .?' Sleeping Beauty bellowed, and well might he ask. At 2.30 of a winter's night on that sleepy road, you'd be as likely to see a giraffe as any other traffic.

6

Next morning – sorry, later the same morning – and did I regret having dossed down so late – I answered the post. Not the bills, just the queries about what toys I had currently in stock. One was from a nutter who wondered if I had a mint boxed Marklin Junkers 52 constructor set of 1939 vintage. I replied '*Nein*' and that his only chance to get one of those was to follow a few international auctions. Even unboxed examples are next door to gold dust.

Then, with a reluctant sigh, I rang the number of Patrick Redstart's home in Bournemouth, which I had learned from Gregory's files. A snooty woman answered and said he was out. I asked if he was at his boat. To which I received a bad tempered, 'Might be. I couldn't say. He doesn't tell me where he's going.'

So I decided to take a chance. I got in the Beetle and went down to Gus's. Needless to say, his place was as quiet (and as welcoming) as a tomb. It took eleven stones to wake him up. I thought the window would shatter before he surfaced.

However, about a quarter of an hour later, Gus yawned into my Beetle and we sped off down the dune road to the ferry.

'Now, Gus, please don't say anything unless I give you a lead, right?'

He snorted. 'I'm not your dog, you know. If you don't want me to speak, why've you hoicked me out of bed?'

'To keep your eyes and ears peeled. You know about boats and all that Jack Tar stuff; I don't.'

'Supposing he's not at his boat. Could be at one of his ruddy junk shops, specially since you say that fancy piece of his lives over one of them.'

'He could be anywhere, Gus,' I said irritably. 'But as his main business is boats, not junk, I'm starting with the best bet.'

Gus sniffed. 'If he was Chinese, he could do both together.'

I pulled up as I reached the short queue of cars waiting for the ferry.

'What on earth are you talking about now, Gus?'

'Well,' he chortled, 'Junk shops must sell boats in China, mustn't they?'

I almost collapsed over the wheel. We didn't speak again until we reached Poole harbour.

For once, the odds favoured me. I saw the red xjs before I had even parked the Beetle. We strolled over to the moored yacht as nonchalantly as anyone with Gus in tow can, for I didn't wish to introduce myself until I'd had a chance to get the feel of the situation.

Here, the odds were against me. There was no one to be seen on the immaculate deck of the *Buccaneer*, though we could detect lights in the cabin. In the sharp winter wind, the clinking of the rigging was almost eerie and did nothing to calm my nerves.

'Well, go on then,' urged Gus, giving me a prod that almost saw me in the harbour.

'All right. Now don't crowd me, Gus.'

He looked around, as if to see if there were any others behind him – an old comedian's gag, but it made me smile all the same. Feeling better immediately, I stepped onto the deck and made for the cabin. I could hear Gus's dainty footfalls right behind me and it must have been those that triggered the shout.

'That you, Abby?'

I just hated to disappoint him.

'No, I'm sorry, I'm not.' (Don't take that literally.)

77

A moment later, the cabin doors opened to reveal an impossibly smart blazer atop razor-sharp white trousers. Atop the blazer was a head that you (or your father) used to see in Brylcreem adverts. Slicked hair, regular features and a neatly trimmed moustache, all adding up to absolutely nothing. Age around thirty-five, I guessed. He looked as if he had stepped straight out of a forties movie, a B movie. I shook my head in disbelief.

'Patrick Redstart?'

He smiled, and even in the November light I was dazzled by his teeth.

'Who might be asking for him?'

''E is,' Gus growled, giving me another of his subtle prods.

'And who might you be?'

'I might be Peter Marklin,' I smiled and stilled Gus from making another helpful contribution.

Redstart's eyes narrowed. 'I don't know you, do I?'

'No, not yet. But then I don't know you yet. I take it, however, that *you* are Patrick Redstart?'

'Marklin,' he repeated, then suddenly his whole expression changed for the worse, as did his voice. 'Peter Marklin. Now I know you. You're the busybody who called on Miss Abigail Gordon the other day, aren't you?'

'I had the pleasure,' I lied.

He came out of the cabin and shut the doors behind him.

'Get off my boat, Marklin. You and that – heavy of yours.'

I laughed out loud at the thought of Gus being described as *a* heavy. Heavy without the preceding 'a', maybe.

'You won't be laughing in a minute, if you don't get off my boat.' As his anger mounted, Redstart's accent started to slip. Dorset was beating Oxford hands down.

'Have the police been round yet?' I tried.

'Mr Marklin, whether the police have been to see me or not is nothing to do with you. For your information, anyone who has the misfortune to have a boat blow up under him, as I did recently, naturally sees the police, amongst others.'

His tone was softening, somewhat. He went on, 'I gather from Abigail you are not really interested in boats, but a Mr Gregory Mann. That correct?'

I nodded but said nothing. I wanted to hear what he had to say.

'Well I, like Abigail, have not laid eyes on Mr Mann for some days. Where he is we have no idea. What's more, we care even less. Mr Mann was an inquisitive nobody who was getting nowhere with his enquiries into my affairs and knew it–'

'Then why did he have another appointment fixed to see you?' I had to interrupt.

'Oh, that,' he smiled. 'I guess it must have been one final fling to try to justify his fee to his client. Who knows?'

I thought for a second, then asked, 'Did you know Gregory Mann was seeing Abigail?'

He frowned, 'Mr Mann met Abigail on one occasion when he was with me – on this boat. He seemed to be attracted to her, so I asked Abigail to see him alone one day, to discover whether there was more to Mr Mann's enquiries than met the eye.'

'Oh, so you knew about their meeting then?'

'Not only knew, planned and fixed it.' He moved towards me. 'Now, Mr Marklin, I have other things to do today than chat to strangers. So if you wouldn't mind. . . .'

'Abigail's due, isn't she? You thought I might be her.'

I wanted to stall, if possible, until Abigail arrived so I could throw her a certain question before Redstart had briefed her on the answer – like was her pub meeting with Gregory planned and fixed by her or Redstart? I couldn't tell from his cold eyes whether he was lying or not.

Redstart came right up to me. The aftershave was somewhat overpowering. I nudged Gus.

'Errm,' Gus began and stood between me and lover-boy, 'we haven't been introduced, have we?'

Redstart looked a little nonplussed. 'Look, that's neither here nor there. Now will you both please get off my boat.'

Gus held out a hand. 'Augustus Tribble.'

Redstart made the mistake of trying to push the hand aside. He was gripped as if by a vice.

'Now we know each other, like,' Gus continued, without loosening his grip, 'how about you telling us where *you* think this Mr Mann has gone?'

'I don't know. I really don't know. Now let me go and. . . .'

'Come on, Mr Redstart, have a guess.'

I was starting to admire Gus's style. Maybe he would make a good heavy after all.

'He could have gone anywhere . . . anywhere. After all, he had the – ' Redstart stopped suddenly.

'Had the what?' I chipped in. Lover-boy's eyes flickered. 'Er . . . had the whole world to choose from, didn't he?'

'That wasn't what you were going to say, was it?' I said firmly. 'Now, come on. Tell me – ' I stopped as I saw Redstart's eyes light up with relief. I looked behind me, then prodded Gus to release the captive hand. For getting out of an all white Peugeot 205 on the quay was the swivel mouthed lady we had been stalling to meet.

'Gus, you might like to talk boats with our friend here for a moment, whilst I chat to Abigail.'

He got the message, bless him, and stood barring the way, whilst I disembarked quickly to catch my quarry before she'd have a chance to change her mind and leave.

'Miss Gordon,' I said, standing by the open door of the Peugeot, so she couldn't get back in. 'I won't detain you long. I would just like to ask you a question or two.'

'God, not you again!' she exclaimed. In the open air, she looked far older and less seductive than she had in the gloom of her shop.

'Yes, me again.'

She made to get on the yacht, but I held her arm. 'No, please, I need to check one or two things.'

She looked daggers at me. 'I've answered enough questions over the last twenty-four hours to last a lifetime. I'm not answering any more.'

'Police?' I queried and knew from her expression that I had hit home. 'I'm not the police,' I smiled gently. 'Just a friend, trying to find another person's friend. I don't care a damn about you or your boyfriend here. I'm just trying to track down where Gregory Mann might be.'

'I don't know anything about Greg – Mr Mann.'

'But I know you and he met alone in some pub, not long before he disappeared.'

She looked nervously towards the yacht. 'We didn't . . . Er, it's not true. I've never met . . . er . . . this Mr Mann alone. Why should I?'

She was really rattled now, presumably in case lover-boy overheard any of the exchange. I let go of her arm. In effect, she had now told me what I wanted to know. Hey-ho, I was now dealing with two liars.

'I don't know,' I said. 'Maybe because you like the way his eyes dance.'

She shook her head and almost tripped in her hurry to get on the boat. I saw Gus move aside from Redstart as she approached the cabin. But he stayed on board long enough to give her a good look up and down. There was life in the old salt yet.

'Thanks, Gus,' I said, as we went back to where I had parked the Beetle.

'That's all right,' he sniffed. 'Find out what you want from her ladyship?'

'Not all I want. But enough to confirm what I suspected. She was two-timing Redstart, or on the verge of it.'

'With old Gregory? But back there, that poncey sod said he knew all about it. Fixed it, he said.'

'He was lying. Probably to save his Brylcreemed pride.'

We got in the Beetle and I was pleased to be out of the wind. It was proving a colder November than I had known in a long time.

''Ere, on the way back,' Gus said, as I turned the ignition key, 'show me where this Gregory fella works, will you? I ain't never set eyes on a detective place before.'

'Okay,' I agreed. 'I was going to drop by and see Sally anyway. Let her know I was "on the job", so to speak.'

When we arrived, Gus was most disappointed that the place was all black glass so he couldn't see in. I was disappointed Sally seemed to be out and the whole place locked up. Still, I should have warned her I might drop by.

Before I left, I popped into the newsagents next door to buy a copy of *Practical Classics*, which a customer had told me was running a series on restoring Daimlers like my own. (Bit late now, really, as mine was already at the top coat stage, but interesting, nevertheless. At least I could read all the things I'd done wrong.) Whilst I was about it, I also bought that week's copy of our local rag. I glanced at the front page. There seemed to be nothing of note except a further spate of burglaries that still baffled the police. That burglaries should be my problem, I thought. At least only things go missing, not people.

As I pulled up the rise after dropping Gus, I saw Sally

Newton's car outside my Toy Emporium. I quickly dumped the Beetle round the back, and ran round to the front to let her in.

'I'm sorry to drop by unannounced, Peter,' she began, but I cut her apologies short by a peck on the cheek.

'I can hardly complain,' I grinned. 'I'd just come back from trying to do the same with you.'

But I could see my *bonhomie* was not working. The only thing she bounced back at me was a double-knitted frown.

'What's the matter?'

'I've had the police again.'

'Whetstone?'

'Yes.'

'What is he asking now?'

'He didn't ask anything, really. It's what he told me.'

I put my arm around her shoulder, opened up shop and shepherded her in. I had a feeling that what she was about to impart, needed a chair not a pavement. And I was, for once, right.

I wouldn't let Sally say anything more until I had poured Scotches for both of us. Then, when we were both ensconced in my modest sitting-room, I kicked off.

'Okay, Sally, so what did Whetstone say?'

Her eyes started to blink in treble-quick time.

'Oh, Peter, I don't know what it all means. . . .'

I transferred my chair to sit next to her on the settee. I took one slender hand in mine. 'Now, try not to cry. Just start at the beginning and tell me exactly what Whetstone said.'

She took a deep breath. 'He didn't say very much, really. They weren't with me long. He just asked if I knew the state of Greg's finances.'

'And did you?'

'I thought I did. I told him that almost everything we earned was going into restoring the cottage, so we didn't really have much besides. In fact, I said I knew Greg was worried about the size of his overdraft at the Midland. He had joked about soon being a "listening customer". It was then the Inspector told me.' She gripped my hand tightly.

'Told you what, Sally?'

'About the ten thousand pounds.'

'What ten thousand pounds?' I asked, somewhat alarmed.

She looked round at me and shook her head. A tear started its run down her cheek.

'I don't know *what* ten thousand pounds. The Inspector said that from enquiries he had made at Greg's bank in Bournemouth, Greg had paid in ten thousand pounds in cash on the Friday before he disappeared. Oh God, Peter, what on earth does it all mean?'

She was now in full flood and I could do nothing but hug her to me.

'Perhaps it's a payment from some client or other.'

'It can't be from any I know about. He's never, ever had a fee that big, anyway.'

'Maybe it's a new client,' I persevered. 'One he hasn't got around to telling you about yet.' I didn't really believe it when I said it and, more's the pity, nor did she.

'He tells me about every client.'

But not about everybody he meets, I thought, though kept it to myself.

'Anyway,' Sally continued through her tears, 'Greg would have told me about a huge windfall like that, wouldn't he? He wouldn't keep it to himself, especially as we have often discussed how much more the cottage was setting us back than we'd thought – and how he really needed a more reliable car than the Stag for his work, but couldn't afford it.'

All I could think of to say was, 'I'm sure Gregory had a good reason for not telling you at the time. Maybe he was saving it up as a big surprise for later.'

She suddenly pulled herself together and sat up straight. Wiping her eyes with a minute hanky, she said, 'You know what I think?'

I shook my head. I didn't know what I thought, let alone what she thought. And her changing from mood to mood only helped to confuse.

'Greg never had any real intention of marrying me.'

'Oh, I'm sure – ' I began.

But she went on, 'No, I've noticed recently that he's been less willing to talk about our wedding whenever I've brought it up. I sort of kidded myself nothing had changed, but it had. I realize it now. Greg was going to do to me what he did to that poor girl up north. I see it all . . . Shit, the bastard.'

Fury now was overlaying distress and the hanky was tucked back in her sleeve. I didn't know quite how to react, but her comments certainly seemed to fit some of the evidence.

'But all this, true or not, Sally, doesn't answer where the ten thousand pounds could have come from.'

'As he didn't tell me about the ten thousand pounds, maybe there are a million other things about which I know nothing.'

'Such as?'

'Other clients he hasn't told me about. Maybe even . . . kickbacks.'

I noticed she hesitated to use the word bribes. Ten thousand pounds in cash, kept hush-hush, certainly felt like some sort of sweetener to me. But from whom? Someone we knew about or someone we didn't? Only the good Lord knew and He wasn't telling right now.

'You surely think Greg is straight, don't you?' I asked, remembering those dancing eyes.

She sniffed. 'I used to think so.'

I put my arm reassuringly round her shoulder.

'Go on thinking so, Sally. We haven't found out otherwise yet.'

She looked up at me. 'He's not going to come back, you know. I can feel it.'

I felt it now too. But not, I guess, for the same reasons or with the same estimation of what he might now be doing. I shivered. My version saw Gregory embraced not by some other lover, but by the skeletal arms of death, for the news of the money had somehow, for me, altered everything. I prayed my instincts were wrong.

My thoughts were suddenly splintered by her next statement.

'Kiss me, Peter.'

I looked at her. Her face was very close, her eyes closed, her beautiful mouth slightly open.

'Sally, I – ' But that's as far as I got, for her tongue made further speech impossible. I didn't respond (voluntarily, that is) and I didn't resist. Thinking herself spurned, I supposed she needed instant reassurance of her own independence, her own sexual attraction.

After a minute or so, she rested her head against my shoulder and said softly, 'Peter, I hope I haven't upset you.'

'No,' I said. 'I understand.'

'It won't make any difference, will it?'

'No,' I lied. 'It won't make any difference.'

By the time I had seen Sally off the premises, grabbed something to eat and fed Bing, it was too late to go to Swanage to get some money from the bank to pay Merinda.

I ferreted in the till in the shop, but didn't really have enough to cover Merinda's painting and give customers change. So my trip to the caravan had to be postponed. I hoped Merinda would understand.

In a way, I was relieved. Sally's visit had unsettled me in more ways than one. And the only way I could imagine I'd get settled again was to get on with finding out what the hell had happened to her boyfriend. So I also put off going to see Jimmy Richardson to review his progress on my possessions and decided to spend what remained of the afternoon with the hairy monster from the Ferndales prospectus, if he would see me.

As I was about to put digit in dial, I realized I might well get more or less the same reception from him as I had from Redstart if I attempted a full frontal: 'I'm enquiring into the disappearance. . . . So I took a leaf from Gregory's notes in his file and gave myself an instant family – and a rather awkward daughter of four-teen, called Tanya. And I discovered what I had sur-mised. There's nothing like the glint of fat fees for instant access to a headmaster's study.

Even in the chill and cheerless grey of a November afternoon, Ferndales impressed. Mind you, rambling Elizabethan mansions set in countless tonsured acres have a tendency to do this. As I parked my Beetle next to a 700 series BMW, I realized my mistake and prayed the hairy one's study did not overlook the interminable drive. For small, seventeen-year-old, yellow cars do not normally signal the kind of wealth needed to incar-cerate a child in these sumptuous surroundings. But it was a bit late then to hide the Volks in any bushes, so I took a deep breath and pulled what looked like a Spanish Inquisition lavatory chain hanging down by the oak studded door.

A moment later, I was met by a middle-aged woman with a dour and doomsday expression who whisked me down a long clattery corridor to the headmaster's study. She knocked, then opened the door.

'Mr Marklin, Headmaster.'

'Thank you, Miss Antrim.'

I stepped forward gingerly and the door was closed behind me.

Jonathan Smythe, the hairy one, proved to be much shorter than the giant I'd been expecting. (I later realized that in the group photograph I had seen in the prospectus with all the staff seated, he had actually been standing up.) His head was large though, or seemed so with all the jungle growing over it. The only bit that was not sprouting hair, sprouted glasses. My initial impression of him was a complete blank. Certainly, if you're male and want to hide, throw away your razor.

We shook hands – he limply, me normally. Formalities over, he put me in a chair opposite his rather gross Victorian desk, and soon got down to brass tacks.

'Have you seen a copy of our prospectus?' He smiled his questions. I could guess why.

I crossed my legs, suddenly very conscious of the cut of my Marks and Sparks trousers, the only conventional pants I possess, jeans or track suits being my usual bent.

'Someone lent me one, yes,' I replied.

'So you are aware of all our facilities and our . . . er, scale of fees and so on.'

I sighed inwardly. I'd been bothered about him seeing my car. But my clothes labels (or lack of them) obviously said more than any car badge, mascot or registration plate.

'Yes, of course, I would like to see all these things at first hand. You know, prospectuses, however good, can only give a glimpse . . .'

'Understandably.' He took off his glasses and started to clean them with a maroon handkerchief from his breast pocket. I had a feeling he had lost interest in me already.

'Would you like me to arrange the full tour today – it takes about an hour and a half.' He breathed on his glasses. 'Or shall we make that another time, perhaps.'

I pretended to consult my watch. Hell, that was another thing I'd forgotten. My paper-thin, diamond-studded Piaget.

'Yes, another time I think,' quickly pulling down my blazer sleeve over my Sekonda. (Gus gave it to me. Said he'd found it in a car park.)

'Your daughter. . . .'

88

'Tanya,' I smiled.

'Tanya, ah yes. Fourteen, you say. Where is she at school at present?'

Like a fool I hadn't prepared for that one.

'Er, abroad,' I said rather too quickly. 'Erm . . . South Africa.'

He replaced his now squeaky clean glasses.

'Ah yes. Over the years, we've had quite a few girls from Africa. Indeed, there are a few here at this present time. So I might well know your daughter's school.'

Hell, I should have said Outer Mongolia.

'I doubt if you will know this one. It's sort of up in the highlands, miles from anywhere.'

He frowned. 'I thought the highlands were in Kenya?'

'They are . . . they are. I use the word highlands in the colloquial sort of way my daughter describes the district. It's not it's official name.'

I was getting a trifle desperate now. If I didn't get round to my point soon, I'd be out on my ear before I had gleaned even a single reaction.

'Anyway,' I continued, 'there are a few questions I would like to ask you, if you don't mind, before I go into the full educational history of my daughter.'

Smythe relaxed back in his chair. 'Fire away, Mr Marklin, fire away.'

I fired. 'Whilst I am extremely attracted to what I know of the very progressive and liberal philosophy of your school – I consider it may be the atmosphere that Tanya has been sadly lacking in South Africa – I did hear a rumour the other day which did rather disturb me.'

'Rumour, Mr Marklin?' he queried. I wished I'd been an instant barber, so that I could have discovered what expression lay under the hair entanglements.

'Yes, rumour, Mr Smythe.' My confidence was on the turn. 'And not an unworrying one where the entrusting of one's daughter is concerned.'

Now he leant forward at the desk, his hairy hands clasped together.

'I cannot imagine what you have heard, Mr Marklin. Our school record is second to none. Pray tell me what is concerning you, so that I may put your mind at rest.'

I wondered if he had put anything else at rest recently. Like Gregory Mann. I looked at him intently, as I went on.

'Well, I may be worrying about nothing, but the rumour has it that Ferndales is under some kind of investigation.'

Drat. Nothing yet.

'Investigation? What do you mean by investigation?'

I shrugged. 'Well, you know how rumours are. Not exactly specific. Someone knew someone who knew somebody else, type of thing, who said they had heard that one of the parents here was employing a private detective to look into what was going on at this school. Naturally, I don't put much credence in such a loose chain of information, but I thought it was worth mentioning.'

'Going *on* at this school?' Smythe queried, playing with a ring nestling in the fur of his finger. 'Private detectives?' He broke into laughter. 'Really, Mr Marklin, I haven't heard such a good one for years. Worthy of television, don't you think?'

His tone and eyes abruptly went serious. 'Private schools, Mr Marklin, have always had to suffer from malicious stories made up by those less fortunate than ourselves. The painful subject comes up year after year at our National Independent School Conferences, but we have never found a solution. I fear there may never be one. Envy, I'm sorry to say, will always be one of the curses of mankind.'

'I dare say you're right, Mr Smythe. And I wouldn't have given the rumour any time of day, had it not been elaborated a little further.'

'Oh?'

As he stopped fiddling with his ring, I noticed his hand shook slightly. Only a crumb, but I was starving for a reaction by now.

'And what else did envy create, Mr Marklin?'

'It created the disappearance of said private eye.'

I thought something blinked under an eyebrow.

'Disappearance?'

'Yes. The man investigating the school is said to have vanished and that the whole affair is now in the hands of the police.'

Smythe rose slowly from his seat and equally slowly came round to my side of the desk.

'Could I see a picture of your Tanya, Mr Marklin?'

The question took me by surprise.

'No . . . I . . . er . . . haven't got one on me. Anyway, I would like to get back to this rumour, Mr Smythe.'

'Are you sure you've got a daughter, Mr Marklin? Or just an insatiable curiosity about affairs that are nothing to do with you?'

I stood up. Short as he was, I felt uneasy at not being on equal terms with him – especially now that he seemed to have rumbled me.

'I am concerned about this rumour, Mr Smythe, and I am not the only one. Do you deny that the police have been to see you about this affair?'

Now he was closer, the anger in his eyes was only too plain to see.

'I have no need to confirm or deny anything, Mr Marklin. Now I would suggest you leave. For whether or not you actually have a daughter has become quite irrelevant. Luckily, we independent schools are still allowed, more or less, to pick and choose our pupils. And I have the distinct feeling your Tanya will never be amongst that select number.'

He reached across to his desk and pressed a buzzer.

'Miss Antrim will show you out. Good day, Mr Marklin, whoever you are.'

'The police have got you that rattled, have they?' I tried, praying that Miss Antrim was too busy practising her scowls to answer the buzzer immediately.

'The police and I have a perfect understanding, my dear sir. Don't worry your pretty head about it.'

'So you admit they've been round?'

He started to herd me towards the door, but I no longer felt sheepish. I tried a long shot.

'Did you get your Board of Governor's agreement before you shelled out the ten thousand? If you didn't, they might spank.'

'What on earth are you talking about now?'

He made to press the buzzer on his desk once more, but, in his agitation, missed. I laughed and left, before Miss Antrim had got her dismissal act together. When I got outside, I saw what looked like a gardener peering at my Beetle. He leaned on his leaf rake, making room for me to get in.

'Like old cars?' I asked.

He nodded. 'Better than they new 'uns.'

I agreed. 'There was a nice Triumph Stag here the other day, I'm told.'

He thought for a minute. 'That's right. Came twice, it did, as I remember. Always liked the old Stag. Belong to a friend of yours?'

'Sort of,' I said.

He furrowed his forehead even further. 'Don't think he will be coming here again, though, somehow.'

I perked up. 'What makes you say that?'

He looked around cautiously, then sidled right up to my door.

'Saw them at it, cats and dogs, I did.'

'Who?'

'The Stag man and Mr Smythe.'

'When?'

'Second time he came.'

'They were fighting?' I asked, incredulously.

This time the wrinkles formed into a smile. 'Not

92

with fists, exactly, but if words could kill,' he chortled, 'they'd both be dead by now.'

I was tempted to tell him he might be half right.

'Hear what it was about?'

''Ere, you won't tell your friend I told you, will you? Might get me into trouble, you see. Don't want to lose my job.'

I heard a bell ring somewhere in the great house, soon followed by the distant sound of young voices and laughter. I knew I couldn't retain the old retainer much longer.

'No, I promise you. Quick, tell me did you hear what the quarrel was about?'

He eyed the house nervously. 'Not rightly. Just bits and pieces. I don't hear so good these days.'

'What were the bits and pieces?'

He licked his cracked lips and put his head almost inside my window. 'I heard Mr Smythe shout that he'd put paid to this friend of yours, if he didn't stop whatever he was doing. I didn't catch the end of it, but your mate replied something like, 'It would take more than shouting to stop me now.' Hammer and tongs, they were. Mr Smythe's got a hell of a temper, you know. I wouldn't want to cross him.'

The noise of children suddenly grew louder and the gardener just as suddenly withdrew from the car and started to rake the odd autumn leaf off the fine gravel.

'Thanks,' I said, then put my finger to my lips. 'I won't get you into hot water. Don't worry.'

He raised his eyebrows and moved with the measured tread of all rural gardeners further along the drive.

I started up my Beetle and crunched back to the main road. It was starting to get dark and the air was icy as it threaded through the gaps in my convertible top. I sighed and donned my gloves. Just everything was making me feel I was in for a long, hard winter.

7

That evening, after ringing Sally to give her an update on my activities and checking on her news (nothing, damn it), I just had to spend a little time 'looking after number one', as my mother used to term it, for I had a swapmeet on the morrow over in Weymouth.

Swapmeets are where all toy collectors gather to buy and sell their beloved treasures. They're big business nowadays and on any one weekend throughout the year, there is usually a choice of three or four to go to nationwide. They are a must if you have to make a living out of your passion. This one meant a sparrow-fart start in the morning to have all my goodies unpacked and displayed on my tables before the doors of the hall opened to the public. So I had to pack up the stock I was taking the night before. It's imperative to take a fairly wide and catholic selection, both in type and price range, so that you end up with a reasonable profit at the end of the day. I've known some traders who specialized too much, ending up by not even covering their expenses in going.

But I must say, my heart wasn't really in what I was doing that night and the task seemed to take forever. Somehow, I felt I shouldn't be toying around, so to speak, when there were much more serious and adult matters to attend to – like what the hell had happened to Gregory Mann and what had triggered his disappearance.

Bing woke me before the radio alarm on Saturday morning. (I'll swear he knows when I have to get up early. And he is less of a shock than the radio. What's more, he doesn't need batteries.) I rose reluctantly, completed the *three* 's's and fed my alarm clock and myself, before the sun had even tipped his head over the horizon.

Then I suddenly remembered I hadn't yet paid Merinda for her picture and banks were shut on a Saturday. (My cashcard was undoubtedly somewhere in the house, but I hadn't set eyes on it for at least two years.) I comforted myself that I would earn more than enough from my swapmeet sales to drop in some cash at the caravan on my way home from Weymouth. The Gregory Mann case was starting to rot my brain. I had a feeling I had better solve it quickly or retire to, as Edna Everage would term it, a home for the bewildered.

With a groan that must have worried shipping in the Channel, I went into my shop to gather up my packages of toys. As I did so, I saw the red of a Post Office Escort strobe past the windows and stop. A second later, the letters plopped onto my door mat. A quick flip through them revealed the usual assortment – queries from toy collectors, queries on old bills that were owing and bright new bills. But the last in the bunch was the best: a well filled envelope with a San Francisco postmark. I looked at my watch. It was still only 7.10 a.m. I had time to linger with Arabella.

I won't bore you with graphic details of the ten pages. Suffice it to say, despite her seemingly hectic schedule, both professionally and privately, working hard, playing hard the all-American way, she still loved me enough to say she would exchange all the blue skies, all the excitement and glamour and material rewards of the sunshine State, just for an afternoon by the fire in a November Studland. (She did add she would like me there too, just to help feed her fire when it needed it.) And in a postscript, she said she was sending separately a parcel of pre-war die-cast Tootsietoys that she had picked up in an old junk shop in a place called Walnut Creek.

Arabella's missive both cheered me up and sorted my brain out a bit, despite my slight concern about the frenzied nature of her leisure hours. Who exactly were inviting her to all these tennis parties, yachting trips, High Sierra weekends and hunting high-jinks in Oregon? I prayed they were all at least a hundred years of age and as ugly as sin. Whoops, perhaps not sin. I determined to pen a reply the second I arrived back from Weymouth.

As, with a somewhat lighter heart, I started to carry my carefully cartoned merchandise out to the Beetle, I heard the phone ringing in the hall. It was the last thing I wanted to hear in my new mood, for ting-a-lings before eight usually turn out to be calls you hate. This was no exception. It was guess who but her voice for once wasn't on the point of cracking. Quite the opposite. She was bubbling with ideas for me to get cracking. Like right away. Waste no time. On with the job. Iron is hot. All that.

'Why, what's happened now?' I asked, somewhat wearily.

'Haven't you heard the radio?' Sally said breathlessly.

'No, I've been a bit busy.'

'At this hour?' she asked, then ignored her own question. 'Anyway, Peter, it's number one on the local news.'

'What is?'

'The raid on the Fellowes Laboratories.'

I scratched my head. 'You mean Gregory's client? The guy who was losing all his animals?'

'Yes, that's right. In the night they lost some more. Four monkeys and some rats. They interviewed Smallbrother, the MD who all but blamed ARAG for the break-in.'

'I thought he didn't want publicity.'

'A policeman came upon one of the monkeys in the road and found the intruders.'

'So what . . . ?' I began, but Sally was in full cry.

96

'I rang you immediately I heard, so that you could get over there right away.'

'Over where? Fellowes?' I stalled, trying to side step committal.

'No, Peter, don't be silly. To Stringle. Robert Stringle, the ARAG founder. If you went right now, you might catch him still with the animals or, at least, when he's not had time to relax and get his alibi straight and well rehearsed.'

I could see her point. But I was not sure if it would really help us to discover her boyfriend's fate. Still, at this stage, I guessed straws were all we could clutch at.

'Shall I come with you?' she offered, taking my agreement to go for granted. Sally Newton was proving to have powers of persuasion I had hitherto not given her credit (or debit) for.

'No. Thanks all the same. I'll try it on my own first – one to one.' I sort of didn't believe what I was saying, which was 'Bye-bye, Weymouth, bye-bye', amongst other things.

'Fine. You've got his address, haven't you? He lives on the far side of Swanage.'

'Yes, I've got it somewhere.'

'Well, good luck. Ring me when you get back. I hope I'm not sending you on a wild-goose chase.'

'No, monkeys and rats are enough for today,' I muttered.

'What's that?'

'Nothing. I'll buzz you later.'

And that was that. No swapmeet, no money for me or Miranda. The only up-side I could see was that I might just be hastening the end of the Gregory Mann saga, and thus the hour when my life could return to as near normal as it ever could be.

As I got in my Beetle, I prayed Stringle hadn't still got the monkeys. The one and only time Arabella and I visited Longleat Safari Park and opted to drive through the dear little creatures' sanctuary, the Beetle emerged sans windscreen wipers, sans mirrors, one hubcap, a headlamp rim, two digits off a registration plate and a partridge in a pear tree.

Stringle's place was not too easy to find. It was up a winding, weed-strewn drive and the house could not be seen from the road. Mind you, the house could hardly be seen at all, even when you were close, so extravagantly had Virginia crept all over it. The windows and doors were like peep-holes in the vegetation and the extensive area around the house, that once, obviously, had been terraced and nurtured gardens, now reminded me of a big version of Gus's briar patch. Stringle was obviously letting his garden do what Ferndales, from its reputation and prospectus, let its children do – run wild and free.

Seeing no obvious signs of monkeys or rats, or indeed, any activity of any sort, I scrubbed around in the creeper and found a bell-button. To my amazement it worked, although it didn't actually produce anybody for a further five minutes – time, I deemed, that might well have been used to magic away a monkey or round up a rat.

The incredibly ordinary-looking man who eventually answered the door took me by surprise. I had been expecting the mad professor type as seen in *Flash Gordon, Tin-Tin* and *Dr Who*. The ordinary-looking man looked at his watch.

'It's eight fifteen a.m.,' he pronounced very carefully.
I nodded in agreement.
'You're not some new postman or other, are you?'
I shook my head.
'You're not a reporter? I've set the dogs on three of those already this morning.'
I gulped. I should have realized professional animal lovers dote on savage beasties too.
'No, I'm not a reporter.'
His grey eyes (a perfect match for his balding hair,

wire-haired pullover and tweedy trousers) fixed on mine.

'So, Mr eight fifteen a.m., what are you and why are you ringing my bell at this hour? Car broken down? Need water? Jump leads? You're too early to be a Jehovah's Witness, Plymouth Brethren, brush- or double-glazing salesman. So what are you, sir? Come on. Come clean quickly or I'll–'

I didn't keep him waiting.

'I'm a great admirer of ARAG,' I lied. 'I just had to come round directly I heard the news on the radio. To congratulate you.' I extended my hand, which he didn't accept at first.

'Your name?'

'Marklin. Peter Marklin. I live over Bournemouth way. Run a modest sort of animal's refuge and hospital. You know, get the oil off cormorants, lead pellets out of swans, snares off rabbits, pump poison out of badgers, that kind of thing. Been following your magnificent crusade for animal rights for months. I meant to have got in touch before, but you know how things are: pick up a phone and another swan could be dying.'

I was beginning to enjoy my charade, but knew I could be in danger of going over the top, so I started to close the curtains. 'But anyway, enough of me and back to the point. Last night's heroic rescue of those rats and monkeys just forced me to come in person and congratulate you. So leaving my little sanctuary in the capable hands of my widowed sister-in-law, I came right over. And here I am, with no apologies for the hour.'

He pursed his ordinary lips. 'What makes you think, Mr Marklin, I or ARAG had anything to do with last night's rescue?'

I put on my 'you're kidding me' look, which was actually quite genuine.

'Well, didn't you, Mr Stringle? Surely you can admit it, as one animal lover to another?'

'I admit nothing, Mr . . . er . . . er – '

'Marklin.'

'Marklin. The essence of an organization such as I have created is to act behind the scenes, not pronounce before the curtains. Do you ever hear an SAS man confessing to a Marine, say, about his deeds? Yet both are, supposedly, dedicated to the same cause, have the same enemies.'

I had to confess, I had not. Mind you I'd never consciously met an SAS man. This Mr Stringle, plum ordinary as he looked, was proving extraordinarily difficult to do business with.

'Talking of enemies,' I tried, 'I've had such suspicious people nosing around my little operation recently. I think I must be one of the suspects too, for releasing animals around the country. Do you get them?'

He at last moved aside from the front door. 'Would you care to come in, Mr Marklin? It's uncommon cold for so early in the winter, is it not?'

'Uncommon,' I muttered and followed him into the house.

Immediately, I regretted that the conversation (was that what it was?) had not been continued outdoors. The interior reeked of cats, dogs, mice, everything, I guess, that urinated and defined its territory. He led me into what must have been a drawing-room before the invasion of the Great Plants. A settee and two over-stuffed chairs were about the only things that were not potted. It was worse than the conservatory scene in *The Big Sleep*. I sat down between a huge palm and the biggest aspidistra in the world. Stringle sat opposite, in the shadow of what looked like a Trifid. Here the urine smells were augmented by the stench of rotting vegetation.

'You mentioned snoopers, Mr Marklin.'

I was so taken aback by the whole place, I had almost forgotten why I had come.

'Oh, so I did. Yes, snoopers. Usually they flee immediately you begin questioning them. But one, a week or two back, was very persistent. He even began to question me.'

I hovered for a reaction, but not for long.

'Did you catch his name at all?'

'Why, do you think he might have been around here too?'

He smiled in the shadows, grey and black. Great camouflage.

'I've had the odd prowler on occasions. That's why I keep my Dobermann Pinschers.'

Hell, I'd have preferred even Alsations.

'I'll describe this fellow to you. About thirty-four or so, but looks younger. Kind of boyish. Oh, and he has very piercing eyes.'

I couldn't really see Stringle's eyes for the shadows. All I got was a 'Go on, Mr Marklin.'

'Well, that's about it, really.'

'Didn't he tell you his name or why he was interested in your sanctuary?'

I took a gamble. 'Come to think of it, he did tell me his name. Now, what was it? It was kind of short and began with an м, as I recall.'

Still no glint from the lee of the Trifid.

'I'll have it in a minute . . . hang on . . . Ah! That's it: Mann. He said his name was Mann. Gerald Mann. Something like that. Might not have been Gerald, though.'

'Gregory,' he offered. A breakthrough at last.

'That's it. Gregory Mann. So it's the same guy who has been pestering you.'

Stringle leaned forward and rubbed his colourless hands.

'He could be. He could be. Did this Mr Mann disclose why he was investigating your operation?'

I knew I was safe now. Or as safe as you can ever be with a fanatic who likes wall-to-wall jungles and Dobermann Biters.

'As I recall, he said something about running a private enquiry business. Lord knows who was his client, though.' I smiled. 'Could even be dear old Fellowes, couldn't it?'

He ignored my offering and rose to his feet. Did I detect a certain nervousness or was I wishful thinking?

'Not seen him recently, have you? Like in the last few days?'

'No, no I haven't. I was sort of expecting to, in a way, but no sign.' He turned to me and gave an ordinary smile. 'Let's hope he has gone for good. Then we can both get on with our separate lives.'

I was not too keen on the way he emphasized the word 'separate'. I took it I was now being invited to leave. But before I could rise from my overstuffed chair, I heard a vehicle outside. Stringle moved to the gap in the Virginia creeper with amazing speed and agility, considering his sixty-eight or so years. He looked out, then sighed.

'I'm afraid I'm about to suffer more snoopers, Mr Marklin. I would advise you to leave whilst you can.'

'More snoopers?' I queried.

'In blue uniforms,' he said, with more than a little venom.

I got up and moved through the overgrowth to the door, Stringle close behind me. But I was a trifle late, for the bell sounded as I traversed the hall. A moment later, I was looking into the tired eyes of my old sparring partner, the overweight and over-prickly Inspector Digby Whetstone, Dorset's Stratford Johns.

'Oh, hello, Inspector,' I grinned sheepishly. 'Just leaving.'

He touched my arm. 'Well, well, well. If it isn't Mr Marklin.'

When a policeman touches your arm, you stick around. They can be as fierce as Dobermann Pinschers when aroused, I'm told. Whetstone's roundly fat face broke into a dubious smile.

'What little pie are you plunging your finger in today? I can't believe you've suddenly become all gooey-eyed about animal rights.'

'I've got a Siamese cat,' I smiled weakly. As a remark, it clearly wasn't up to scratch.

His expression hardened. 'It might be wiser if you didn't go out again this morning, Mr Marklin. Play with your toys awhile in your shop. I may want to have a talk with you later.'

Hell! That meant I couldn't even turn up at the Weymouth swapmeet late. But I took comfort in the opportunity it might provide to discover what the blazes the police thought of Mann's disappearance and what progress they might have made.

'All right, Inspector. I'll stay in until lunchtime, but I can't guarantee to be around after that.'

'It will be before lunch, Mr Marklin. Don't worry,' he smiled unctuously, then turned to Stringle, who was, by now, looking at me with the utmost suspicion.

'Mr Marklin been bothering you with his amateur sleuthing, Mr Stringle?'

I didn't hear the reply for two good reasons: one, the Inspector had disappeared into the house with its owner, followed by a stalwart constable with a tough guy moustache; two, and more importantly, I was down the steps and into my Beetle at supersonic speed, for fear Dobermanns might soon be on my heels. There's nothing quite as ironic as having one's cover blown by an officer of the law, is there?

The only real consolation on the drive home was the fresh air I was again breathing. Cold as it was, it was a fair exchange for the odours in Stringle's house. I wondered the Dobermann Pinschers didn't go on strike.

Once home, I phoned Sally, who was truly grateful

that I'd been, but as disappointed as I was at how little I had gleaned, and that Digby Whetstone had made further calls on Stringle more or less impossible. However, by way of thanks, she did invite me to pop over for a drink and some lunch, but with Digby's visit in the offing, I took a rain-check on it, as they say over the water in Arabella-land.

So I had time to kill, or so I thought. I opened up shop and unpacked all the parcels I had intended to take to Weymouth; not particularly helped by Bing who attacked all the string as I tried to undo the knots.

However, half an hour later saw toys back on shelves, in stacks each end of the counter and, the more expensive ones, in display cases. I had hardly finished, when the bell went clang and a scholarly-looking gentleman strolled into the shop, the cut of his overcoat a cut above the average. The usual 'Can I help you?' was followed by the unusual, 'Yes, I think you can.'

Thereupon followed further evidence of the uncanny grapevine that seems to be at work amongst old toy collectors, however hard one may try to hide one's discoveries.

'Word has it that you may have a rather fine Carette rear-entrance Tonneau car? Would the word be correct?'

'The word is correct,' I replied, somewhat amazed.

'Good,' he said with satisfaction. 'Would it be painted pale cream with black wings, have a silver roof with a red luggage rack, all pin-striping carried out in gold or red?'

Hell, I thought, can this be the original owner of the toy, and the car-boot seller a light-fingered thief?

I replied hesitantly. 'I believe those were its original colours. It was very chipped and faded.'

'Was?' he said with alarm. 'Does that mean you have disposed of the car?'

'No, no. Not yet. I use the past tense because I have

taken it to be restored. By now it could well be on its way to its original glory.'

He sighed with relief. 'Thank goodness for that. Who are you using for restoration?'

'Richardson. Jimmy Richardson. He's about the – '

'Best there is,' he smiled. 'Good. And may I ask when it will be ready?'

His affability seemed to dispel the thief theory of mine.

'Not quite certain. A week or two yet, I would think.'

He reached into an inside pocket and withdrew a fine leather notecase, embossed with a gold monogram.

'I would like to place a deposit on it, sir, if that is in order with you. Returnable, of course, if the Carette does not fully live up to expectations.'

I held onto the counter. 'But I haven't as yet fixed an asking price. I was intending taking it up to Christie's.'

'Good idea. You do that. Get them to value it, because their judgements are nearly always too conservative by half with toys. I'll give you half as much again. Saves you all the fuss of an auction. Saves me having to go to it. I'm off to Saudi Arabia in about a month, so I might well miss it anyway. I'm down here just visiting my brother's family over Dorchester way. That's how I heard about your Carette.'

He opened his notecase, peeled off ten fifty-pound notes, and handed them to me.

'There. That should be a reasonable deposit.' He looked at my face. 'Don't look so surprised. I want that particular Carette, you see.'

It was a deal I couldn't possibly refuse. I started, with a shaking hand, to write out a receipt for the five hundred pounds.

'May I ask, is there any particular reason why? I mean, beyond its rarity and its delicate sort of beauty.'

'Of course, you may. I have been a vintage toy collector for some years now, and have been building up, a bit like the famous David Pressland, a collection centred upon vehicles and aircraft made before the Great War. The Carette is, of course, a car that I have been after for quite some time but my desire to own one was considerably quickened by a discovery of mine in Paris earlier this year. Would you believe I came across its box? Empty but in perfect condition. No tears. No damage. Just some minor discoloration through time.'

He put away his now thinner notecase. 'So now I have box and contents. I doubt there'll be another rear-entrance Tonneau so complete and perfect in the world, wouldn't you agree?'

I agreed. He reached into another pocket and took out his card, which he placed on the counter, picking up my receipt at the same time. I saw the first word was 'Lord'.

'Now, sir, don't let anyone steal that Carette from you before you deliver it to me, will you? My brother had a break-in only the week before I came down. Poor chap lost half the family silver. I don't know what Dorset is coming to. Used to be such a sleepy county. Now my poor brother tells me that burglaries round here recently have become as common as rats in a barn. Ah well, maybe they've got the right idea in Saudi Arabia, who knows. If thy right hand burgles, lop it off.'

He waved a now immaculately gloved hand and made for the door. As he went out, he pointed to the locks.

'When my Carette is back with you, keep 'em bolted, won't you?'

After his lordship had gone, it took me a few minutes to recover from his whirlwind visit. I even picked up the money to check that the last few minutes had actually taken place. I opened the till and put in all but sixty pounds. Fifteen for myself, and, at last, forty-five for Merinda. Once Digby had gone and I'd had something to eat, I could take it round to her. I rather looked forward to it.

I went into the kitchen to make a Nescafé special. I felt I needed something and the non-existent sun was not sufficiently over the yardarm to warrant anything stronger. (I do have a backbone sometimes.)

It was whilst I was stirring in the granules, that there was another ding of the doorbell. I cursed under my breath and trudged back into the shop all ready to face Digby Whetstone. But it was not his Michelin-man figure that stood among the toys, but Gus's granite variety. I didn't know whether I was relieved or not.

'Morning,' he coughed.

'It's not a good morning,' I retorted.

'Isn't raining,' he said.

'It is in me,' I moaned and went into my sad Saturday so far. I naturally made no mention of the only bit of sunshine – the sale of the Carette. For I've never really dared to break to Gus that toys sometimes fetch thousands of pounds. I've only just got him used to the idea that they might cost hundreds. Besides, Gus is not exactly ace at keeping confidences. He tends to open up like a clam.

His reaction to my activities was brief and amazingly to the point.

'Well, look at it this way, old son, you've now seen all Mann's main suspects.'

I hadn't realized that truth, so sudden had been my visit to the ARAG man. I was slightly cheered.

'Yes, I suppose so. Still, I'm no nearer finding Gregory, am I?'

''Aven't got any facts or anything, I'll grant you, but what's your gut say? What's that fancy word you and that Inspector Blake always used to use?'

'Intuition,' I guessed.

'That's right. Well, what's that say, then? Who is more likely to be mixed up in his disappearing act? That smarmy sod, Redstart, or the headmaster fella or the animal man? You must have a feeling.'

The trouble was, I should have had, but I hadn't

really. Not gut feeling. That was what was bothering me. They all seemed capable of being mixed up in the affair. They all shared a common interest in Mann disappearing from their respective scenes. And Redstart was a shady character anyway. The headmaster, no doubt, would hate to lose his comfortable living in a vast mansion, surrounded by at least a hundred nubile girls (nearly half the school) and, by the looks of things, a brand new 700 series BMW to boot. And the Dobermann Pinscher man was clearly a fanatic who would no doubt fight to protect ARAG the way he fought to protect animals.

It all came down to the question as to which one had so much to hide that he would go to the lengths of arranging Gregory's vanishing act. Which, in fact, probably meant his death. For none of them, I felt, would be likely to have incarcerated him away somewhere. But if he was dead, where was his body? And where, for that matter, was his ruddy great Honda bike? Pitched into the sea by Redstart? Hidden in those expansive Ferndales acres? Or somewhere in the undergrowth of Stringle's garden? All possible, I supposed, but how was I going to find out? Searching without a warrant was hardly the simplest of endeavours.

'I just don't know, Gus. Not in my gut. But my reason would suggest the answer may lie in that ten thousand pounds that Gregory banked without telling Sally. Don't forget it was cash. Legitimate deals of anything like that size are normally handled by cheque or bankers order, aren't they? Cash smells a bit, don't you think?'

'Only if it's other people's,' Gus smirked. 'But any of that lot could probably raise ten grand, if they really wanted to. Redstart is bound to have that sort of loot. That poncey school must be rolling in money. And, who knows, the animal man may have saved a fortune over the years he worked as a, what was it, a scientist? After all, he's never married, has he?' He looked at me knowingly. 'You can save quite a lot if you don't marry, old son.' (Good old Gus. Loves women but hates spending.)

'Thanks Gus. That's helped us a lot,' I grinned. 'They all could have paid it.'

'Well,' he shrugged, 'I was only trying to – '

'I know. Thanks.'

We both sat silent for a moment, then I said, 'I wonder what that money was about. I mean, was it payment for doing a job, or for *not* doing a job?'

'Could be either, couldn't it?'

'I suspect, being cash, it was a sweetener of some sort, rather than a fee. If it was, and it's connected at all with his disappearance, it doesn't make sense.'

Gus frowned, his forehead more full of lines than Clapham Junction.

'Well, Gus, if you've paid somebody off, you don't then turn round and kill him, do you? There's no need, is there? The sweetener should have already done the trick.'

'Yeah, s'pose so. But that sort of means the money and his disappearance *aren't* connected, then.'

I threw up my hands. 'We go round in circles, don't we?'

'Not the right ones,' Gus laughed. 'But then I never have.'

I smiled. Suddenly I was glad Gus had called round. He drives you insane in such a nice way.

'Maybe we're barking up the wrong trees altogether. Maybe Gregory is still fit as a fiddle somewhere, shacked up with some new girlfriend or other. Or on some hush-hush case on which he was sworn to secrecy. Or – '

'Or rubbish,' Gus broke in. 'You don't believe any of that, do you?'

'Not really. You're right. You just don't roar off on a Honda in winter with no luggage, no goodbyes, no nothing. What's more, if he knew he was going to bugger off like that, he surely wouldn't have paid the ten grand into a bank round here, now would he? He'd have more likely banked it where he was going.'

Gus looked at me sadly. 'You told Sally that?'

'Of course not. But she's a bright girl. Its significance won't have escaped her.'

It was at that point I saw a dreaded shape in white and red glide to a stop outside the windows. Gus looked round.

'Well, here he comes,' he muttered. 'Digby bloody Whetstone. I'd better be off.' He moved behind the counter, towards my back door, with a turn of speed that belied his size and age.

'Good luck, old son. I'll down a pint for you.'

Now, wasn't that nice of him?

Digby Whetstone hadn't really changed. Maybe he weighed a few pounds less, there was a trace of grey now in the ginger of his tubercular moustache. But his manner was still as subtle as a sack of potatoes, and his temper as endearing.

After the usual unpleasantries, I invited him through to the sitting-room. One might as well be comfortable with a discomforting visitor. But he declined.

'I haven't come here, Mr Marklin, for a cosy chat.'

So we stayed in the shop. At least this gave me the buffer of the counter.

'Then what have you come here for?' I asked, not unpleasantly. I didn't want to antagonize him before I'd learned what I wanted.

'I'm here primarily because of a complaint about your recent activities, Mr Marklin. But maybe I would not have come in person had it not been for our meeting at Mr Stringle's house.'

'Let me guess,' I said. 'Would the complaint have come from a certain Poole Harbourite who seems to blow up at the slightest thing?'

He actually smiled. 'If you are referring to Mr Patrick

110

Redstart then your guess is correct. I'm glad to note you remember whom you bother.'

'What did he say about me?'

'Nothing very nice, I'm afraid.' Whetstone picked up an unboxed Dinky *Queen Mary* liner from my counter and looked at it as if he had never seen a toy before. He turned it over and read the price.

'Twenty-two pounds,' he said. 'What I would call daylight robbery.'

I ignored his barb, for right then he probably had robberies on the brain.

'To put the record straight right now,' I said, 'I only asked him about the missing private detective – you know, Gregory Mann of Ask Force over in Sandbanks.'

'He did mention that, but he also complained that you had some "heavy" with you, who behaved in a most intimidating manner. And that you had also been worrying a friend of his, a Miss Abigail Gordon.'

I smiled. 'The "heavy" who accompanied me that day, Inspector, was the ruthless, pitiless Gus Tribble. You've met him. I wonder you allow him to walk the streets. And as for either of us worrying anybody, well, questions only worry someone if that someone has got something to worry about. Wouldn't you agree?'

He put the *Queen Mary* down. 'So you weren't worrying anybody, intimidating anybody, just asking questions. Okay. So let's turn to what you were doing this morning at Stringle's house. Asking more questions? Mr Stringle told me you had spun him a web of lies about running an animal sanctuary in Bournemouth.'

He scratched his podgy nose. 'Come clean, Marklin. What the hell are you up to?'

'Same thing you should be up to,' I said. 'Trying to find out what the hell has happened to Gregory Mann.'

'You a friend of his, then?'

'Not exactly. I'm a friend of a friend.'

111

He gave a leery chuckle. 'Friend of Miss Sally Newton?'

'No,' I said firmly. 'A friend of a friend of – '

'Bit remote, isn't it, for you to get so obviously het up about his going missing?'

'I'm not het up. I'm concerned, that's all. Aren't the Dorset constabulary?'

'Bournemouth,' he corrected me. 'Naturally we are concerned about anyone who goes missing. Our files are full of missing persons we are concerned about. We are doing our best, in case you don't reckon so, to trace the fates of every one. Gregory Mann is no exception.'

'I'm glad to hear it.'

He leaned across the counter. 'I'm glad you're glad to hear it. But what I'm *not* glad to hear is that you are sticking your face, yet again, into affairs that not only are best left to the police, but which *must* be left to us professionals to deal with. I'm asking you to desist forthwith. It's people like you who can foul up the most carefully planned police operation in a split second by crossing lines, alerting the guilty, confusing the innocent and God knows what else. All inadvertently, maybe, but all unnecessarily. Leave it to the pros, Mr Marklin. By all means, let us know any theories you may entertain at any one time. Who knows, they might be useful. We police do not pretend we have a corner in brains. But I must insist you leave all action to us. It will be the simplest, safest, speediest way to trace Gregory Mann, I assure you.'

I didn't comment. After all, he might well be right. In theory, he had to be. But in practice? I still remembered the Lana-Lee case during which I had first met Digby Whetstone last year.

'Okay,' I said. 'Tell me how you pros are getting on with Mann's disappearance. You know vaguely what I've been doing: interviewing a few of the people from Mann's office files who might just have an interest in his vanishing from their lives.'

'How does Abigail Gordon fit in that category? We have got copies of the Ask Force files, and she herself was not under investigation.'

I hesitated, then said, 'I believe she and Mr Mann might have been seeing each other. I mean, without Redstart knowing.'

He raised his ginger eyebrows. 'And who told you that?'

'I heard it around,' I prevaricated.

'Miss Sally Newton did not tell *us* that,' he smiled.

I should have told you. Digby is by no means a total fool.

'Maybe she was a bit embarrassed.'

'But she's obviously not embarrassed with you, Mr Marklin,' he leered once more.

'Look, Inspector, I have no relationship with Sally Newton other than that of a friend trying to help out. So please, out with any innuendos. Okay? Now, let's get back to my original question. What progress, if any, have you made in your investigations?'

He cleared his throat. From the gurgly sound, he'd either got a bad cold going or coming. Either way, I had a feeling I'd catch it. It was that kind of day.

'Let's put it this way. We haven't found him yet, but it's early days.'

'It's the seventh day,' I muttered. 'People just can't vanish off the face of the earth for seven days.'

'Seven years and more sometimes. Look at Lord Lucan. And, on occasion, missing persons are never found. But tracing people nowadays is made a little easier by national computer link-ups from force to force, data banks, finger-print – '

'All right, all right. So I take it every computer in the country is programmed to find Gregory Mann. Now tell me what human beings are doing.'

'Our best, Mr Marklin,' Digby retorted. 'We have naturally followed very much the same route as yourself and carried out interviews with all Mann's main clients

113

and the various persons into whose activities he was probing.'

He moved closer to me across the counter. 'By the way, Miss Newton hasn't, by any chance, confided in you what exactly Mr Mann was trying to discover at Ferndales has she? It was a bit vague in the files.'

'No, she hasn't. She doesn't know. Nor did Gregory.'

'You use the present tense for Miss Newton, I notice, and the past tense for Mr Mann. Does that mean you believe Mr Mann to be dead?'

'Do you?'

He shrugged his round shoulders. 'Hard to say, isn't it? Mann missing, large, heavy bike missing, no reported sightings, no trace of his clothes or personal effects, nothing at all since last Sunday morning, when he is supposed to have gone off – '

'Suppose?' I cut in irritably. 'He *did* go off.'

'Did you see him?'

'No, I didn't, but – '

'Ah, well, there you go. That's the difference between a trained professional and an amateur. We like our evidence to be corroborated.'

'But surely the people in the newspaper shop next door would have heard his Honda depart.'

'Bikes and cars go by on that stretch all day. No one can remember one particular bike.'

'Okay,' I said reluctantly. 'So what are you saying? That Gregory Mann never left and is hiding away somewhere in the flat above the offices.'

'Don't be ridiculous, Mr Marklin. Think a bit harder. Think a bit deeper. We gather that the last time Mr Mann was seen, other than, apparently, by Miss Newton, was some ten hours before his reported trip on his Honda. A neighbour saw him pull up outside the flat in his Triumph Stag with Miss Newton, about twelve thirty or so at night, she said. Saw them both clearly under the streetlamps.'

'So you are implying that Mann could have disappeared before Sally said he did.'

'I'm not implying anything. I'm just trying to prove to you that our investigations are far more complicated and complex than any amateur could possibly imagine. That's why amateurs should, capital K, Keep, capital O, Out. Get my message?'

He took a deep breath and his stomach overlapped the edge of the counter. Boy, what Jane Fonda could do with him; not that she'd want to.

'But back to my question just now. You used the past tense about Mr Mann. Do you think he is dead?'

I thought for a moment. 'If he had just decided to vamoose of his own accord, for some reason we do not know, then why deposit ten thousand pounds in a bank round here? Wouldn't he place it where he was going?'

'Oh, so Miss Newton has told you about the ten thousand. Yes, the same thought bothers us. So you . . . er . . . think he must be either held against his will somewhere or dead. Is that right?'

I nodded reluctantly. ''Fraid so.'

Whetstone pursed his blue-ish lips. 'Would it interest you to know that it is not the first time Mr Mann has deposited a large sum in cash and then left the area without too many formalities?'

I could not hide my surprise. 'When? How?' I mumbled intelligently.

'Up north. Our inquiries show he deposited eight thousand pounds immediately prior to leaving a certain lady waiting at the altar.'

Oh boy, that kind of befuddling information I needed like a hole in the head. I thought the case was complicated enough already.

'Gets around, does our Mr Mann,' Whetstone smiled. 'See, I use the present tense. The professional never assumes anything is a fact until it's proven so.'

I sighed. How could anyone be so perfect?

'So, what are you going to do now?'

'I've told you too much already, Mr Marklin. But only to show you we are taking the case seriously and need no outside help from untrained sources.'

'All right. Well, thanks for the reassurance.'

Digby Whetstone buttoned up his c&a overcoat (I saw the label) and made to go.

'Now, heed what I've said, Mr Marklin, and we will get on fine. Meanwhile, I have a mountain of work I've ignored back at the station, just to visit your . . . toy shop.' He peered at another price sticker, this time on a mint boxed Spot-On Morris Minor. 'Seventy pounds!' he whistled.

'I only rob in daylight, Inspector,' I grinned.

He waved his hand. 'Don't talk to me of robberies. These days, that's a whole mountain of work on its own.'

And with that, he left. But where it left me, I now had no idea. So while my Birdseye quiche was in the oven, I got pen and paper and started on a long reply to my dazzling overseas correspondent.

8

Before I left to take the forty-five pounds round to Merinda, I phoned Philippa, brought her up to date and asked her if she knew about Mann's little cash transaction up north. But she was as surprised as I had been.

I said, didn't she think it was a bit of a coincidence? She agreed but pointed out that life can be full of coincidences, most of which are entirely meaningless. Anyway, he did not disappear without trace up north, did he? I asked her what she knew about the jilting at the altar. She said that as far as she knew, he had just buggered off without a word and gone abroad for a holiday. Soon after his return he'd closed his detective agency and moved lock, stock and barrel down south. I said he can't have done that this time – gone abroad, I mean – because Sally told me he did not take his passport. The conversation ended with us both thinking it all very peculiar. I did not tell her about my warnings off from Whetstone. Philippa was too nice a lady to worry.

So, well muffled up (the day had grown even colder and Beetles have lousy heaters even when the seams in the roof don't leak), I motored up the Corfe road to the track that led up to where the caravan was parked. It all looked so very different in the daylight. I was amazed how kempt the whole area looked around the van. John-John and Merinda were certainly not despoiling the environment. As I pulled to a stop, I was glad to see a glow of light emanating from one end of the van, for the sun might have already set for all the light it was shedding on that bleak November afternoon.

It was Merinda who opened the door. She expressed no surprise at my visit and immediately invited me in out of the elements. Coat, gloves and scarf doffed, I sat down opposite her on the bunks.

'John-John not here?' I asked, stating the obvious.

'No. He had to drive up north to see his mother. She was hit by a car crossing the road.'

'Bad?' I queried.

'No,' she smiled. 'More shock than anything else: cuts and bruises and slight concussion, apparently. John-John thought he ought to check for himself. He will be back tomorrow.'

I was glad it was no longer. I handed her the money.

'Here. I'm sorry I'm so late with it.'

'Don't worry. I knew you would come.' As before, she looked rather too wonderful in the soft glow of the gaslight.

'Like something to drink or anything?' she offered. 'I was about to make some coffee when I heard your car. Only instant, but I'm afraid I sort of need it after the last lot of visitors.'

'Who were they? The people who want your caravan moved on?'

'No.'

I could see now that her eyes were not as serene as they normally were.

'Want to tell me about it?'

She rose from the bunk. 'I'll make the coffee first, if you would like some.'

So that's what she did. When the steaming mugs were on the table between us, she said, 'Are you sure you want to know?'

'If something is troubling you, yes . . .'

She sighed. 'Well, the visitors were the police. They only left about twenty minutes ago.'

'Snap,' I said, then told her to ignore my interruption.

She looked down at her slim, almost boyish fingers.

'They were here for what seemed like hours. They searched everywhere, everything. In the van, under the van, around the van, in the hedges around. I thought they would never leave.'

'What on earth were they looking for?' I reached across and touched her hand.

'Stolen property. They said they had reason to believe John-John and I might have been involved in . . .' She did not seem to want to go on, so I came to her aid.

'. . . the spate of robberies round here?'

She nodded. 'When I asked what evidence they had, they wouldn't say. But one of the constables let slip that they always check on what he called 'you hippies' when there's any trouble in the district.'

I squeezed her hand. 'My God, no wonder you need the coffee.'

She smiled weakly. 'I didn't mean to trouble you with – '

'You're not troubling me in the slightest. Now, tell me, when they left without finding anything, did they apologize or anything?'

'No. They just seemed disappointed and drove away.'

'Did they ask where John-John was?'

'Of course. I had to give them his mother's address. I'm worried that they might imagine John-John went up north just to get rid of whatever they think we've stolen.'

'Can't you ring him to warn him?'

'No, his mother is not on the phone. Anyway, it might look a bit suspicious if I warned him, don't you think?'

I groaned. I guessed that to some policeman the very fact that you chose to have an impermanent address in a caravan was cause for suspicion.

'What an awful experience – '

'I wouldn't have minded so much', she interrupted, 'if I'd been alone when they called.'

'You had somebody with you?'

'Yes. And someone who wouldn't really understand what was going on. She looked really scared.'

'Who was that?'

'Tom Sweet's daughter, Molly. You know the thatcher.'

I knew the thatcher.

'Whew. Were you looking after her or what?'

'Yes, I do occasionally now. We've got to know Tom and Molly a a bit since the rethatching started. So I offered to keep an eye on her every now and again to save Tom either leaving her alone at home, or taking her along with him when he works.'

'Where is she now?'

'Tom came and picked her up soon after the police had left. He's finished work for the day now.'

'Did you tell him about the police?'

'I had to. Molly was still looking so scared; I had to have some explanation. Besides, Molly knows who policemen are, even if she's not really sure what they do – except frighten people.'

'Hell.' I sipped my coffee, but didn't really taste it. 'Did he say anything?'

'Not really, though I don't think he will be too keen on my looking after Molly again.'

'Think not?'

'No. Whilst he didn't say anything, his face showed his concern.'

I reached across the table again for her hand.

'I am sorry, Merinda.'

She took a deep breath and smiled. 'There was a vicar who used to call on my mother when I was a child. When anything bad happened, like when I broke my leg, or another time when my mother scalded herself, he would always say, "These things are sent to try us." ' She laughed. 'I guess I've just been tried.'

'But hardly a fair trial,' I commented. 'You've been adjudged guilty before the proceedings have even opened. All because you and John-John have chosen a nomadic life instead of opting for some sober semi in suburbia.'

This time she patted *my* hand. 'I'm glad you came,' she said.

'I'm glad too.'

'Like another cup of coffee?'

'Thanks, but don't get up. I'll make it. I'm a dab hand with spoons and jars. I was voted Stirrer of the Year by the Brazilian Coffee Planters Association.'

For the first time, she smiled a proper smile.

'Which year?' she asked.

'The same time I won the Liar of the Year award.'

She laughed again. It was a good sound.

I guess I spent around two hours or so with Merinda. It seemed no time at all. She was one of those rare people who was as good at listening as she was at keeping other people interested in what she was saying. What's more, her inner calmness (it did return) created an atmosphere that made any inhibition totally evaporate and one talked as if one had known her intimately all one's life. That's how she got to know all about me. And Arabella. And the kind of limbo land I was in at the moment. I didn't bring up the problem of Gregory Mann for obvious reasons. She needed cheering up, not depressing. But, just before I left, she mentioned him herself.

'Lady Philippa tells me you're helping look for the man who was at the Guy Fawkes party – Gregory Mann.'

'Yes,' I sighed. 'I'm helping, I suppose, but not really making any forward progress.'

'What do you think has happened to him? Anything? Or could he have just taken off – a bit like John-John and myself, I suppose – leaving all his troubles behind?'

I shrugged. 'I'd have thought he would have been seen somewhere by now if he'd just taken off.'

'So you think he might be . . .'

'Dead?' I helped her. 'It would fit, wouldn't it?'

She shuddered. 'I was hoping . . .' She stopped.

'What?'

'. . . he might, maybe, have just gone off with, perhaps, another girl.'

I saw something in her expression I had to explore.

'Got any reason for saying that?'

'Well, I hate speaking behind people's backs, but something happened that Guy Fawkes night that made me a bit suspicious of his intentions to marry Sally Newton.'

'Tell me,' I said, eyes glowing in the gaslight.

'He, er, sort of got me cornered late in the evening. Behind the barn.'

'Made a pass?'

'He tried to kiss me, gave me, I suppose, the usual kind of chat: never met anyone like me before, etcetera. I won't bore you with it all.' She smiled self-consciously. 'Must have been the drink talking.'

'No, I'm not bored. I'm so out of clues right now,' I grinned, 'I need every iota of information about him that I can lay my ears on.'

'Well, there's not much more. I said I had heard Sally Newton saying earlier in the evening that they were to marry soon, so what was he doing trying to make love to me? He said I wasn't to listen too much to what she said because she was "wedding-bell mad" – that was his phrase. I asked about the cottage she had also mentioned, that they were soon to move into once all the inside work and rethatching were finished. And he said he was thinking of selling it again at a profit directly the inside was finished and that he would forget about the rethatching.'

'Hell,' I sighed. 'Mr Gregory Mann, hour by hour, is turning out to be a rather different animal from the one I set out to help find.'

Merinda looked very concerned. 'Oh, I hope nothing

122

I've said is putting you off helping trace him.' She touched my arm. 'He was probably just spinning me a tale to get me to . . . Nobody's perfect, you know.'

'I know. People aren't like toys, more's the pity. There don't seem to be many mint ones – most of us turn out to be chipped in one way or another, once our boxes are opened.'

Some ten minutes later I was in the frigid chill of my Beetle, reversing down the track. She waved until I was out of sight. At the main road, I was about to turn left to go home, when I hesitated. It was dark, it was cold and bleak, and somehow I was not in the mood for going straight back. I was too full of thoughts, and not about the philandering and maybe backhanding Gregory Mann. So, with mental apologies to Bing, I turned right and accelerated away towards Corfe and Wareham. I badly needed a fix of antique toys and old Daimlers.

Thank the Lord, Jimmy Richardson was in. And what's more, he was working on my Carette and opened the door with a brush in his hand.

'Heard your car,' he said hastily. 'Come on in to my workroom. Can't stop, sorry. Paint'll dry before I've finished.'

The next three-quarters of an hour was the greatest therapy in the world, watching Jimmy coachlining that old Carette with a brush so fine you could hardly see the tip. Sans roof, sans windscreen, sans wings, sans passengers, the little car still looked wonderful, resplendent in its new cream paint with the red coachlining already finished along the short, blunt bonnet and one side. I remarked on the fantastic quality of the gold that ran around every edge of the main body.

'How the blazes did you do that, Jim? Can you have tinplate "brassed"?'

'Not, brass, old love. I thought of having it treated in some way like that, then decided on the real thing.'

'Real thing?' I queried.

'Gold leaf. I had some over from another job, so don't fret about the cost.' He grinned at me. 'You can do me a favour some time.'

He went back to his pinstriping, his hand as steady as a surgeon's. (But not the one who removed my appendix. I've forgotten his name but by the wiggly nature of my scar, it must have been Magoo.) His restoration was so perfect, you would swear it was the original lithography. I decided that if I were to find Gregory Mann alive, I would take him to Jimmy to be brought a little nearer to the condition his Maker no doubt intended. Mind you, I could do with a bit of touching up myself. (Don't misunderstand me, though.)

At last, he set the Carette body aside and asked if I would like to see my Daimler. I went out with him to a lock-up shed, with Jimmy carrying the biggest torch I've ever seen; it looked as if it must run off car batteries! Shed doors opened, its candlepower almost floodlit my old car. Not that I should use the adjective 'old' about what I saw. For there was what seemed a totally new vehicle, its silver-grey paintwork scintillating in the beam of the torch.

'Came out rather well, I think,' Jimmy remarked, making the understatement of the year. I knelt down and inspected a door panel with delight. The lustre was as deep as the Pacific, with not a trace of 'orange peel'.

'Fantastic,' was all I could murmur. My Daimler had suddenly lost twenty years and was back in its showroom awaiting its first owner. (Well, as far as the bodywork was concerned, anyway. Don't forget I'd muddled around with the mechanics.)

'You can pick it up tomorrow. The paint should be hard enough by then, even if it rains. But don't polish it for about three months, will you?'

I promised not to and we repaired back into the warmth of his house where, in a trice, he magicked up a couple of Carlsbergs.

'Can I pay you for the Daimler tomorrow?' I grinned. 'Deposit on the Carette.'

He looked at me in astonishment. 'Sold it already?'

I nodded. 'A Lord Staverton has earmarked it, sight unseen. Apparently, he has got its original box.' I explained my stroke of luck.

'Hey, hey. It couldn't happen to a more rotten bastard,' he laughed and raised his glass in salute.

I'm afraid we kept on raising glasses for quite a bit that night. It was just as well that Jimmy Richardson's better half was spending the night at her sister's in East Lulworth, or we would have suffered a domestic version of 'Time, gentlemen, please'. By the time I was ready to leave, around midnight, I would have walked home had Jimmy lived nearer. As it was, I had a feeling I would burst any balloon offered me by a passing boy in blue. But to get a taxi would have taken ages and meant I would then have *two* cars to pick up on the morrow. So I'm afraid I risked it and after waving farewell, meandered to my Beetle and started up.

It was as I was turning out from Jimmy's yard that I saw, or thought I saw, a figure mounting a motor cycle just outside the house next door. Now I would have taken no notice of such an everyday occurrence, had the house next door shown any lights at any windows or the motor bike any lights in its lamps. Besides, I thought something about the figure was familiar but, in my befuddled state, I couldn't quite think what. Anyway, I stopped the car, wound down the window and shouted at the figure that he had forgotten to turn on his lights. But by now, the revving of his motor was drowning my effort to be helpful and a second later, figure and bike disappeared into the wild black yonder, still without the sign of any lamps, white or red variety.

I sat there for a moment, my only companions now the phutting of the old Volks engine behind me and the hoot of an owl out front. I looked at my Sekonda. It was the bewitching hour of 12.12. Now I wouldn't really have worried too much about the whole incident, had Jimmy not once told me that his neighbours were in their early eighties and frail as all get out (or, I suppose, all stay in). So the biker was unlikely to be some lover leaving a warm bed to sneak home, for instance – the only explanation my be-lagered brain could rustle up for that hour of the morning. So if he wasn't a carrot-eating lover, who was he?

I shivered when I thought of another explanation. A moment later, I was knocking on Richardson's door once more.

We tried not to make a noise as we Pink Panthered round the outside of the neighbours' house. But like many elderly people who can no longer do much gardening, they had laid gravel and paving stones where beds and grass had once been, so we could not avoid coming to the odd crunch. We prayed that their age might have brought with it a degree of deafness, for we did not want to alarm them unnecessarily. As neither woke up during our prowl, I guess it had.

To our great relief, there were no obvious signs of a break-in. Every downstairs window was intact, every latch seemed secure. We even peered into an outside lavatory but, in retrospect, what we expected to find stolen from it, I cannot imagine.

'Well, maybe the guy's motor bike just conked out,' I said rather sheepishly. 'You know, wonky electronics or something. It would explain his lack of lights too.'

'Maybe,' Jimmy whispered. 'Still, I'll just check the upstairs windows.' He swung the beam from his huge torch across the curtained mullions, never lingering very long at any one for fear the light might wake up the occupants. But all, again, seemed hunky-dory. We tiptoed around the back and flash-checked those too. Same thing.

'Sorry, Jimmy,' I whispered and in that split second,

126

collided with something hard, rounded and rather damp. In the stillness of the night, the impact sounded like HMS *Hermes* hitting a harbour wall.

'Shit, Peter. What are you doing?' my friend succinctly asked.

I felt around me. It wasn't a huge woman, after all. It was a water butt. Jimmy flashed my way. It was then we noticed it: there were lengths of straw lying on the wooden lid of the butt and a few more pieces around its base on the ground. There were no prizes as to where they had come from. I pointed upwards and Jimmy flashed his torch to the lower eaves of the thatched roof. There were more lengths of straw dangling from one edge.

'Well, that could be it, couldn't it?' I said with some relief, anxious that my suspicions should prove unfounded. 'Someone trying to get on the roof to get in an upper window.'

I pointed upwards. 'Keep your flashlight over there. See that ledge? By climbing up the thatch a bit he could have got onto that ledge and along to the side window.'

Jimmy had a look. 'Could be. That's their spare bedroom, right the other end of the house from where they sleep. They would probably never hear anyone getting in that window.'

There was only one thing worrying me.

'But they wouldn't hear anyone getting in downstairs either, would they?'

'That's a thought,' Jimmy pondered, then whispered, 'Lots of people have safety locks on their downstairs doors and windows, but not upstairs. Maybe the burglar fellow was counting on that.'

'Maybe.' I walked towards the road and looked back. 'There could be another reason for choosing that window,' I said on my return. 'It can't be seen from the road, or anybody's garden, for that matter.'

'Well, there you are then,' my friend said, with the satisfaction of a Sherlock Holmes at solving time, and switched off his searchlight. 'It's too bloody cold to stay out here any longer. I'm going to get to bed before I get a touch of the brass monkeys. I'll tell the old folks in the morning. After all, it may just turn out to be rats.'

I followed the steam of his breath back to my car. By now, I was feeling a degree more sober, if fifty degrees colder.

'Mind the police,' he said with a wave.

'No, not really. Most of them do a good job,' I smiled and accelerated away towards home, sweet home.

Some hundred yards down the road, I remembered to turn on my lights.

9

I awoke later that morning, circa 8.30, feeling surprisingly chipper considering everything. I even sang in the bath, much to Bing's chagrin; he walked out of the room in the middle of my rendering of 'I'm in the Money' from the show *42nd Street*, which Arabella and I had seen in London the week before she left.

It was not until after my muesli, toast and Golly marmalade, that I realized I had nothing much to sing about – except the Carette and the beautiful work Richardson had done on my Daimler. I was no nearer finding Gregory Mann, despite my recent news about his devious and reprehensible ways. What's more, I was more than annoyed at what had happened to Merinda.

Just as I was about to go round to Gus to ask him if he would drop me at Jimmy's so that I could pick up my old/new car, the heavens opened and all points of the compass seemed to promise more. So, instead of twiddling my thumbs, I rang Sally Newton, not that I was quite sure what I was going to discuss with her. Boy, did I start the day on the wrong foot.

Sally was in some state – but not depressed and weepy. Flamboyantly aggressive is the nearest description of her mood. Not against me; against life, I guess. Life, right then, in the form of Gregory Mann's parents, who had descended from Shropshire unannounced the previous evening and had spent the time more or less blaming Sally for his disappearance. She hadn't managed to get rid of them back to their hotel until two in the morning. I tried to cheer Sally up by explaining that people in pain tend to lash out in all directions and

129

what they say at such times shouldn't be recorded on condemnatory tablets of stone, but I'm afraid my words fell on stony ground. She even went so far as to say that she no longer really cared what had happened to dear Gregory and that he and his whole family could take a running jump. You can imagine the rest. So what did I do? I said I'd come over.

She was a different girl by the time I pulled up outside her black windows. Don't get me wrong, she still regarded the whole Mann family as having crawled out of the bowels of Salop but she was no longer upset or belligerent about it. She was all smiles and Opium perfume. I was starting to get used to her changing moods.

I accepted her offer of coffee, and she asked me what was new.

'Have you spoken to Philippa?' I queried. 'Yesterday or today?'

She shook her head. 'Why?'

I decided I'd better go the whole hog now that Sally was in an anti-Mann mood.

'Well, I told her yesterday about something I discovered from Digby Whetstone.'

'Oh? What's that?' Her big, beautiful eyes widened.

'Gregory, apparently, made a significant cash deposit into his bank shortly before jilting that girl up north.'

She took a deep breath and expelled it slowly.

'Cash?'

'Cash.'

'Eight thousand.'

'Ten thousand this time.'

'Right.'

She thought for a moment. 'It doesn't surprise me. Not now.' She looked at me. 'Don't look so apprehensive, Peter. I've been doing a lot of thinking, sitting here alone day after day. I've come to the same conclusion that I guess you have.'

I didn't say anything. She had to say the word.

130

'Gregory bloody Mann is an out and out bastard.'

There, she'd saved me.

'Looks a bit like it,' I concurred quietly.

'Looks a hell of a lot like it. I always knew he was not exactly the most faithful of types – his track record shows that – but I always assumed he was straight in business. But those cash deposits can't be anything else but back-handers, can they?'

'Well, they could, but certainly from where I sit they look a bit dubious.'

She took my hand. 'Always the soul of tact, aren't you, Peter?'

'No, not really. I can be leaden footed often.'

'Not what Philippa says.'

'I don't wear my lead boots over in Owermoigne,' I smiled and removed my hand as if to scratch my nose. There's tact for you.

She pursed her rather over-red lips. 'To think, Peter, I've lived with this man for all this time without really knowing him at all. Isn't that awful? Now I'm not sure whether I will ever want to find out where he has gone or what has happened to him.'

'Yes, you will. You can't wipe out those years just like that.'

'He was going to.'

'We don't know that for sure.'

'We know it near enough, don't we?'

I shrugged and refrained from letting her in on Merinda's back-of-the-barn revelations.

Her hand was back on me. My arm, this time.

'All I'm saying is, if you want to call it a day, it's fine with me. You've been marvellous to bother about Gregory's disappearance at all. God knows how I'll ever repay you for what you've done already.'

As she spoke the last words, her eyes were transmitting a rather different message.

'No, as Magnus Magnusson says on *Mastermind*, I've

started, so I'll finish. You will feel differently about Gregory once you're over his parents' visit and all that.'

She reached across the settee and kissed me on the cheek. I could have killed Saint Laurent.

'All right, Peter,' she said rather too intimately, 'what's your next move?'

I had to fight myself not to be closer to her on the settee.

'I think I'll see Abigail Gordon again.'

She frowned. I knew why.

'What do you expect to find out from her?'

'I'm not sure, but as Patrick Redstart is the most obviously corrupt of Gregory's list and is the most likely to be able to lay his hands on large sums of cash, I thought I would have another go at his weakest link. I got nowhere with a full frontal.'

'You think Gregory may have confided something to her?'

I shrugged. 'I don't know what her role is in all this – even if she has one. But for such a brash and confident lady, she was rather rattled when I saw her on Redstart's yacht.'

Sally laughed and was back touching me again.

'Ladies like Abigail must get rattled quite often, don't you imagine?'

I laughed awkwardly and looked at my watch.

'If I left now, I could fit her in before lunch, maybe.'

She looked hard at me. 'You're afraid of me, Peter, aren't you? After the other day, I mean. When I kissed you like that.'

'No, of course not,' I lied.

'Taken an oath of celibacy while your girlfriend is away in America?'

'No.'

'Well, then.' She leaned towards me once more, only this time more than her mouth made contact. I was about to – to be honest, I'm not quite sure what – when I was saved any decision-making by the bell, a telephone bell. The nipple pressure left my shirt as Sally sat up straight and came out with an unlady-like word. She hesitated for a moment, then raising her eyebrows at me, got up and made for the hall.

From her initial few exchanges, I gathered the call was from Mum and Dad Mann, apologizing for their hastiness of the night before. While Sally was working out whether to continue being hurt and belligerent or move towards some *rapprochement*, I sidled past her and with a whispered, 'See you soon', made my escape.

But once back in my Beetle, I worried about my decision, for now I would never know whether I, or British Telecom, had fought with Opium and won.

The rain followed me all the way to Lyme Regis, wrapping up the road in the grey fog of its scurries and penetrating the pinprick holes in my rag-top as only West-Country downpours can. So by the time I arrived at the Cob, I was not only still sexually frustrated but now damp with it.

Being a bleak winter Sunday, Lyme Regis High Street looked as deserted as Dawson City – the only difference being you can park in Dawson City (or so I'm told). The pub car park by the Cob was almost empty, so I sighed, reversed into a space and cursed the fact that I didn't have a chauffeur called James or whatever chauffeurs are called these days.

Pushing my dirty raincoat collar as high up over my neck and head as it would go without the coat actually leaving my shoulders, I exchanged the occasional dripping of the Volks for the incessant splatting of the wild outdoors. The raindrops hitting my exposed flesh felt like ice picks, as I broke into a run and started up the vertical climb towards The Wood Worm.

By the time I actually reached the shop, my blood pressure must have been at least four million over two million, and my weight, at meanest guess, some eighty gallons. The shop, of course, was shut and dark as a tomb when I peered in, but to my relief, I could see lights in the windows immediately above the premises. I peered around for another door and, at last, found one down a tiny arched alley.

There was no bell, but an obnoxious knocker in the shape of a dolphin. I roused its head and rapped. The noise seemed hardly louder than the racket the raindrops were making on the pavement, so in my general frustration, I rapped really hard three or four more times – this time, to some effect. One, I reckon the noise would have woken Abigail even if she'd been dead, but two, the dolphin came off in my hand. It was thus, clasping a brass fish and/or mammal, that she discovered me. The sodden sight must have been enough to make anybody's mouth swivel around, let alone hers.

'What the hell . . . ?' she began and then recognized who the blotting paper was. '*You*?' She said the word as if it had four letters.

'Yes, it's me. I'm sorry about damaging your knocker.'

She looked down at the dolphin and then back up at what she could see of my face.

'Look, go away. I don't want to see you.'

She made to close the door, but I inserted my size nine waterlogged canoe.

'I'm here to help you,' I said quickly. 'You can't go on for ever hiding behind Redstart.'

'I'm not hiding,' she persevered, but her eyes said otherwise. 'I've got someone here, that's all.'

She tried to squidge my toe-cap with the door.

'I only need a minute.'

At that second, I heard a male voice call down from upstairs. It wasn't Redstart's.

'Who is it?'

She hesitated, then shouted back. 'Marklin. Peter Marklin. That snooper fellow I told you about.'

There was silence for a moment, then I heard footsteps descending the stairs, followed by the opening and closing of two doors. Whoever it was must have made a quick exit via the shop.

'He's gone,' I smiled, licking the rain-water that was running off my nose. 'Can I come in now? I'm really trying to help.' I proffered the brass knocker. 'And if you tell me the going rate for dolphins . . .'

Her mouth and eyes flickered their indecision and then I felt the door pressure ease off my toe-cap.

'I'll give you just five minutes,' she said and held out her hand, not for the knocker, but for my eighty-gallon raincoat. We went upstairs, leaving it emptying on an art nouveau coatstand, marked with a seventy-eight-pound label. I wondered what Abigail's price tag was.

The room she shepherded me into was surprisingly pleasant. The furniture, a combination of Scandinavian and antique, seemed carefully chosen and I didn't see another price label on any of it.

Abigail sat down on a black leather and chrome chair and left me standing, quite literally.

'Hurry up, Mr Marklin, say what you've got to say and then be on your way.'

I took out my handkerchief and dabbed the water off my face. It didn't make much difference. There were still gallons ready to dribble down from my hair.

'All right,' I said and took a real flier. 'I'll begin with the jackpot question: why did your friend Redstart give Gregory Mann ten thousand pounds? What is he so afraid Mann will expose?'

She crossed her up-to-the-chin legs but even so, I caught the surprise in her eyes.

'What . . . what are you talking about?'

I sat down opposite her. I was glad to take the weight off the pools of water in my shoes.

'You know – or maybe, you don't. Maybe dapper Mr Redstart doesn't tell you everything any more than you tell him all about your affairs.'

'How do you – ' she began and I started to think that just maybe my last statement had been bang on the button.

'Mann paid it into his Bournemouth account just before he – disappeared. Now, come on, Miss Gordon, there's no need for you to get caught up in the nasties of your boyfriend. What's he up to, eh? You must have some idea.' I pointed downwards through the carpet. 'Is the shop downstairs on the level or is it some kind of front for stolen goods, or drugs or God knows what? It hasn't escaped me that all sorts of goodies can be smuggled under the guise of a seemingly legitimate antiques business.'

She moved uneasily in the leather chair and it squeaked against her leather skirt. (I forgot to mention she was wearing the full bit.) I knew she was trying to work out whether I was more of a threat thrown out into the street or kept awhile seeping in her sitting-room. She obviously threw her luck on the latter.

'I don't know where you've got all those ludicrous notions from, Mr Marklin, but I would advise you to keep them to yourself. Mr Redstart has taken people to court before for slanderous statements they couldn't sustain.'

'I didn't think I was talking to Mr Redstart, Miss Gordon. I thought I was talking to you. Or is it really the same thing?' I smiled. 'I was hoping for your sake that it wasn't.'

I think she was starting to recover. Her face's big asset began to swivel.

'Mr Redstart and I are not business partners, just friends, pure and simple.' I had grave doubts about the 'pure and simple' bit, but let her continue. 'I don't own this shop. I just run it as a manageress. I don't even keep the accounts. But I do know that every stick we sell, every item we have in stock, has been legitimately bought and has paperwork to prove it. So, Mr Marklin,

136

now we've destroyed that absurd theory of yours, have you got any others? If not – '

'Yes,' I interrupted. 'I've got others. Let me try this one on you. You and Gregory Mann were on the verge of starting an affair, weren't you? Maybe, you were already lovers.'

'How could we be?' she snapped. 'Greg . . . Mr Mann was soon to marry Sally Newton.'

I laughed. 'Gregory Mann wasn't soon to marry anybody and you know it. Now don't try to pull my other leg. It doesn't have bells on. Just answer this. What did your pal Redstart say to you that day I met you at the boat? He didn't know you were seeing Mann, did he? So I'm afraid I must have landed you in it that morning.'

She squeaked around on the chair again. 'All right, so I saw Gregory once or twice. There was no harm in it.'

'How do you know there was no harm in it? Redstart doesn't exactly come over as the forgiving type. And he's too much of a dandy to let his ego get dented by what he would regard as a dumb private eye.'

'He doesn't own me.'

I leant forward until I could smell her fear.

'So if he doesn't own you, don't act as if he does. It makes people suspicious. Not just me. There's the officers of the law.'

The threat didn't seem to work. The swivel started up again.

'Mr Marklin, I think it's time you left.' She looked at her over-shiny watch. 'You're beaten by the clock.' She squeaked up from her chair.

'I'm not beaten by anything yet, Miss Gordon,' I retorted, with paper-thin confidence. I got to my soggy feet and she ushered me to the door. As I went out on the landing, I turned back to her. 'If you liked Gregory Mann enough to start something with him, how come *you* are not looking for him? It just could be because you know what has happened to him, couldn't it, and you're too scared to do anything about it?'

My lance did not seem to strike to her very vitals. She just waved me on across the landing and down the stairs. With a sigh, I did as I was bid, but then had a thought. Once in the hall, I did not proceed onwards to the front door as she was expecting, but doubled back into the house.

As she cried out to stop me, I found a door that I guessed must lead into the shop. I opened it and my hunch, for once, was right. The man I'd surprised her with had not really left. He was sitting beside a grand-father clock, hidden from view from the street windows, and looked mightily surprised to see me.

'Sorry,' I said. 'I thought you had gone.'

He instantly put his hand up to his face but not before I recognized him.

'I thought people hid from the police, not police from the people,' I quipped, but by then Abigail Gordon had pulled me back from the door. I knew better than to be seen by the law fighting with a woman, so I tipped my wet hair and left.

But not before I'd remembered to leave three fivers for the damaged dolphin on a hall-stand marked a hundred and twenty-five pounds.

I wondered I didn't get pneumonia that day. I had to wait over an hour in a shop doorway a hundred yards or so up the street before he left. And then paddle after him, dodging in and out of doorways, so he wouldn't see me. Didn't do me much good though, except the trail led me back to where I had parked my Beetle – and where he had parked a Lada that looked overdue for the great scrap-yard in the sky.

A moment later and he'd gone. There was not much point in tearing after him in the car. After all, I would always know where to find him when he was wearing his constable's uniform. That is, when he wasn't accompanying Digby Whetstone on his rounds, which is where I had first seen him – at Stringle's urine palace, standing on the steps, pad in hand, tough-guy moustache a-quiver.

I shivered all the way home, anxious to dry my outside and warm my inside with some overdue lunch. And all the way I wondered what the hell Abigail was doing with a lowly constable, even if he did sport an SAS moustache. She didn't appear to me to be the type who looked for the inner man. She was an 'outer' girl, if ever I saw one and, even with the best will in the world, the constable's exterior could not be compared with a Redford, Stallone or even a Joe Bugner. He wasn't a terrier type, like Bruce Willis of *Moonlighting* either. More like a Ronnie Corbett on stilts than any of those, and without Ronnie Corbett's money, what's more.

So, if dear Abigail wasn't consorting with him for corporal or financial reasons, just what was going on? He was obviously more than embarrassed at seeing me and had done everything to avoid it, except get *in* the grandfather clock. So what was bugging him? He obviously couldn't have been on any official assignment, otherwise he would not have acted that way, nor been in plain clothes and driving a clapped out Lada rather than a sprauncy police Ford. So . . .

I never got farther than 'so' before my Toy Emporium hove into view. I parked the Volks, fed a justly complaining Bing, stripped off, had a bath, downed a couple of Heinekens and devoured a frozen sweet and sour chicken for four without noticing there should have been enough for three other people. (Just how thin do frozen food companies think their customers want to be?)

The mechanics of sustaining life out of the way, I was about to settle down in my favourite armchair and ruminate à le Sherlock Holmes, but sans pipe or hookah, when I noticed the skies had lightened and the rain had stopped. Thunderstruck, so to speak, I plucked up courage and instead of ruminating, rambled down to Gus's. He was in, watching the Sunday afternoon movie, *The Magnificent Seven*.

It took a bit of doing to transport Gus back to reality and England (a six-pack, actually), but eventually we were ensconced in his Ford Popular and banging and bouncing our way over towards Jimmy Richardson's to pick up my Daimler.

En route, to take my mind off the hazards of the journey (Gus's driving), I brought him up to date on the Gregory Mann saga. Typical Gus: he did not seem surprised by anything I told him. I think if the sandwich-board man's warnings were ever proved to be correct and the end of the world actually came nigh, he would only shrug or see how much he could down before it happened.

'Well, you can never trust a woman like that, now can you? Might have it away with anybody – especially if she wanted something.' He took a huge hand off the battered steering wheel from which the horn button hung out on its wire and prodded me in the ribs. 'You'd better watch out yerself next time.'

Gus's remarks gave me a thought.

'Maybe that's the explanation: she wants something from old macho moustache. Like, maybe, his silence about something . . . or something.'

I smiled innocently across at Gus.

'What do you think?' I prompted.

'You mean she's obliging him to keep his mouth shut?' He laughed and added, 'Except when he's obliging her, that is.'

'Well, could be, couldn't it?'

'Orrrr . . .' Gus prolonged the word until I wasn't sure whether he was about to give an alternative or be sick, '. . . rrr might be the other way round, with him doing the forcing. You know, "Drop 'em or I'll drop by old Whetstone's office and spill the beans".'

'What beans?'

'Lord knows. What ever he may have found out about her or Redstart.'

'H'mmm,' was all I found to say.

'Going to mention it to Whetstone?' he asked with a grin.

'Oh sure,' I nodded and closed my eyes as Gus missed an old lady on a bike by the denier of her Lyle stockings. 'That would put me in well with him, wouldn't it? "Digby dear, I think one of your constables is guilty of laying a lady in Lyme Regis." '

Gus chuckled.

'That's all I can accuse him of, isn't it?' I went on. 'And laying ladies in Lyme Regis isn't yet prohibited by law. Should be, with that hill, but it isn't.'

Gus took his eyes off the road again to wag a thick finger at me. 'So what are you going to do, old son? Sit on the information and hope it'll hatch?'

It was then I saw her. 'Gus, look OUT!' I screamed and leaned across to grab the wheel from him. By some miracle, four hands on the wheel managed to slew the car across the still slightly damp road, without either hitting the girl, or the car ending up on its roof. However, we were now well and truly stuck in the fast flowing ditch. I could see the water welling in through the collander of Gus's door.

I got out quickly, no easy task with the crazy tilt of the car, and ran back to the girl. She smiled with recognition as I neared her and I saw it was Molly, the thatcher's daughter. I took her by the hand.

'Are you all right?' I asked anxiously.

To my relief, she gave me a broad grin.

'Toys,' she said quite distinctly. 'Toys . . . toys . . . toys.'

Five minutes later, Gus and I were plodding up a muddy and slidy track towards what we imagined must be the thatcher's house on the top of a steep ridge.

141

Certainly, it looked a fine advertisement for him, with its crowning glory of fresh golden reed, thick and splendidly fashioned, with a distinctive scalloped edging to its ridge, and surmounted at each end by small, straw peacocks.

But as we ascended the track, we could now see that the building was a large barn and not a house. Molly pointed ever onwards.

'More, more,' she smiled and pulled at my hand.

Another twenty paces or so and we saw the stone cottage. It nestled in a slight dip and was, curiously, smaller than the barn and with a less recently thatched roof, the reed having matured to a pale-ish grey. We strode down to it and soon were in the small cobbled yard which immediately fronted the cottage. Gus made to knock on the stable-type door.

Molly shook her close cropped head. 'Out, out,' she grinned.

Gus tried all the same, but no amount of rat-tatting could raise a soul.

I looked at Molly.

'Do you know when your Daddy will be back?' I asked slowly.

'Back?'

'Back home. Here.'

'Not home,' she smiled, then shook her head. 'Not home.'

Gus tried the handle on the door. The top half opened. 'We can get in,' he observed, stating the obvious.

'It won't help us,' I said. 'Tom Sweet must have left Molly indoors and she got out and down to the road. We can't risk that happening again.'

Gus closed the door again.

'So what have you got in mind, old son? All of us hanging about 'ere in the bitter cold until dad comes home, or sitting in the ditch in me car?'

I thought for a minute.

'Look, Merinda's caravan isn't far up the road. Maybe we could leave Molly there. She knows Merinda, thank goodness, and it would give us a chance to think how we're going to get your car out of the ditch.'

Gus sniffed. 'Know already how I'm going to do that, matey.'

'Oh? How, pray? You and I can't manhandle it out of there. It would be an eighth labour of Hercules.'

Gus pointed to the barn. 'Saw an old Fordson tractor in the back of there. A man like Tom Sweet is bound to have some rope or chains around. While you take Molly round to Merinda's, I'll get the old thing going.'

'Gus,' I shouted, 'you don't mean to tell me you are going to borrow somebody's tractor without a say-so, are you? Anyway, he won't have left the keys around, I don't suppose.'

Gus threw his arms in the air. 'You don't know about boats. You don't know about old tractors. They don't *need* bloody keys. Dear, oh dear. What do you know about – 'cept old toys?'

'Toys, toys, toys,' Molly repeated, her eyes wide and gleaming.

'Cor,' Gus went on. 'There you are with a ruddy shop full of toys and I bet Molly here hasn't been given a toy since she – '

He stopped and looked away. I knew what he was going to say, 'since she grew up'. But he was right, was old Gus, as he often is, though I hate to admit it. Sixteen or so she might be, but Molly would always be a child, however much grown-ups might like to gloss over or ignore the fact.

I took her hand once more.

'Have you got any toys, Molly?'

She nodded, and began pulling me up towards the barn, whither Gus was already now plodding. I went along.

Whilst Gus was fiddling around in the back of the barn with the tractor (I couldn't stop him. Once he gets

143

a bee in his bonnet, or someone else's bonnet in this case, you have to let it buzz around until it drops.) Molly led me to a little side door that, once opened, disclosed a ladder into what was obviously a hay-loft. She mounted the rungs, continually looking back to check that I was following.

The first thing I did in the loft was to check on the density of an oak beam with my forehead. Molly laughed and led me across the straw-strewn floor to a corner, where five or six bales of straw had been arranged to form a kind of miniature corral. She invited me inside; I accepted.

This was, quite obviously, where Molly spent a great deal of her time, for arranged against the inside of the bales was a wide and varied collection of what were plainly her treasures. To the right, there were half a dozen dolls of various sizes, each one neatly dressed in Victorian rather than modern style. (There were no Barbies or Cindys, thank the Lord. Indeed, two or three of the dolls, china-faced and cherubic, were of considerable vintage, probably hand-me-downs from previous generations and worth considerable sums today.) To the left were stuffed animals of every sort, teddies, Rupert Bears, dogs, cats and some obviously home-made and knitted farm animals, cows, ponies, pigs and the like.

In the centre (I almost trod on one of the pieces), carefully arranged, was an assortment of miniature farm animals and agricultural machinery that I instantly recognized as being of Britains Ltd manufacture: donkeys, sheep, pigs, cows, horses, chickens and tractors, bailers, ploughs and even a red combine harvester.

Molly sat down cross-legged amongst the dolls.

'Toys,' she grinned, picking up the oldest of all the dolls and rocking it to and fro so that its curly lashed eyes opened and shut.

'Toys,' I repeated and knelt down carefully opposite her. From below, I could now hear a clanking of chains, as Gus rummaged amongst the thatcher's possessions. I picked up a Britains' Land Rover that I had almost knelt on.

'Car,' she beamed. 'Car.' She pointed at me. 'More cars . . .'

'I've got cars, yes,' I smiled.

'Like cars.'

I nodded. 'So do I.'

She took the Land Rover from me and pushed it along the floorboards. 'Vroom.'

'Vroom.' I suddenly had a thought that would please old Gus's heart. 'Molly, I've got a car at the shop that you would like.'

She sat looking at me with eyes like saucers, as if I were some god.

'It goes along and keeps a little ball up in the air.'

I could see I had lost her a bit with the description.

'I'll bring the car next time I'm over this way.'

'Bring car?'

'Yes. Promise. You'll like it.'

I rubbed my hands together; it was pretty cold even though we were out of the wind and our breath showed it.

'Aren't you cold?' I asked, but she shook her head.

Curiously, she looked warm as toast, even though she wasn't wearing a coat. Perhaps she was so used to playing in the barn that she did not notice what the temperature was. From what little I had seen through the window of the inside of the cottage, it looked highly unlikely that anything as sophisticated as central heating had ever been dreamt of – electricity, I reckoned, was the latest wonder there – so I guessed she had to make do with the obvious warmth of her personality to see her through. (As you may gather, I was starting to fall under the spell of Molly's disarming simplicity. With all her problems, she looked happier than any of us. Where the hell did we all go wrong? By kidding ourselves we'd grown up, maybe?)

145

'Would you like to go to Merinda's? Remember, the caravan?'

'Cavan,' she smiled, Cheshire cat style.

'Yes. If your daddy isn't back by the time we leave, I could take you there,' I said slowly.

The grin stayed and she took my hand. I was right. She was warm as toast and her contact warmed me.

It was then I heard the success of Gus's cheeky endeavours, the phut-phutting of what I took to be the Fordson's engine. Molly looked slightly frightened.

'It's all right, Molly. My friend has just started your daddy's tractor, so that we can tow his car out of the ditch.'

I didn't know whether she fully understood, but she got up and led me back to the ladder.

'Down,' she said.

So down I went. As I did so, I looked back at the little world in the corral of straw bales.

It didn't look half bad to me.

Twenty minutes later, the Popular (misnomer of all time) was out of the ditch and parked by the thatcher's gate. Except for a crushed right wing, a cracked head-light glass and a water garden for a floor, it was the wreck it always had been, at least in my memory.

'Strong, these Fords,' Gus had observed, rapping his huge knuckles on the damaged headlight, which promptly sagged to the side.

'Talking about the structure or the smell it makes?' I laughed, at which Gus took umbridge, whatever that is.

'Well, it was good enough for you to want to ride in to pick up your ruddy Daimler,' he grumbled and he was right.

I looked at my watch in the now rapidly fading light.

'My God, yes. I'd almost forgotten why we came out here. We had better get going, because I would rather not drive the Daimler back totally in the dark, and you have your broken headlight.'

I took Molly's hand.

'Would you like us to take you to Merinda in the caravan? I'll leave a note on the cottage door to say where you are.'

'Yes. Cavan. Minda.'

So it all looked settled. But as I was scrubbing around in Gus's Popular trying to find a scrap of paper on which to write a note for her father, I heard a motor cycle coming along the road. Molly recognized the sound instantly.

'Daddy. Daddy come,' she said.

I looked up and in the distance could see a figure all in black astride a rather old-fashioned looking bike, which turned out to be a Norton. It was not until he was right up to me and had flipped the visor on his black helmet that I saw that Molly had been right, and it was Tom Sweet.

I smiled and moved towards him, before I had seen the look in his eyes.

'What are you lot doing here?'

He dismounted and took off his gauntlets. He looked pretty angry.

'Peter Marklin,' I said. 'Remember? We met at Lady Philippa's.'

He ignored my remark and looked around. It was then he spotted his tractor that Gus had yet to put away. He strode over to Molly and stood in front of her, as if Gus and I might be some kind of rapists or child molesters.

'What are you doing here?' he repeated.

He turned to Gus. 'And who's this?'

'He's a friend of mine, Gus Tribble. He was giving me a lift in his car when . . .' I hesitated, because I didn't want to get Molly into any trouble. After all, she was probably under strict instructions never to venture into the road.

'. . . the car seemed to go out of control and we landed in the ditch.'

He looked even less enthralled with my story than I was. I pointed at the muddy and crumpled wing. 'See for yourself. That's the side we landed on.'

He came nearer me.

'That's as maybe. But who gave you permission to come up here and use my tractor?'

'No one. I'm sorry,' Gus intervened and I was thankful for the diversion of the thatcher's gaze. 'We went up to yer 'ouse, see, but no one was in – but your daughter 'ere, that is.'

'Molly in the house?' He laughed. 'Not if she can be in the barn, where I left her.'

'Molly came out of the barn, that's right,' Gus said hastily, much to my relief. 'Yer. Must have 'eard us tramping by up to the cottage.'

'So when you found nobody around, you just took the liberty of pinching my tractor to pull your car out. That it?'

'Didn't mean any harm. I thought round here neighbour helped neighbour,' Gus smiled.

Tom Sweet didn't smile back.

'You're no neighbour of mine. And I don't lend no tractors to to one, either. Neighbour or not.'

Gus fiddled in his pocket. 'Anyway, I've said I'm sorry.'

He took out a battered billfold and extracted a fiver. I looked around for the moths. ''Aven't done no harm to it. But here's something for having borrowed it.'

The thatcher gestured the money away, then strode slowly around us, Molly in his wake.

Eventually he said, 'I'm not letting you two go, until I've checked on what else you might have been up to. There have been too many burglaries around these parts.'

I guess he thought we might have been out to burgle

148

his place and was checking we hadn't any loot on our persons.

I shook my head. 'We haven't been up to anything, honestly. We just borrowed your tractor to get our car out.'

He crooked his finger. 'Maybe you're telling the truth. Maybe you're not. Any road, come on back up to me house. I said you're not going until I've had a good look round. I've had stuff pinched before by people like you. How do I know you weren't just about to make off with my tractor?'

I started walking. I had no option with the Thomas Hardy archetype. But I flung out a last plea, all the same.

'But you've met me at Lady Philippa's. You know I'm not a – '

He didn't even let me finish.

'I don't know anything. All sorts of people drop by at her nurseries. Her ladyship has to be friendly with all of them, doesn't she, otherwise she wouldn't sell enough to keep a cat alive.'

He had a point, so I frowned at Gus to obviate any further argument and we dutifully trekked back up the hill to stand freezing in Tom Sweet's cobbled yard, whilst he went over the cottage and barn with a fine-toothed magnifying glass to see if we had half-inched anything.

As a result, it was freezing hard and darker than pitch by the time we actually rolled up at Jimmy Richardson's. And by the time I'd rolled back home in the Daimler, having kept a wary eye out for Gus's single good headlamp in my mirror all the way, I was bushed, Bing was belligerent and Sunday, dear Sunday, was well and truly blown.

10

I opened up shop on Monday morning. I had to, otherwise collectors would imagine I had won the pools and no longer needed their custom. But before I turned my 'Closed' sign over and slipped the bolts, I made one phone call. It took about ten minutes to discover what I wanted: the name of the constable who had accompanied Digby Whetstone that morning at Urine Palace. Ultimately a very helpful policewoman replaced an unhelpful sergeant and informed me, from the description I gave her, that he was likely to have been a PC Oliver Smart. Naturally, I couldn't go so far as to ask where he lived, so I thanked her and hung up.

Now armed with a piece of information I could as yet do little about, I threw the Toy Emporium open to the public. For the first couple of hours the great British public looked the other way, for not one punter came in, not even to browse.

I was busying myself rearranging the window (an operation I carried out fairly frequently, mainly to pretend my stock turns over with lightning speed), when I spied a crumpled wing and a broken headlamp out of the corner of my eye. A moment later and Gus had ting'd his way into the Emporium. I clambered out of the window just in time to prevent him bumping into a stack of mint-boxed Dinkies and Corgis that I had just removed from display.

'Tartin' up your front, then?' he sniffed, with not so much as a 'Good mornin'.

'Yes, I'm tarting up my front, Gus, as you so delicately put it. To what do I owe the honour?'

He saw me look at my watch. 'No, I know the blinkin' sun's not over the yardarm, old son, but I've been thinking.'

I scratched my head and went back to the counter.

'About what, Gus?'

'Us,' he said, for all the world like some dissatisfied wife talking about her marriage.

'Us?' I laughed.

'Yeah,' he persevered, ignoring my merriment. 'You are getting all the fun again, aren't you?'

'What fun, Gus?'

'The sleuthing lark, you great berk. You know what I mean.'

I sat down, elbows on counter. 'Come on, Gus, you just tell me what fun I've had on this whole Gregory Mann saga.'

He shrugged his big shoulders. 'Well, you . . . er, I mean . . . get to see some fancy bits of stuff, don't you? That there Sally Newton is more than a bit of all right and even that piece over at Lyme, I wouldn't throw that out of bed.'

I laughed again. 'Gus, don't tell me you are jealous of my seeing someone like Abigail Gordon?'

'Naah. Not jealous, you pillock. But it's more exciting than sitting on your bum round here on a cold and rainy day, isn't it?'

I suddenly had an idea that might help me – and not just by ending this stupid conversation.

'Gus, if you think I'm getting all the fun, and you're not, then pin back those ears of yours and listen to this. I'm glad you've dropped by today,' I invented, 'because I've got a job for you. And from all you've just said, you will love it.'

Dear old Gus. He tried to hide his interest by turning away from the counter and pretending to inspect a Chinese made tin-plate Karmann-Ghia.

'What's that, then? I'm a bit busy along now, but – '

'I want you to drive over to Lyme, park your car

well away from the High Street and keep a watch on The Wood Worm shop and the flat over it.'

'How do I do that then, without me brass monkeys falling off with the cold?'

'There's a small café opposite.' I went to the till and took out a tenner, which I handed to him. 'Here, this is to cover coffee, or whatever, and then some lunch. You can always pretend you are waiting for somebody who doesn't turn up if the owners of the café think it's all a bit funny.'

'What am I supposed to be watching, then?'

'Who comes and goes.'

He turned back to me. 'You mean you're expecting that policeman fella to come back.'

'Maybe. By the way, I've found out that his name is Oliver Smart.'

Gus chuckled. 'He wasn't very smart that day you caught him at Abigail's.'

'No, that's why he may be foolish enough to return.'

'Give me his description, then.'

I did so and Gus continued, 'Anyone else you're expecting?'

'I don't know. Redstart may well come, but that's to be expected. It's the unexpected I'm looking for. There's obviously something going on and I want to know what the hell it could be.'

'What are you going to do, then, while I'm sitting like a spare prick in that café, gorging myself to death. By the way, I 'ope to 'eaven they've got a licence.'

'They have got a licence. But don't drink so much you miss what might be going on over the road.'

He gave a scout's salute. (At least I like to think it was a scout's salute.) 'As to what I am going to do, I'm going to sit here and try to make a living this morning. This afternoon, who knows? I might call round at that school again or see that animal crank. I shouldn't put all my eggs in Redstart's basket. After all, PC Smart having the hots or whatever it is for

Abigail Gordon may well have nothing to do with our missing detective.'

'Well, you just watch out, then. Don't trust schoolmasters any more than I do Dobermanns.'

'You haven't seen much of either, have you, Gus?' I laughed. He ignored me, as he should.

'Well, I'd better be on my way,' he said, limbering up his shoulders, as if he were about to step into the ring with Mike Tyson.

'You watch out, too,' I smiled. 'Just stick to keeping a note of who goes in and out of both the shop and the flat. For goodness' sake, don't get involved in anything more. Don't follow anybody or go into the shop, or intervene whatever happens, just – '

But I was speaking to a brick wall. He had turned at the door, smiled, then left. I watched his Ford Popular shudder out of sight and immediately started to worry about having sent Gus off to Lyme at all. I had just crossed my fingers when I heard the phone ring; so they weren't destined to be crossed for long.

It was Sally. And she had some news that certainly cut down my options for the afternoon.

'I was in the newsagent's next door,' she said, excitedly, 'because they delivered the wrong paper this morning, and the lady there was chatting to the woman in front of me about Ferndales school. Apparently, it all happened last evening.'

'What happened?' I asked, 'and how does your newsagent know about Ferndales?'

'Her sister works there as a part-time cleaner. Anyway, let me tell the story. When this lady got to the school this morning, she found that Jonathan Smythe had been taken off by the police last night, together with his matron, the Mary Withers mentioned in Greg's file. And the rumour going round the kitchen staff is that the headmaster and matron are being investigated following a complaint made by one of the senior girls.'

153

'What kind of complaint?' I asked. '*News of the World* type?'

'You guessed it, Peter. The police have been back this morning and, so the gossip goes, have found a two-way mirror at the back of matron's surgery. I couldn't hear all that the woman in the newsagents was saying, but it would appear that this Withers character was indeed a bit butch. Whatever the real facts of the case, the headmaster and the matron were kept over-night down at the police station, where they still are, and the schoolgirl has, apparently, left the school in the care of her parents. So now you see why I rang you, Peter. This must be what Mrs Teddington's daughter had been on about – what she asked Gregory to investigate.'

'Yes. She wasn't lying after all, it would appear,' I said reflectively and Sally castigated me for not sounding as excited as she was.

'I'm sorry, Sally, it's just that Jonathan Smythe's stay with the police doesn't really help us any, does it? You see, I was planning to drop by his way again this afternoon, beard the beard in his den and come out in the open with the real purpose of my visit.'

'Well, you can't right now – '

'Exactly. And now we know that Smythe *did* actually have something to hide. Maybe something he might have – '

'Killed for?' she offered. 'Peter, don't pussyfoot any more about Gregory. What we've learned about him since his disappearance has, bit by bit, built a protective cocoon round me. I can't be hurt that much any more . . . I hope. But it doesn't stop me being curious about what may have happened, though.'

'I know.' I thought for a moment. 'Look, Sally, all we can hope for with Smythe right now is that the police will look into more aspects of his activities than just the ogling of naked schoolgirls in Matron's surgery, or gay rompings or whatever. After all, Digby Whetstone now has the perfect opportunity to grill Smythe as deeply and widely as he wishes, which he could hardly do before. I wish I was sitting in on that.'

'To see he asks the right questions?'

'Something like that.'

'You don't reckon him, do you?'

'I reckon any policeman has got a bloody hard job.'

She chortled. 'So we will have to forget Mr Smythe for a bit.'

'And concentrate on the other two, Redstart and Stringle.'

'Why don't you let me try Stringle?' Sally suggested. 'I can tell him I'm a pussy lover.'

'No. I'll take on the Dobermann Pinschers,' I replied, doing my best to ignore her come-on. 'I've seen *Crocodile Dundee*. I'll just make with the fingers and eyes like Paul Hogan.'

'I like Paul Hogan,' she said softly. 'Now, if you bought yourself a hat like his – '

'I'd better grab some lunch and get off,' I said quickly. 'I don't want to be at Stringle's when it gets dark. Dobermanns tend to merge with the night.'

'So do I,' she said.

I'll swear the receiver quivered in my hand.

I parked the Volks about a hundred yards from Stringle's house, around a bend. Yellow Beetle convertibles aren't two a penny round Purbeck way and, for that matter, nor are Peter Marklins – so I played as safe as I could.

I pulled my anorak collar up around my head and twisted a scarf round the lower part of my face, as if to protect me from the bitter cold of the day. I know Sherlock Holmes would have perfected a somewhat more fiendish disguise, but there you go. Approaching the house with considerable angst, I tried to work out from the layout of Stringle's overgrown land, where best to make a Dobermann-free entry, for I reckoned, before making any official visit, I might as well do a recce of his garden and outbuildings first, in case I was thrown out the instant I rat-tatted on his front door.

The decision was risky, I know, but as my old mother used to say, nothing ventured . . .

I eventually climbed in over a low stone wall surmounted by a wire fence about two hundred feet from the only side of the house that did not have windows – just a forbidding-looking door. Keeping low, I made my way through waist-high rotting nettles and vegetation, which made me wet in no time, towards a thatched stable-like building some distance from the back of the house.

As I went, I cast my beady eyes across the land to see if I could detect any signs of recent soil disturbance. But there was none. Just limp wet weeds and grass that had obviously not met a tending hand for many an old season. Here and there, to my dismay, I saw tracks through the undergrowth that spoke of animals with sharp teeth, but so far I had neither spotted one nor, seemingly, disturbed one. I licked my finger and held it in the air. I was, purely by accident, downwind of the house. I decided to try to keep it that way.

Proceeding round the back of what actually turned out to be stables, I tried to find some way of getting in without having to go round the front and thus risk being spotted. The only opening I could see, however, was high up above my head and I could not even reach the rotting sill. I looked around for something on which to stand or climb up, but ladders, barrels or boxes were there none. I came out with my favourite expletive that covered situations like this, then saw a jumble of logs half hidden amongst some blackberry bushes. I sighed and set to work.

Three minutes or so later, I had traded a certain amount of blood to the blackberries in exchange for a rather unstable pile of damp wood just high enough, I considered, for me to be able to reach the window. I clambered up on them and found I could now clutch the rusty metal bar that divided the unglazed window down the middle. After a great deal of heaving, I managed to get my stomach up on the sill; next, my whole body in the opening – and then it was only the work of a split second to fall like a stone some ten feet into God knows what.

After I had checked all my limbs to see if they bent and extended like they used to, I looked around in the gloom. I seemed to be lying between two banks of cages. As I struggled to my feet and my eyes got used to the lack of light, I saw other eyes watching me. The cages were full of animals: rabbits, guinea pigs, some asleep, some sniffing, scratching, others just sitting there peering at the clumsy fool who had just dropped into their world. I suddenly realized what an idiot I had been. The stables could well have housed far less cuddly animals – and there would have been no way any Paul Hoganism would have saved yours truly.

It was as I was dusting myself off, that I heard the first bark. Almost instantly, a second dog joined in and I guessed the Dobermanns must have heard my fall or shuffling around in the stables. I instantly looked back at the window from which I had fallen. It seemed even higher from inside. Desperately I looked round for something to climb on and, to my immense relief, discovered an old ladder resting against the far end of the stables. As I propped it up against the wall, I heard the barking increase in volume – and it wasn't an extra dog joining in. It was the same dogs getting nearer.

I scrambled up the ladder with the speed of light and pulled myself into the opening. As I crouched there, looking at the ground, I realized a jump down onto a pile of slippery logs was a far more hazardous undertaking than climbing up from them. I could see myself lying with a broken ankle or worse, surrounded by Dobermanns salivating for the fresh meat that used to be Peter Marklin.

I looked upwards. The opening was only a foot or so from the thatch. If I could get up there, at least I might be safe from the fang fraternity, if not from their fanatical master. As I hesitated, my mind was made up for me by the appearance of the first slavering, barking darling. I literally clutched at straws, as the dog stood on all fours on top of my pile of logs, so that I could almost feel its breath. Luckily, the thatch being thin and old as the hills meant there was precious little overhang and a fairly shallow pitch helped me as I stood on the sill and clawed my way up, holding on to the withies that seamed age-old patches over the whole roof. I didn't stop until I was sitting astride the crown, if that's what you call the damp and rotting ridge of thatch that ran across the centre of the roof. I could no longer see the dogs now, just hear them, of course, but I had a generous view of everything else, as Stringle, if he were about, would have had of me.

I waited for the inevitable with my heart in my mouth, and tried to work on excuses for being discovered on the roof of the stables, having clearly climbed in and out without so much as a nod to the owner. But although the dogs still barked, the house itself remained quiet as a tomb. After five minutes, I reckoned Mr Stringle must be out or been afflicted with total deafness since my previous visit. I opted for the former and surveyed the ground all round the stables from my lofty perch to see if there was even the slenderest chance of escaping without suffering the death of a thousand fangs.

At first, I could see none, but then noticed that at the end of the stables farthest from where I was, there seemed to be a long wire enclosure which I assumed was some kind of run for Stringle's assortment of animals.

I started to inch my way along the ridge, legs still astride, to get a better view of the run and, as I did so, my left foot dug into what I thought was a decayed piece of thatch, and I almost lost my balance. Looking down, I saw to my disgust that I had dislodged the rotting carcase of a crow, its body alive with creepy-crawlies. The sight was all my spirits needed right then.

From the vantage point at the end of the roof, I could see the netted run would give me protection from the Dobermanns for quite a way up the overgrown garden; but, sod's law, it ended with a door some ten feet or so from a wooden fence that ran around the front of the house, obviously to keep the dogs from savaging postmen, milkmen, dustmen and other visitors Stringle and his Urine Palace might attract. Now, I figured the fence was just about climbable – at least by somebody whose alternative was being a dog's dinner – but the ten-foot gap was something else. I could not think of any way of distracting the dogs long enough to make a run for it. That is, until I remembered the dead crow.

I still wake up at night, sweating and shouting aloud at the remembrance of those next few minutes. Suffice it to say, the stratagem would never have worked if: a) Stringle had decided on owning three Dobermanns rather than two; b) the crow had been dead twenty-four hours more; c) my shoe hadn't come off in lieu of my foot; d) one snarling Dobermann hadn't attacked the other snarling Dobermann in order to get more of the running and climbing food; e) I'd cared how I landed the other side.

However, on that last point, I certainly started to care once I *was* over. Care quite a bit, for my left ankle hurt like merry hell or rather, very sad hell. At first, I thought I must have broken it, but thankfully, it passed the acid test of bearing an ounce and a quarter of my weight without either turning over or causing me to pass out. But sprained it badly, I certainly had.

With my heart still going a thousand to the dozen, I started to hobble back to where I'd left the Beetle, clothes wet and streaked with mud and dirt and my face, no doubt, a study in pain and disappointment.

For, seemingly, I had gained sweet Fanny Adams from my visit to Stringle's; except an ankle that badly needed strapping up. It wasn't until later, much later, that I realized I had actually learned rather a lot.

I had to drive the Volks home without using the clutch and I was quite proud of my clutchless gear changes (a technique I had perfected years before on my father's old Jowett Javelin). After my débâcle at Stringle's, I had to find some achievement, however modest, to restore my spirits. By the time I reached the first few houses in Studland, I had the next hour or so all mapped out to restore the rest of me: for instance, long bath, followed by inspection of ankle, followed by either strapping up (I had a good first aid box), or a limp round to the doctor's surgery. But as my Toy Emporium hove into sight, and I saw Sally Newton's car parked outside, I guessed the Marklin restoration scheme would have to be drastically revised, if not cancelled.

She waved as I passed her to park around the side and by the time I was at my front door, so was she.

'My God, Peter, you're limping,' was her first comment. 'And look at your face and clothes. Oh, Peter, what on earth happened?' Her face displayed genuine horror and concern.

I let her in and she gently helped me off with my anorak, as if I were as frail as a Chelsea Pensioner.

'Don't worry, Sally,' I smiled. 'It's not as bad as it looks. Just a sprain and the odd bruise or two.'

'Did you have a fight with Stringle, or what?'

'No. I didn't even see him.'

'Then how . . . ?'

'I had a running argument with two of his four-legged house guests,' I began and told her very briefly what had happened.

'Hell, Peter, I should never have let you go,' was her verbal reaction when I had finished. Her physical reaction was to hug me tight, her lovely head on my shoulder. (The sensation was, however, slightly spoiled by the hug aggravating the odd bruise.)

From that moment on, my life was taken completely out of my hands. For Sally Newton was determined to fulfill the multi-function role of nurse, mother, mental and physical therapist, wife, mistress and all round good egg. To tell you the truth, in the state and mood I was in, I sat back and indulged in her reassuring and comforting attentions. About the only thing I did insist on carrying out alone was my bath but, even there, she sat right outside the bathroom door (which she made me promise not to lock) in case I might need assistance.

Thus, within the hour, the Marklin restoration process was, after all, completed and I was lying on the settee, ankle crepe-bandaged, with foot on a cushion and a stiff Scotch and soda in my hand.

Sally, her hair rather deliciously over one eye from her exertions, looked down on me with a certain satisfaction in her smile.

'Can I light your fire?' she asked, pointing at the dead ashes in the grate.

I refrained from the obvious, that she could light anybody's fire, and said, 'That would be nice. There are some sticks in that log basket. Paper and matches in the kitchen.'

So, within two shakes of Bing's tail, she had the fire ablaze, in front of which Bing immediately plonked himself.

'It's just as well I was too impatient to wait for you to ring me, isn't it?' Sally smiled from the armchair opposite me.

'I'm only too sorry I've got nothing really to report.'

'Oh, it's enough to know you couldn't see any newly turned soil,' she smiled kindly. 'You know, maybe we should leave it all to the police from now on. After all, I gather that Jonathan Smythe and his butch matron are still down at the station and I tremble at the thought

161

of you ever visiting Stringle again. So that only leaves Redstart and the charming Abigail. And maybe that policeman you saw is really a tail appointed by Digby Whetstone to keep tabs on the lady and her boyfriend. The police may be more acute than we give them credit for.'

'Maybe,' I said without too much conviction.

'Anyway,' she continued, 'you will have to rest that ankle of yours for a few days until it gets better, so further sleuthing is out for a bit.'

'Maybe.'

'Maybe nothing. I'm going to see you don't move from this house until you're better.'

I was a little alarmed at how she planned to achieve such an aim, but let it ride for the moment. I sipped some more Scotch and said, with a jaunty smile, 'It doesn't stop me having agents in the field.'

She raised her lovely eyebrows.

'What agents? What field?'

'A mature and experienced emissary of mine is, as of this moment, in Lyme Regis keeping track of all the comings and goings at The Wood Worm and Abigail's place.'

'My goodness, who's that? You didn't tell me you were going to employ others.' She looked terribly concerned. 'I owe you enough already, without you dipping into your pocket again for – '

'I haven't dipped in any pocket,' I said reassuringly. 'It's only Gus Tribble. He asked me this morning if he could get into the act a bit, so I asked if he would like to keep a watch over in Lyme.'

'Wow! Poor old Gus. He'll freeze to death on a day like this.'

'No, he won't. Least, I hope he won't.' I explained about the café, then looked at my watch. 'He will probably be darting in and out of pubs very soon, if he's not on his way back already.'

'How long did you ask him to hang around?'

'I didn't. Anyway, Gus has his own ideas about time. Mostly he ignores it altogether.'

She laughed. 'I don't know why you and Gus bother with my weird problems – especially now it looks as if Greg isn't really worth finding, anyway.'

'Everyone is worth finding.'

She sipped her G and T thoughtfully, then said softly, 'I think he must be dead, you know.'

I didn't comment, for I sort of agreed with her verdict. The whole affair was certainly smelling that way at that moment.

'And I think that Redstart is more likely to be the . . . murderer than the other two. And he's the most likely to have coughed up the ten thousand pounds that Greg banked, don't you agree?'

I shrugged. 'I suppose so. That's why I'm still probing his weakest link – Abigail. Or rather Gus is.' I finished my Scotch. 'The only thing that troubles me is whether jealousy is a strong enough motive for Redstart to murder a man to whom he had, if we're right, only just paid ten thousand smackeroos. And somehow, also, I'm not sure Abigail is the kind of woman you murder for. I would imagine her sexual track record is as varied as his own is supposed to be. He doesn't come over as a man under anybody's spell, either. And I would have thought that to murder for someone, you have to be a bit under their spell.'

She rose and came over to kneel by my settee. I offered my empty glass to her extending hand, just in case it had other operations in mind.

'Besides another drink,' she said, huskily, 'would you like something to eat?'

She looked quite delicious as she knelt there and I was sorely tempted. . . .

'That would be nice,' I managed to reply. 'But I'm not sure there's a great deal in the house. I should have done a bit of shopping today, really.'

'All my fault,' she smiled, rising and managing to

show more than a glimpse of thigh through the slit in her skirt. 'You stay here and I will go and have a ferret round. If your cupboard is as bare as you say, I will pop into Swanage and maybe get a Chinese take-away or something.'

As she walked out into the kitchen, I realized, to my surprise, that I wanted there to be enough in my cupboards, for I had no wish for her to leave, even to go to Swanage. Not right then. What really bugged me though, was that I sort of knew why.

I made to switch off the television but she shook her head and got up and did it herself.

'It was hardly worth waiting up for, was it?' she smiled. 'You should have gone to bed ages ago.'

'I'll survive,' I smirked.

'Not if you insist on watching many more Jean Luc Godard films, you won't. You'll die of boredom.'

I laughed, not at her sally, so to speak, but because she did not know the reason I had insisted on watching what I knew would be a boring experience – to encourage her to leave before things got rather too late, if you understand my meaning. But here she still was, bright eyed and bushy tailed. (And boy, was she bushy tailed.)

I looked at my watch. 'It's twelve twenty-five. I'm surprised Gus hasn't dropped by. He should have been back ages ago.'

'I know it's late, but why don't you ring him, if you're worried?'

'Gus doesn't hold with the phone. Says he has enough ringing in the ears without a machine to add to it.'

She came and sat on the edge of the settee not filled by Marklin. Opium had definitely not finished its last pulse for the day. Taking my hand, she said, 'Would you like me to walk down to Gus's place and check if he's back? You say it's only just down the road.'

I shook my head. 'No, it's cold and dark, a mugger's night, if ever I felt one.'

She squeezed my hand. 'No, come on, Peter, be serious. Tell me where the cottage is. I promise I'll run all the way and all the way back. It's the least I can do, after all you have done for me.'

In the end, I had to agree. Sally Newton is a tough act to argue with. Besides, once dressed in her coat and gloves, she might decide it wasn't worth taking them all off again, and having reported on Gus, might get in her car and go home. Seemed like a good wheeze to me – that is if I really, *really* wanted her to go at all. But there was one thing I had left out of my calculations – the weather.

She came back, ten minutes later, looking like the most fetching drowned rat you've ever laid eyes on. The wet had even percolated through her coat into her sweater and skirt.

'I didn't realize it was raining,' I said pathetically.

Sally tried to wipe away the rivulets from her hair with her hand.

'It isn't. It's damp, sleety snow.' She looked down at her sweater, where the nipples were well delineated through the wet wool. She caught me looking at her. 'Christ, I'm cold, Peter. Can I go in your bathroom and grab a towel to help dry off?'

'Of course.' I was relieved when she ran out. Man (and woman) has his (and her) breaking point. But to my amazement, she was almost instantly back in with the towel. She moved past me and knelt before the fire.

'Mind if I take these wet things off in the warm?'

What could I say: 'No, I'd rather you caught pneumonia'? Besides, by then, she was already doffing her sweater.

'Gus isn't back, by the way. There were no lights on, no reply to my banging on the door, and no sign of his old banger in the garden.'

She turned round to me, as she fumbled for the belt at her waist. She wore no bra and made no attempt to conceal her nudity.

'You're not embarrassed, are you, Peter?' she asked quietly. 'Imagine I'm on Studland beach.'

I couldn't have, even if I'd tried. I could only see her, lying back on the silken sheets of a bed, her full and rounded breasts awaiting the touch of a lover. . . .

I shook my head to get some sense into it. 'No, I'm not . . .' But I was, so I stopped. And I was even more as she stepped out of her skirt to reveal the sucker punch of all time, a suspender belt.

'They will dry in front of the fire,' she smiled and eased herself to the side of my settee. Neither of us spoke for quite a while. In retrospect, I think both of us knew what was about to happen and wanted to work out our own separate reasons for our needs. I am sure now that it was not for each other, but for others far, far away. Not a need so much as a test, may be, an exploration of each individual self and not each other.

After a while, she gently took my hand and put it round her breast.

'Can I stay the night?' she whispered.

My hand gave her the answer and she reached across and took my head in her own hands.

'That's nice,' she breathed into my mouth and all further communication from then on was distinctly non-verbal.

It cannot have been many minutes after I had, at last, dropped off, that I was woken by what sounded like the Third World War going on downstairs. Once I had pulled myself sufficiently together to realize it was unlikely that Mr Gorbachev would chose my Toy Emporium as his first target, I eased myself out of bed slowly, so as not to waken the sleeping beauty, and limped out onto the landing, where I almost tripped over Bing. From there, I could hear that it was someone rattling the shop door with considerable force. I turned on the landing light and went down the stairs, step by painful step, for I knew there was only one person it was likely to be and that was Gus. I wasn't annoyed at the absurd hour of his visit, so much as relieved he had at last surfaced. For, even while heavily engaged with Sally, the love-making had not obscured the unease I had been feeling about Gus's non-appearance.

I slipped the bolts on the shop door and let him, and a strong smell of beer, inside.

'Wotcha,' he said, raindrops dripping down his face.

'Christ, Gus, do you know what time it is?'

I took his wet anorak from him and propped it up on the door mat. 'And anyway, why didn't you ring, rather than rattle the door off its hinges?'

'Didn't want to wake your ladyfriend,' he grinned. He pointed to Sally's car outside. 'Or did her car break down and you take her home?'

I ignored the wink and asked, 'How can rattling a door be better than ringing a bell.'

'Bells wake me up more than rattles. Hate bells. That's why I don't have – '

'A telephone. I know.'

'Had enough rattles, have you then, tonight?' he winked again.

'Gus, I hope you haven't just called to make racy remarks because – '

'Making any coffee?' he cut in, rheumy eyes as bright as they'll ever be.

'Yes, I always make coffee about two thirty in the morning. It helps me sleep,' I muttered, as I peg-legged into the kitchen.

I sat him down at the table and put the kettle on.

'What's wrong with your leg, then?' he asked.

'I sprained it climbing a fence at Stringle's,' I said. 'Nothing serious.'

'Discover anything there, did you?'

'No, not really. Except his dogs are fierce.'

'Oh,' he said. 'Thought you knew that already.' He wiped his wet hair with a torn handkerchief. 'Want to know all about my day, then?'

'Yes, of course, Gus. But maybe the morning would have done. Anyway, you haven't just come back from Lyme, have you?'

He sniffed. 'I'll start at the ruddy beginning, old mate, not at the end. Otherwise, I'll lose myself, won't I?'

I guessed he would. For his eyes, voice and breath spoke of enough Heinekens to enable Victor Borge to retire.

'Okay, I'm listening.'

He reached in his trouser pocket for a scrappy piece of paper that was covered in his pencil scrawl. He began reading from it. 'Well, there were quite a number in and out of The Wood Worm. I'll start with them. First there was a short, bald man, clutching a clock. Then a fat old lady with a kind of beret on, only it had a feather. She didn't take anything in or anything out. Then there was a chap, looked like a Yank with a bow-tie and all. He didn't take anything in but came out with what looked like a little statue or something wrapped in paper. Then there wasn't anybody. Then there was a young woman with red hair and a scarf who looked in the window for ages before going in. She came out with sod all. Then there was – '

At this point, I had to interrupt. 'Gus, all this is wonderful. Well done. But seeing the hour, could you let me know just about any people you think might be important? We can go through the others later on today.'

He took a deep breath, then grinned. 'All right then, I'll get to the meaty bits.'

'Thanks. So there *were* meaty bits?'

'P'raps. First off, just after lunch I saw that Redstart turn up. He went up the alley, so I ran out of the café and hung around near where I'd seen him go in. Wasn't long before I heard him and that Abigail going at it hammer and tongs. Couldn't hear what they were saying, but it was a row and a ruddy 'alf. Then I heard what sounded like a scuffle and she screamed. Then there was nothing, until he came out again, face all screwed up with rage like you wouldn't believe.

'Didn't hear anything more for a bit. Thought he might have killed her. But then I heard someone coming down the stairs, so I went back to the café in case I missed anyone else.' He laughed. 'They were pleased to see me again – thought I had nipped off without paying.'

'What else?' I asked, for I could see from Gus's face he had other goodies to impart.

'Nothing else really for quite a bit. The odd customer, that's all. Then a youngish guy turned up, all sneaky like, and he had one of those tough-guy moustaches like that prick Magnum on telly. I thought, "'Ello, 'ello, 'ello, he might be that policemen fellow you told me about." '

'Did he go to the alley or the shop?'

'He seemed to 'esitate but, in the end, went up the alley. I nipped out again but couldn't hear anything. 'E left after about quarter of an hour or so and sneaked off down the hill. He was wearing a brown mack, but his trousers underneath looked mighty like police issue to me.'

'Yes. It was probably Oliver Smart.'

'Thought of following 'im, but remembered you said not to get involved,' he grinned, as if he expected me to pat him on the wet head for his obedience.

'Anything else?' I queried.

He looked back at his scruffy piece of paper. 'Only other important thing, s'pose, was that that Abigail woman shut up shop round about four thirty – early I thought – and then left a few minutes later. Even from across the road, I could see a whacking great bruise on her face.'

'So Redstart *can* be quite violent when he wants to be,' I reflected.

'Looks like it, doesn't it? Nasty piece of work, he is.'

169

'I wonder what their argument was about. The policeman fellow, or what?'

Gus shrugged. 'Kettle's boiled,' he said.

I broke off, limped to the cooker, and made us both a cup of your instant coffee. Gus slurped at his right away. He must have a larynx with a boiling water guarantee.

'Anything else?' I asked over the slurps.

'Well, as the shop was shut and no lights on above, I took a bit of a walk. Stretch me legs. Then it was opening time. So I went in The Feathers, had the odd pint and kept nipping out to see if any lights had come back on. Did that till closing time, I did. But still no lights.'

'Okay,' I said. 'So what on earth have you been doing in the countless hours since then?'

He looked at me with a blanker than usual expression. 'Ermm . . . I've been . . . in me car.'

'What do you mean, in your car? Where on earth did you go? Land's End?'

'No,' he said, self-consciously. 'Not that far.'

'Then where?'

'The car park by the cob.'

I couldn't believe it. 'What the hell are you saying, Gus?'

He sniffed again. 'I'd had quite a skinful by then you see, what with drinking all through me lunch and then in The Feathers all evening. And I didn't have no meal in the pub, you see, 'case I missed the lights going on, and that.'

'So?'

'I fell asleep the ruddy second I got behind the wheel to go home.' He laughed. 'Just as well, really, I suppose. Feel better for it altogether. Might have fallen asleep going along otherwise, mightn't I? Still, you can't blow up balloons when you're asleep, can you?'

I could have killed him. Here he was waking an injured man up at the dead of morning to spout information that could have waited, when he had already had four hours or so kip under his belt. I got up from the table.

'Thanks a lot, Gus, but goodnight.'

He put down his coffee, looking most hurt.

'I knew it was late, but I only really knocked you up because I saw Sally Newton's car outside – and I thought something important might have happened. Has it?'

'Not the way you mean, Gus. No. Now I really must get back to bed. Thanks again for all the work – I'll see you later.'

He slurped the last of his coffee, then got up and looked hard at me.

'Not too bad a girl that,' he said quietly. I knew what he meant: she wasn't Arabella.

I patted him on the back as I limped with him to the door.

'It's all right, Gus, I haven't forgotten America.'

He looked back at me, now with a big smile on his still beery face. And I suddenly realized the real reason he'd knocked me up so late at night. He was trying to preserve me for the only member of the female sex for whom I've ever heard Gus express time; he and Arabella used to get on like the proverbial blazing building.

'That's good,' he said and winked, but now without a leer, ''cos I might break your other leg if you do.'

11

I had a struggle to get out of bed at all when daylight at last penetrated the curtains. It wasn't because we made love yet again, because we didn't. It was just that Sally said I should stay in bed all day to rest my ankle and she would be head cook and bottle washer and whatever other role I wished for her.

After a lot of argument, I managed to convince her that my proposed programme for that morning was not over-arduous for a sprained ankle, if she would only be so kind as to act as chauffeur unpaid. So I made it down to breakfast, which she insisted must be fried egg, fried bread and fried Spam instead of my measly muesli. That inside me, I made first mention of our rather sudden circumstance.

'I'm glad you came,' I said.

She reached across the table for my hand.

'I'm glad you were here.'

'You still love Greg, don't you?'

She looked surprised, then squeezed my hand and nodded.

'How could you tell?'

I shrugged. 'Don't worry. It was nothing you did or didn't . . .'

'Good,' she murmured, then added, 'You still love Arabella, don't you?'

I smiled awkwardly and she laughed. 'It was nothing you did or didn't, don't worry.'

'Well, that's great. Here we are after a night of love – and Gus Tribble – confessing we're dotty about two other people.'

'Perhaps everybody should do what we've done.'

'But risky,' I smirked. 'Not everybody is like us.'

'They should be.'

'Crazy, you mean?'

'If that's what we are.'

'That's what we are.'

She sighed with satisfaction, then abruptly changed the subject.

'So, Mr Peter Marklin, what are we starting with this morning? Opening up shop or what?'

'Or what, I think. Remember what I told you Gus said last night, about Abigail and Redstart.'

She frowned. 'I don't think you should get involved in anything like that; at least until you're in one piece again.'

'You still love Greg.'

'I know. It's dreadful, isn't it? I can't forgive him for his lying and deceit, yet I can't stop loving him.'

'So – we shouldn't waste time. He may still be alive, though God knows where.'

'And God probably doesn't care about someone like him.'

I refrained from getting into any theological argument.

'Can you chauffeur me over to Lyme?'

She nodded and I got up from the kitchen table to hobble into the shop.

'Why not go out the front door?' she asked.

'I'm going to get a toy I promised I'd drop round to Philippa's thatcher's daughter. We can pop in *en route*.'

'Tell me where it is and I'll get it.'

And she did, while I phoned Philippa to check whether Tom Sweet had, by chance, taken Molly with him to thatch her barn. He hadn't, but I was quite relieved to hear that he himself was hard at work at his trade, trying to finish the barn before the real snow of the season started. I had no wish to be thought trespassing again.

173

So off we went in Sally's Mini, with me in a passenger seat for a not particularly welcome change. The ice on the road, thank goodness, had melted in the snatches of morning sun and we were soon at the end of the track leading up to Sweet's cottage and barn.

I turned and picked up the tinplate car from the rear seat.

'Got its ball?' Sally smirked.

I nodded.

'Let me take it up. Save your foot.'

'No, I'd better go. Molly doesn't know you. She might be shy.'

We both got out of the car, though, because Sally insisted that I needed a crutch (her) until I got to the barn or cottage, or wherever Molly had decided to play. Luckily, as I was expecting, it turned out to be the barn and she answered to my call without my having to peg-leg up the ladder.

'I've got the car, Molly, the one that blows a ball up in the air and keeps it there. Remember?'

She was down that ladder in a flash and only hesitated when she spotted Sally beside me.

'Friend,' I said. 'Sally meet Molly.'

'Hello, Molly.'

But she ignored the greeting and came right up by my side.

'Car,' she said. I handed it to her. I thought her eyes would burst with excitement.

'Ball?' she queried.

I reached into my pocket and took it out.

'You mustn't lose the ball,' I said. 'It's special. You keep it somewhere safe.'

She took it from me. 'Keep it safe.'

'That's right.'

The pleasure in her face was so rewarding that I felt like forgetting running a business and giving all my antique toys to her.

'Let me show you how it works.'

I persuaded her to let me have the car once more and Sally and I cleared an area of the barn floor free from straw and muck. I started to wind up the toy.

'See, that's how you do it, Molly. Turn the key.'

'Turn the key.'

She watched intently and gestured with her own hand as if it were she herself who was winding.

Once wound, I placed the car on the floor, let it go, then placed the ball carefully over the trumpet-like chimney in the roof of the car. To the 'oohs' and 'aahs' from both Molly and Sally, the ball remained suspended about three or four inches above the car as it moved along.

'That's sensational,' Sally enthused. 'Why don't they make toys like this now?'

I shrugged. 'The world has got too sophisticated, I suppose.'

'I haven't,' Sally grinned. I looked at Molly. I could have drowned in her smile.

Our demonstration ultimately lasted more than a quarter of an hour and Molly looked very sad when we said we had to go.

'Remember,' I reminded her, 'turn the key, but not too far. And look after the little ball. Keep it safe.'

'Keep it safe,' she repeated, and somehow I just knew she would.

As we left in the car, Sally observed, 'I saw the price ticket on that car, when I took it off the shelf.'

I didn't comment.

'You had got it marked up at a hundred and twenty-five pounds.'

Still I kept mum.

She reached across for my hand. 'Greg would never have done anything like that. Getting five pounds out of him was something of a miracle.'

I pointed ahead. 'Just up there to the right is where Merinda and John-John have their caravan.'

She looked up the track as we passed it.

'All looks very neat, a bit like a park.'

'It wasn't like that before they came.'

She smiled. 'If they're not careful, they'll give hippies a good name.'

I noticed the little dig but let it pass. I guess Merinda was just the calm and naturally beautiful kind of girl of whom other girls could well be jealous, even if they had no wish to emulate the life-style.

It didn't take us too long to get to Lyme Regis and I asked Sally to park by the cob.

'Why?' she queried. 'Let me drop you off by The Wood Worm, then you won't have to lump up the hill. Then I'll come back to the cob and park, so you'll know where the car is.'

'Where will you be?'

'Why not where Gus spent a lot of yesterday? In the café opposite the shop.'

Once dropped outside The Wood Worm, I saw immediately that the shop was still shut and I hoped that this did not mean that Abigail had not returned at all overnight. I hobbled up the alley and was amused to see the broken dolphin knocker had still not been replaced. I banged on the door with my fist. It took three bangings, so to speak, to raise any life. But much to my relief, I eventually heard footsteps on the stairs and, a moment later, a very downbeat Abigail opened the door just a crack.

'Oh, it's you.'

She was about to close the door, when I quickly said, 'I'm not a bent policeman.'

The door slammed and I was about to issue a silent expletive, when it opened again but still only a crack.

'What do you want?'

'To talk to you.'

'What about?'

'You know what about.' (Which right then was more than I did.)

Again she hesitated, then stood aside and let me in. I followed her up the stairs. There was no spring in her step now. Winter had definitely set in for Abigail.

Once in her living-room, I could see the bruising on her face that Gus had mentioned, despite her attempts to hide it under a foot of make-up. She saw me notice it and turned the other cheek towards me.

'You don't strike me as a masochist,' I said, 'so why did your Patrick turn violent? Find you were up to more with PC Smart than he'd planned?'

She did not reply, nor did her eyes display anger at my remark – or anything. They had a dead look today, like you see in survivors from an earthquake. I suddenly felt mean being so aggressive, but I knew I had to go on.

'Is your tame policeman the reason that Redstart has got away with his . . .' I hesitated, because I didn't want to use a word that betrayed to her that I didn't actually know what the hell Redstart was up to. I finally opted for '. . . operations for so long? Inside information that enables him always to keep one step ahead of the law?'

She turned away and stood by the door. Even so, I could see she was trembling.

'Bent policemen have a tendency to own up, you know, once the going gets tough – especially if the carrot of leniency is dangled in front of their macho moustaches.'

Still not a spark out of her. I tried another tack.

'Look, Abigail, I'm not the law. I'm not interested really in what you and Redstart are up to. That's for the boys in blue to discover, not me. I'm only here because I want to know what you and your boyfriend have done with Gregory Mann.'

That did it. She spun round, her eyes exchanging death for fear.

'We haven't done anything with Gregory. Why don't

177

you believe me? We don't know what has happened to him any more than you do.'

She spoke with such intensity that I didn't know whether to believe her or not, but then, even without her swivel, she could just be a better actress than I'd given her credit for. I decided to try a full frontal.

'Why did Redstart give Mann that ten grand?'

Her eyes flickered, but that's all.

I went on, 'I'll answer for you. To keep Gregory's mouth sealed tight about what he had discovered about your little games. But Redstart couldn't be certain he wouldn't decide to blab one day or, perhaps, ask for more and more money to keep quiet. So your boyfriend decided that there was a better way of silencing Gregory forever, didn't he? What's more, he was worried how matey you and Mann were getting. So he would kill two birds with one stone by arranging secretly to meet Mann on that Sunday morning, maybe on his boat somewhere, and then killing him and dropping bike and rider into the deep blue sea. Come to think of it, he might even have persuaded you to make that secret assignation on that Sunday morning. Gregory Mann would have fallen for that, hook, line and sinker, wouldn't he? Little would he know that the only bed he would dip into that day would be that of the sea – '

'Shut up! Shut up!' she shouted, her eyes now flooding with tears. 'I didn't do it. I didn't do anything, *anything*.'

She collapsed into a chair, her body quivering and racked with her crying.

'If you didn't, then somebody else did. Gregory Mann had to be silenced. You knew that much, didn't you?'

She suddenly looked up at me, her make-up ploughed by her tears. 'I only knew about the money. Nothing else, just the money.'

I took a deep breath. I had, at last, made a breakthrough. I pulled up a chair next to her and sat down, as much to relieve the throbbing pain of my ankle, as better to interrogate her dear self.

'So Redstart gave Mann ten grand to silence him. Why? What had he found out?'

'I can't tell you,' she muttered into the cushions of her chair.

'Why? Afraid Redstart wouldn't stop at his fists if he found out?'

More sobbing was all I got. I took a diversion.

'What was your bent constable doing here last time I called? And yesterday? Must have been something pretty important, otherwise he wouldn't risk his little neck being seen too much around you.'

Again, no response.

'Redstart did not like it, anyway, did he? And somehow, I don't think it was because he was jealous. There was some other reason, wasn't there? What was naughty Oliver Smart up to – besides his neck in trouble?'

Abigail slowly turned her head and looked across at me.

'Look, why pick on me? Do you prefer to bully girls – is that your turn on? Or are you afraid to try your bullying tactics with a man?'

She was wrong, but she was right in one sense, and I knew it. The questions I was asking her had to be asked of Redstart too. Whatever little games of her own she was playing, it was her boyfriend who was in charge of the master game.

'I don't mean to be a bully. If only you would tell me the truth.'

She hunched up in the chair, like a baby in the womb.

'I have . . . about Gregory Mann.'

'That you know nothing?'

She nodded, then murmured into the chair, 'I'd sort of like to know what's happened to him, too.'

I got up to go. I felt there was little more I would achieve right then. But I did drop my Toy Emporium card in her lap, just in case she ever felt like talking some more.

'I'll let you know if I ever find out,' I said, then added as I got to the door, 'I'd move out of here if I were you. If your boyfriend has killed once, he might be tempted to try a repeat performance.'

I couldn't see her reaction to my last remark, for the chairback was in the way. But I hoped it might bug her enough to reach for my visiting card in the not too distant future.

We sat in the café opposite for around half an hour before we set off back, just in case Abigail reacted by leaving the premises; in which case, we planned to follow her. But she didn't surface, and in the end, we gave up and Sally went and got the car to save me hobbling down the High Street. As we set off, I noticed the rear seat of the Mini now sported a box of assorted groceries.

She caught my expression.

'We've got to live, haven't we?' she grinned. 'I bought them on my way up to the café.'

On the way back, I went over and over what I had managed to worm out of Abigail, and Sally seemed inordinately pleased that we had at last tracked down the donor of the ten grand.

'I thought you might be a little upset,' I observed.

'Why? Because it confirms what we had suspected, that Greg is not exactly a mint specimen of a hero?'

I nodded.

She went on, 'It fazed me when I first considered the possibility that Greg was not exactly straight. It doesn't any more, curiously. I guess because I asked myself the question – would I have fallen in love with Greg if I had known from the start what he is actually like. And the answer I have come to is, yes, probably. So . . .'

Logical lady, but the pain had to be there all the same. I changed the subject.

'What worries me is that if Redstart is involved in

180

Gregory's disappearance then he could have spirited him off anywhere in one of his boats – even taken him to France or wherever.'

'Or dumped him overboard,' Sally added. 'That's what you really meant to say, isn't it?'

I didn't deny it. 'But then he would have to get rid of the motorbike. I suppose that might be at the bottom of the English Channel too or lost in the shady end of the motorbike trade.'

'It would be far easier for Redstart to get rid of the bike than for our two-way mirror headmaster or the Dobermann freak.'

'Unless Dobermanns eat bikes for breakfast,' I semi-smiled. 'Their teeth look capable of devouring anything.'

We were both silent for a moment, not because of my bad joke either.

Then Sally said, 'I don't think you should see Redstart. You should leave that to the police. Tell them what you have learnt from Abigail and they can pick up the lead.'

She reached across for my hand. Whilst her driving was pretty good, Dorset roads weren't all built by the Romans and I'd have preferred two hands on the wheel to cope with the wiggly bits.

'I don't want you risking your neck any more for me.'

'I won't go in the dark,' I smiled. 'And I'll try to fix a meeting-place that's not on a headland or a boat.'

'How about Trafalgar Square?' she quipped. 'I wouldn't trust Redstart unless there were plenty of witnesses.'

'Know anywhere round here with pigeons?' I asked, and we both laughed.

The sun deigned to come out from behind a cloud and the Dorset countryside was deep etched with light and shadow, and, in the distance, the towering ruins of Corfe Castle were silhouetted against the sky like some silent sentinel keeping watch over us. In that moment, all problems seemed to slip away and I relaxed back in my seat, even my ankle keeping its throbs to itself.

'Penny for your thoughts?' Sally said quietly.

'They're all about country matters,' I smiled.

'Country-type country? Or Hamlet-type country?' she queried, laughing.

'The green variety,' I assured her.

The next second there was an explosive jolt and I was only prevented from cracking the windscreen by my seat belt.

'What the . . . ?'

As Sally struggled to regain control of the Mini, I looked back. Behind us was the low, predatory shape of a red Jaguar XJS – and I only give you one guess as to who was at the wheel.

Once I had told her who was playing bumper cars, Sally's instinct was to try to keep going until we entered the comparative safety of Corfe village, but I cautioned her to stop.

'If he pulls alongside, he can have us off the road in a second.' I began and then saw out of the corner of my eye that was exactly what Redstart was now about to do. I cursed my ruddy ankle and longed to be behind the Mini's wheel, for though out-paced and out-classed by the twelve-cylinder Jaguar, there are still wonders you can achieve with a baby car that no grown-up car can emulate. Handbrake U-turns on a sixpence for one, and a dodgem ability round tight corners, up narrow tracks, through tight gaps . . . I hadn't seen *The Italian Job* for nothing.

Suddenly I saw a muddy lane leading off on our left. I pointed.

'Swing up that lane, but don't slow down. Leave it to the last bloody minute.'

Sally timed it to perfection. The Mini leaned over so far as she swung the wheel, that had she had her

182

window open, we would have swallowed the hedge. The front wheels spun crazily, trying to find an iota of grip in the mud, and bracing my feet against the toe-board to prevent myself landing in Sally's lap caused me to groan with pain. I looked back as soon as the Mini had regained a ha'p'orth of equilibrium, but of the xjs there was no sign.

'Have we lost him?' Sally shouted over the din of the screaming motor and thuds of the rubber suspension.

'Keep going,' I shouted back and then saw, to my dismay, what a silly, goddamned statement I'd just made. A hundred feet ahead of us, now just showing around the bend, was a five-barred gate – and it was well and truly closed. I looked frantically around, but there was no escape. We were bounded by high hedges on both sides all the way to the gate, which I could see was chained and padlocked. Sally slewed to a stop.

'Shit,' she said.

I looked around in trepidation. And the man she had just so aptly described was now to be seen aiming his red projectile up our exhaust-pipe some hundred yards behind.

I pressed Sally's hand reassuringly and forced a smile.

'Look on the bright side,' I said. 'It saves us all the petrol of going to see him.'

I had planned on staying in the Mini, but it didn't work out that way. Redstart made a bee-line for my door, wrenched it open and pulled me out of my seat. I swung at his stomach, but my foot (guess which one) caught in the framework at the base of the seat, thus putting an end to any significant resistance and we began our interchange on the high note of me crying aloud in pain.

I can only remember odd phrases through my red mist but they all seemed to be in the category of 'You interfering bastard, Marklin' – certainly that will suffice for this narrative.

I, at last, managed to support myself by leaning back against the warm bonnet of the Mini and thus could take some weight off the leg that was, in its way, shouting louder than he was.

When I could get a word in any which way, I began, 'Don't be more of an idiot, Redstart, than you have been already . . .' But that's as far as I got. He grabbed me by the neck of my anorak and bunched it up in his fists so to make breathing, let alone speaking, rather a luxury.

'It's you, Marklin, who are being an idiot. I saw you coming out from bothering Abigail and going over to that café. I'd have caught you sooner had I not had to calm her down from the state you left her in.'

'How did you calm her down, Redstart? With your fists, like last time?'

He thought I shouldn't have said that. Now my face hurt almost as much as my ankle. I heard Sally scream from inside the car. By hitting me, he had at least relinquished the stranglehold on my anorak.

'Stay in the car, Sally,' I screamed back.

He hit me again, his usually dapper hair now flopping over his forehead, reminding me a little of that guy who died in the bunker.

'Is this how you went to work on Gregory Mann, before you killed him?' I ventured, reckoning I was in for a battering anyway, so I might as well earn it.

Half a dozen or so knuckle encounters later, he let up long enough to say, 'This is just a warning, Marklin. You interfere with me or Abigail again and you'll find life can get a load nastier than this.' He looked around at Sally. 'And not just for you, either, ladies' man.' He kicked at the Mini door and the car shook.

'Why don't you pick on a car your own size,' I managed, as I tasted blood from my nose and mouth.

He combed his hair from his forehead with his hand, before hitting me again. But at least, this time I managed a little retribution.

As he was recovering from his swing, I edged myself onto the bonnet of the Mini, so no weight was on my legs, and then let fly with the good knee. It hit him where only the devil aims and he doubled up, his knees slithering in the mud. But it took me two blows on the chin to get him to lie down really properly. I looked at him. Boy, would his tailor and laundry be mad at him when he eventually got home. White, blue and slimy brown just don't make a mix-and-match combination.

I signalled to Sally and she got out of the Mini. A couple of minutes later and we had dragged his semiconscious form out of the way of the wheels. I hobbled back to his Jaguar and by dint of its being automatic gear change, managed to reverse it back onto the road, where I left it parked.

Sally supported me – nay, more – *put* me into her car. I felt like a Humphrey Bogart to her Ida Lupino.

'Oh, Peter, I feel so dreadful. I should never have got you involved in all this. He could have killed you.' She started to dab at the blood on my face with her handkerchief and give me little kisses.

'It's all right, Sally.' I tried to smile, but one side of my face wouldn't let me. 'It's all in a day's work for intrepid heroes.' She looked at me in surprise, before I added, 'Trouble is, I'm not one. So let's get home, where I can scream without scaring the living daylights out of the wildlife.'

12

It was soon after we had taken the Corfe-Studland Road
and Sally and I were arguing about whether or not I
should go to the police about Redstart's assault (she
thought I should, I thought not. I didn't relish Whetstone's wrath at my continuing interference.) that life
was taken out of our hands again. As we neared the
site of John-John and Merinda's caravan, we came
across the boys in blue whether we wanted to or not.
And not just one flashing Rover, but two.

At first, I thought there must have been a car accident, but as we neared, I saw another police car up by
the caravan. I signalled to Sally to stop by the nearest
Rover, beside which stood a towering constable. I held
a handkerchief up to my face to hide the blood and
bruises and wound down the window.

'What's going on, constable?' I asked.

'Would you mind moving on, please, sir.'

'Yes, I would,' I said rather sharply. 'The people in
the caravan happen to be friends of mine and I would
like to know what three police cars are doing here.'

He looked around as if to find a colleague from
whom to ask advice and I took the opportunity to get
out of the car. But the long arm of the law soon
restrained me.

'You can't go up there, sir, I'm afraid.'

'Why not?' I asked, but then I saw why not. Four
policemen were now coming down the track from the
caravan, two each side of a very bewildered-looking
John-John and Merinda.

'What the blazes are you lot doing?' I exploded. 'Why are you taking my friends away?'

I suddenly felt a tap on my shoulder. I spun round expecting, maybe, to see Sally. What I saw was a ginger moustache atop the flabby form of Inspector Digby Whetstone. He must have been in the second Rover, parked by the roadside.

'Mr Marklin, why on earth can't you just stick to selling your toys?' He smiled patronizingly. 'It's something you, no doubt, have some flair for.'

By now, Merinda and John-John and their escort were within ear-shot, so I ignored the Inspector's barb and shouted across.

'What's happening, Merinda? Why are they taking you away?'

She looked up and recognized me, but winced as she saw the condition of my now handkerchiefless face.

'I don't know,' she shouted back. 'They say they have found – ' But the rest of her words were drowned in the siren from another police car.

I looked back at Whetstone, who now was studying the condition of my face with a wry smile.

'You've found *what*?' I snapped and licked some blood off my lips from my bleeding nose.

'May I ask first, Mr Marklin, how you came by the damage to your face. Has someone else taken offence at your interfering ways?'

I looked on helplessly as Merinda and John-John were escorted into separate Rovers, to be driven away.

'Where are you taking them, Whetstone?' I almost grabbed his overcoat collar, but thought better of it. 'You can't have found anything. I know those two – they're incapable of doing anything criminal.'

He gave a laugh. 'Old friends of yours, are they? Known them many years?'

I felt Sally take my hand and squeeze it reassuringly.

'No, but – '

'How long have you known them, then?'

I didn't bother replying. Ten days is not actually a lifetime.

'All right, Inspector, what do you claim you've found? Let me guess. From the last time your men called round here, I would suggest you reckon you have discovered some stolen property. That it? Well, if that's your claim – '

He touched my arm. 'Mr Marklin, the British police do not come and take people away for questioning without good reason. We're not living in some South American police state, you know. This is Dorset – '

I cut his lesson in geography short.

'Okay, okay. So just tell me what the hell is going on?'

'We don't really know ourselves until our questioning has been completed.'

As he spoke, two policemen in Wellington boots came past us from the direction of the caravan, one carrying two spades, the other a large black plastic bag full of Lord knows what.

It was Sally who reacted first.

'Is that what you found?' She pointed at the bag that was now being loaded into the boot of a Rover.

'What's inside?' I demanded roughly.

Whetstone shook his head. 'Look, I'm sick and tired of standing here being interrogated by you, Mr Marklin. Now I've got some questions I want *you* to answer. How did you come by that face and . . .' He looked down at my peculiar stance, '. . . what looks like a leg injury of some sort?'

'I fell off a stool laughing at the mistakes policemen make,' I countered, despite Sally's fingernails digging into my hand.

The Inspector looked back at the cars.

'I had better be going now, Mr Marklin. And I would advise you to do the same.' He turned to go, then looked back. 'And I don't want to see you ever again trying to interfere in police business.'

I looked at my watch. 'Half past three suit you?'

'What . . . er . . . ?'

'Half past three, English time. Not Paraguayan time, Chilean time, Nicaraguan time, but your old Greenwich mean . . .'

His eyelids flicked their continuing incomprehension.

'This afternoon,' I explained, with a smile, 'I will come to your office. If you're not in, I'll sit there resting my injured foot until you do turn up.'

'May I ask, Mr Marklin, why on earth you want to see me?'

I pointed to the two Rovers which were now starting to move away towards Studland and, no doubt, the ferry to Bournemouth.

'I'll tell you when you've told me why you want to victimize people who live in caravans.'

He looked the proverbial daggers and was about to retort when Sally stepped in.

'Make it three o'clock then, Inspector,' she said, her voice oozing placatory balm. 'I will see he's on time, so you won't be kept waiting.'

Digby Whetstone adjusted his shoulders self-consciously, like Del Boy in *Only Fools and Horses*, then after a moment's hesitation, turned and moved off.

I looked at Sally. 'Thanks,' I said.

'For what?' she asked, somewhat surprised.

'For – ' I began and then she laughed and offered me a clean handkerchief for my bloody nose.

Ever felt five years old again?

Instead of going straight back to my place, Sally insisted we drive on to Sandbanks where she claimed she had a better first aid box than mine, with a more supportive bandage for my leg, some kind of special healing ointment for my facial abrasions and a 'sniffer thing' to help stop the bleeding in my nose. What's more, she said, there was a chemist two doors away in case I needed anything further; and being at Sandbanks rather than Studland meant I would be that much nearer Digby Whetstone's blue lamp for my appointment. All pretty compelling arguments, although we had to wait ages for the ferry because the police had commandeered the next sailing for the Rovers we had seen at the caravan.

Once ensconced at Sally's place, she not only performed her Florence Nightingale act on me superbly well, but also made a near perfect Delia Smith clone by serving me up a scampi concoction that made me totally rethink the role of crustacea in the scheme of things.

But, withal, as they say, I remained in a pretty low mood, for complication was piling on complication and I suddenly had two major problems to confront: Gregory Mann's disappearance *and* Merinda and John-John's apprehension, if not arrest. And to add to it all, sodding Digby's digs about how short a time I could have known my friends kept coming back to me. I had not known them any time at all. I didn't, in reality, *know* them from Adam and Eve, nor anything about them except what they had told me. And that was next to bugger-all on which to make a definitive character assessment – a judgement on which one could bet one's life. And yet . . . and yet . . .

To stop my mind disappearing up its own doubts and anxieties and to fill in time before my three o'clock appointment, I asked Sally if she would dig out Gregory's files and diaries again, just in case we had missed anything that might be relevant the previous time we had been through them. It seemed a forlorn hope, but I desperately needed something more than I'd got if I was to nail something on Redstart or, at least, trick him into some kind of confession. It had been clear from his full-frontal ferocity that unprovable assertions of the payment of ten grand were not likely to faze him. Besides, I could hardly reveal the source of my assertion without putting Abigail into considerable danger of physical harm, if not of losing her life.

Pore as I might over the files, they seemed to offer us nothing more than we had already noted, with our unholy three still the only real suspects. In the meantime, Sally had popped into the newsagent's whilst I was beavering away and had come back with the news that the headmaster of Ferndales and his dubiously sexed matron had been released pending further enquiries, but the governors were not allowing them back to the school until these had been completed – the assistant headmaster being appointed acting head in the interim. Floreat fair play and all that.

So my only hope lay in the two diaries, Sally's and Mann's own. I started with the latter and went back meticulously to 1 January and followed each day through, noting every appointment, lunch date, weekend note and doodle. I even started to inspect innocent deletions for hidden meaning. Again, there seemed nothing we had not observed before and dismissed.

Dispirited, I kept flipping over the pages for the week preceding and the week following Gregory Mann's disappearance, but couldn't see anything that could give us a further nail for Redstart's coffin. In the end, I took refuge in looking again at the only mark against the Sunday of his disappearance – the art deco 4. I showed it again to Sally.

'I know Gregory tended to doodle in his diary, but are you happy that this four is just an attempt to arrive at a style for the letter-heading for the new cottage?'

She looked at the figure for quite some time, then said, 'I know what you mean. It looks a bit ragged at the edges, doesn't it?'

'Right. And you must have noticed from the other doodles in the diary that they are pretty precise; the strokes and outlines are very definite.'

'Well, I guess striving for a style and just doodling are different processes. The first is bound to be a bit tentative.'

191

She had a point and maybe I was just clutching at straws.

'Have you got that *Savoy Cocktail Book* that you said so impressed Gregory?'

'Yes. It's in a cabinet on the landing. I'll go and get it.'

We went through it page by page. It taught us little, I'm afraid, except that in the 1930s, one had some splendid ways of getting pie-eyed. Sally pointed out the kind of lettering the doodled 4 seemed to be emulating and I saw what she meant. Lots of thin lines together contrasting with a single thin line to make a letter or numeral.

I shut both cocktail book and diary with a sigh.

'Pity your cottage number is four. If it hadn't been, we might have thought we were on to something, but God knows what. Even so, it might be worth throwing at Redstart.'

'What, for Christ's sake?'

'Oh, you know, something like, "Own up, Redstart, I know all about the magic four." '

She laughed and she was right. It sounded even dafter spoken aloud.

'Okay, but I'm willing to try anything at this stage.' I smiled and winced. My bruises and abrasions hurt most when I laughed. I looked at my watch. 'I should be off to see old Digby now.'

She saluted promptly.

'At your service, sir. The Mini is at the door. Destination – lion's den.' She extended a hand and helped me to my foot.

'You've got your fingers crossed,' she observed.

'Oh, really,' I said, adopting the most innocent of expressions. 'I hope I'm not starting arthritis.'

At the stroke of three, I was ushered into Digby Whetstone's office with a speed that was well nigh indecent.

192

There was no question I was expected to be as quickly out.

'Sit down, Mr Marklin,' the Inspector barked, without taking his eyes (or paws) off the papers on his desk. 'But don't think you're stopping. I'll give you ten minutes max, and that only because I want to know how you got your limp and your facial.'

He looked up and rubbed one freckly hand on the other. 'So we'll start with that first, shall we?'

I had no option, really. We started with that – *all* of that: what I had learned from Abigail, the ten grand, Constable Smart, Redstart's bumper-car antics and the fight at the O.K. Corral. After all, I reckoned if I didn't share my knowledge with Whetstone, I could hardly expect him to share his knowledge with me. I prayed that what I'd discovered was sufficiently interesting to fudge the issue of my interference in police business. Certainly, from his initial reaction, it seemed it might have.

'I cannot condone your methods, Mr Marklin, or your attempt to be Dorset's Clint Eastwood or a Purbeck version of the Beverly Hills Cop. However, I am at least pleased that you have decided to come clean with me about your, er, amateur activities. I hope this means that from now on you will be leaving the action in professional hands.'

I did not comment, but asked, 'Well, what do you think of what I've told you? Shouldn't you be getting Redstart in?'

He creaked back in his chair and clasped his freckles together.

'There you go again, Marklin (I noted the drop of the 'Mr'), trying to do my job again. Won't you ever learn?'

'You could give me some reaction.' I phrased my next question carefully. 'For instance, how much of what I've just told you did you know already and how much – ?'

'You must know I cannot divulge any information at this stage of an enquiry,' he cut in. 'Suffice it to say, not all of what you have said is unknown to us.'

I tried again. 'Is PC Smart still on regular duty?'

Whetstone slammed his flabby fist down on the desk. 'Marklin, I've given you more than ten minutes already. I think it's time you – '

'I think it's time now I had a little quid pro quo, Inspector, don't you? And I'm not leaving until I get it.'

He raised his beady eyes to the ceiling. 'So. What "quo" do you reckon you've paid a quid for, Mr Marklin?'

'The caravan "quo". Why've you taken Merinda and John-John in for questioning?'

He smiled unctuously. 'Oh, I think I can tell you that now. You see, our questioning is finished.'

'And you've released them?'

'No. Arrested them.'

'Arrested? What the blazes for?'

'Burglary.'

I stared at him in disbelief.

'Merinda and John-John are no more burglars than Mother Teresa is a terrorist. Can't you see that?'

'What I see is very clear, Mr Marklin. Buried at the back of their caravan, we found a haul of items that have been stolen over the last few weeks, not just from one burglary, but from five or six. All small objects easily concealed – jewellery in the main, miniatures, small silver items, even a Fabergé egg. Merinda Scott-Jameson and John Fredericks will be appearing in court in the morning.'

I was about to explode once more, when he held up his hand. 'We have been watching their activities for some time because their arrival in the county coincided too neatly with a rise in the burglary curve in this area.'

'But you've searched their van and that area before, and found nothing. What made you search again?'

'We received certain information that – '

'A tip-off?' I interrupted.

He wouldn't say yea or nay.

'If it was a tip-off, then has it occurred to you that cache could have been planted there?'

'What motive would there be in that for anyone? Come, Mr Marklin, don't scrape bottoms of barrels.'

'So it was a tip-off?'

He rose ponderously from behind his desk. 'Time, Mr Marklin, please. I've interrupted my work schedule enough already to humour you. Thank you for your information. We'll consider its implications in the Gregory Mann case, if, indeed, it proves to have any.'

I suddenly had a startling brainwave. 'Hang on a second, Inspector. When you next interview Patrick Redstart, would you ask him two questions for me?'

He rested back against the top of his desk.

'I'm listening,' he smiled.

'First, check whether the figure four means anything to him and note his response or reaction carefully. Second, ask him why he's trying to frame my friends from the caravan.'

'Redstart framing those two?' Whetstone laughed, his chins doing a rumba. 'You must be joking. What on earth makes you say that?'

'Intuition. The thing you policemen used to rely on before you buried your heads in computers.'

'But intuition has to be based on some kind of evidence, however slender.'

Painfully, I got up to go. 'I'll leave you with this passing thought, Inspector. Have you ever recovered any of the property stolen in the recent robberies, except that found buried by the caravan? I haven't read or heard that you have, despite the rewards offered.'

'Go on.'

'Well, from what I gather, there's quite a load of loot from all those burglaries. Surely some of it should have turned up by now. At jewellers' or antique shops, auctions or via fences, or however hot stuff is disposed of. Well, if none of it has so far, don't you sometimes wonder where it has all gone?'

'So?'

'So Redstart has a fleet of boats, doesn't he? If not the actual burglar himself, he might well be the brains behind the men carrying out the robberies and the man who can dispose of the loot with the most ease – over the water in France, Holland, Belgium, you name it on the Continent. Or even, for that matter, transfer it at sea to ships going much further afield.'

'We have considered many possibilities in our enquiries, rest assured.' He chuckled. 'But tell me what makes you think anyone, whoever he or she or they may be, would think it worthwhile to suddenly try and frame two hippies dossing down in a caravan?'

I didn't answer because I didn't know the answer. All I had was a glimmer of a gut feeling.

'And just before you go,' he went on, 'what's all this about a figure four? Sounds like you've been reading far too much crime fiction to me.'

'I don't know,' I came clean. 'You've seen Gregory Mann's appointments diary. He had what looks like a figure four doodled against the Sunday he disappeared.'

'I believed there was something marked on that day. From what I remember, your friend (he pronounced the word 'friend' like *Time* magazine uses it), Sally Newton, thought it was probably something to do with the number of the house Mann had just bought.'

'I know, I know,' I said quickly. 'But supposing it isn't, and the four was some kind of reminder for Gregory Mann of the appointment he had to keep that Sunday morning?'

'Moses supposes his toeses are roses . . .' Whetstone began. I didn't wait for the end. I hobbled out and left him to his erroneous line of thought.

That evening, back in Studland, I wasn't exactly the life and soul of any party, though I smiled in the right places so as not to drag Sally down to my Slough of Despond. Even the sight of her suddenly launching into a Jane Fonda work-out session, for which she had brought the tape over from Sandbanks, on my sitting-room excuse-me-for-a-carpet did little to divert me – for it just reminded me of how out of shape I was physically.

Half-way through puffing, stretching, bending, blowing and burning, Sally said over the music, 'Don't be so down. You did your best with Whetstone.'

'That's the trouble,' I shouted back. 'I didn't. I just flailed about, clutched at straws, scraped barrels, made wild guesses, put two and two together and either made nought or a hundred and twenty-five.'

She laughed and looked up at me from under a knee. 'At least that way, you may have expanded the Inspector's imagination a bit. You say he needs it.'

I shrugged. 'He didn't seem very surprised at anything I said. Sat there like a Cheshire cat, or rather, a ginger tom, even when I was telling him about his own constable's dubious antics.'

'Maybe he had put him up to those antics?' she suggested and resumed her self-torture.

Maybe he had. Maybe he hadn't. Since Merinda and John-John's arrest, I didn't seem to know anything for certain any more.

Five minutes' perspiration later, she said, 'Well, at least the Inspector will have to see Redstart now, if only about his Mini bashing. So that will save you seeing him, won't it? By the way, I'm going to send that belligerent bastard a bill in the morning for a new rear bumper.'

'Do that,' I said, and she stared at me hard. With her chin on the floor and her legs doing the splits behind her, she looked for all the world like a giant (but very attractive) fly.

'I'm not risking you going to see Redstart again, d'you hear?'

I heard.

'Promise,' she shouted.

I shook my head. 'I've got to go to see him – one more time, anyway. I'll promise I will be careful. I didn't get anything from him last time – '

She pointed to my bruised face.

'You got plenty,' she cut in. 'And if he did kill Greg, he's quite capable of killing you too. This morning was only a warning.'

We didn't communicate again until Jane Fonda had tired herself and Sally out. And when she at last turned off the tape, it was funny speaking at a normal decibel count once more.

'I'm going to take a bath now,' she announced. 'Want to take one with me?' She saw my expression. 'We needn't do anything.'

'I might not be able to stop myself,' I smiled. 'Last time I took a bath with a lady and didn't do anything, I was two.'

'Late developer, eh?' she grinned. 'Suit yourself. I make a mean wave and if you've got any toy boats, I'm great with torpedoes.'

I blew her a kiss. 'You're great, you know that?'

'*I* know that,' she said, exiting for the bathroom. 'But does the world?'

We were very good. We slept in separate rooms that night, for Gregory and Arabella were still very much around, and we had no real wish to lay their ghosts, so to speak. And curiously, I think we were starting to enjoy each other's company more this way, frustrating though the experience was.

Surprisingly, I slept like a log, albeit a damaged and chopped about log. As a result, I didn't wake until I felt Bing almost sitting on my face – his subtle way of announcing that some breakfast wouldn't come amiss. I washed and dressed as quietly as possible, so as not to wake Sally, then went downstairs and actually prepared a cooked breakfast – well, if you can call boiled eggs and toast a cooked breakfast. I then got my sprauciest tray, a silver-plated job that I had inherited with my house from a loving great-aunt, and daintily arranged two eggs and the toast on my best crockery (Clarice Cliff – normally never taken out of its display cabinet), and peg-legged upstairs with the trayful for the sleeping beauty.

But the tragedy was, she wasn't sleeping. When I'd knocked and opened the door, I found a beautifully made bed, but no beautifully made occupant. Just a note lying on the pillow. I put down the tray and read it. The message made me blanch.

Darling Peter,
Have decided that Ask Force needs reactivating, under the sole proprietorship of yours truly. So what better time to start than now – file marked 'Gregory Mann'? I couldn't go on being a sleeping partner, now could I? We proved that last night. So am out sleuthing. Don't worry, Sally Newton knows which side's up. Should be back for lunch. If not, there's a couple of scotch eggs and some coleslaw in the fridge.

I'll try and pick up some more news about your caravan friends on the way back, so take this magnificent chance to put your feet up, chin up, spirits up and ketchup.

> Bye for now, Bathtime Pooper,
> Sally.

Hell, I suppose I should have seen it coming. Now that Sally was out of the worst of her boyfriend blues, her nature was far too bouncy and ebullient to allow her to take a back seat whilst others did all the work. I kicked myself all the way downstairs and then sat at the kitchen table trying to work out where she might have gone and what I could do about it, anyway.

The four boiled eggs seemed to stare me blankly in

199

the face, so I ate two, but it didn't really help. There were really only four places she could have gone unless she had dreamt up some new fancy ideas of her own. Ferndales, Stringle's Urine Palace, Redstart's house or yacht, or the police. For that matter, she might try to go to all of them, but it needed no crystal ball to guess with whom she would start.

I looked at my watch. It was almost 10.30. The gloom of the November day had made it seem much earlier. I decided I could not hang around any longer or I'd go spare with worry. I'd just have to try to chauffeur myself without a clutch.

Before I left, I went into the shop and turned the lights on. At least that way the Toy Emporium looked as if it were open for business, even if it wasn't. There was a pile of post, which I left till later, but also a very neat parcel with lots of American stamps on it. I quickly opened it to reveal four mint-condition thirties Tootsietoy die-cast cars: two very rare La Salles, the coupé and the saloon; a Graham town car and roadster – all from guess whom. And withal, a nice long, Arabella-type letter, which I put next to my wallet to enjoy when my mind could settle long enough to dream.

Somehow, with that letter next to my heart, I felt warm and a trifle invigorated, and didn't notice the bitter chill of the wind as I hobbled out to my Beetle. I had a bit of a struggle reversing (the screaming understatement of the year), but once on the open road down to the ferry, I even took a certain pleasure in the slickness of my clutchless gear changes. Once the clanking ferry had disgorged me, I headed straight for Poole Harbour. If I struck no joy there, I planned to go to Redstart's home.

I was rather relieved, for once to see the police. Two of their white and red Rovers were stationed at the quayside beside Redstart's yacht, but there was no sign of Sally's Mini. I parked where I could and hobbled over. But as I neared, a third Rover followed by an ambulance sirened their way past me to slew in by the other two cars. Now my hobble turned into a run, but to no avail. I was stopped by a hefty constable whilst still some yards from the yacht.

'I'm sorry, sir. This area is restricted at the moment.'

'Why? What's happened?' I tried to peer past his arm, but other than a brief glimpse of a stretcher party and the odd helmet, I could see nothing.

'I don't know as yet, sir. We've just been told to keep everyone back.'

As he spoke, two other constables started taking some rope out of the boot of the Rover obviously to begin cordoning off the area by the yacht.

'Look, I must see whoever's in charge here. There's a friend of mine who might have been visiting this yacht this morning and I need to know if she's safe.'

He looked at me intently and I saw his eyes run over the bruises and bumps. 'Your name, sir?'

Before I could reply, a voice saved me the trouble.

'Marklin. Peter Marklin.'

I looked round into that ginger moustache yet again.

'Look, Inspector, you must help me. Sally Newton may have come to see Redstart this morning and I must know what's happened.'

'I don't really know what's happened myself yet. Like you, I've only just arrived.'

I pointed to the ambulance. 'But you must know who has been hurt, or – '

'Yes, I know that much.'

'So tell me, for God's sake. It's not Sally, is it?'

He sighed. 'You'd better come on board with me, I think.'

We ducked under the cordon and gang-planked up onto the yacht. Three other policemen made way for us, as we approached the cabin doors. I was so frantic with worry, I didn't even notice the pain in my ankle.

'You wait here,' Whetstone said and I didn't like the look of sympathy expressed in his face. He disappeared into the cabin and it was a full agonizing five minutes before he surfaced again.

'I'm afraid, Mr Marklin, I cannot let you see Miss Newton at the present time.'

'She's here? She's hurt?'

'Physically, she seems to be fine.'

'Then what has happened? Who is the ambulance for?'

'The man she apparently came to see – your fountain-head of evil, Patrick Redstart. He's dead.'

I just didn't believe what he was saying.

'Dead? How? Who killed him?'

'He appears to have been stabbed. There was a paper-knife near the body. As to who killed him, it's far too early to – '

'My God! Did Sally find him like that?'

'So she maintains.'

I looked at him angrily. 'What do you mean by that? Don't you bloody believe her?'

He put his hand on my shoulder. 'Now, now, now, Mr Marklin, don't go jumping to any conclusions. I'm not, so you shouldn't. All we know is that a constable was passing along the quayside when he heard a scream from the yacht. He came on board and found the man dead in the cabin, a knife by his body and your friend, Miss Newton, standing over him.'

I tried to push past him. 'You must let me see Sally. She'll be in a state of shock.'

But Digby Whetstone was not as flabby as he looked. By the time I had freed myself of his arm, two other constables were at the ready.

'Shit, Whetstone, let me see her.' I blazed.

'I will, no doubt, in due course. But for the moment, you must be patient. Remember, this is not just a case of a missing amateur detective any more, Mr Marklin. It's a full-blooded case of murder.'

202

13

I crunched quite a few gears on my worried way back
to Studland. And was relieved to see, as I negotiated
the last bend, Gus's Popular drawn up outside the Toy
Emporium. I had no wish to be alone with my now
despondent thoughts.

Gus noticed my look of doom immediately.

'What's 'appened, old love? You look as if the bailiffs
have been.'

Ten minutes later, Heinekens in hands, I'd brought
him up to date.

'Ruddy hell! Poor girl. No bloody sympathy for 'im,
though. He's got his just come–uppance. But 'er . . .'
He ruminated for a moment, then expressed my fear.
'You don't think she got Redstart to confess to killing
her boyfriend, and then picked up a knife to . . . ?'

I gave a sepulchral sigh. '*I* don't think so, but Whetstone may.'

'What about the fingerprints on the knife? That
should tell him one way or the other, shouldn't it?'

I pointed out the window. 'It's cold enough to freeze
them off, Gus. Sally was probably still wearing her
gloves.'

'Bloodstains?'

I shrugged. 'I don't know. Whetstone wouldn't tell
me anything more than that Redstart was dead, killed
by a knife. And a constable had found Sally standing
by the body.'

Gus slurped some more lager. 'We should look on
the bright side, old lad.'

'What bloody bright side?' I exclaimed. 'Even if

Whetstone absolves Sally from any involvement with Redstart's death, that sodding knife may well have put paid to us ever knowing what's happened to Gregory Mann.'

'There's that Abigail woman.'

'Now her boyfriend is dead she may shut up like a clam.'

'Or open up like one.' Gus wiped some froth off his upper lip. ''Ere, it might be 'er who killed him, mightn't it?'

'It might.'

He looked at me. 'You don't sound as if you think so.'

'I don't really. Corrupt she may be, nymphomaniac she may be, but I don't see her as a murderess, somehow.'

'You don't have to be cut out to be a murderer to pick up a knife in a quarrel and lash out, old son. Almost anybody could do it, I reckon.'

Gus had a point. I had been thinking more of premeditated murder. Redstart's killing might well have been spontaneous.

'All right then,' Gus sniffed. 'If that Abigail didn't stick the knife in, who did?'

'Oh Lord, Gus, it could be anybody at all. This murder is a whole new can of worms. Someone like Redstart must have made a million enemies over the years. It could be someone he cheated in business at some time, or a partner in crime, or an outraged husband, or some girl's father, or another smuggler or ship's captain . . . You name it, Gus.'

He didn't. He raised his heavy eyebrows instead. Then he reached into his pocket.

'S'pose now you won't really want to go through all these other people I noted down what went into Abigail's shop.'

I tried to smile. 'Not right this minute, Gus. I

couldn't really concentrate. You said they didn't seem to you to be very important.'

''Ave it yer own way, old lad.' He took his hand out of his pocket. 'Some other time.'

I suddenly had a thought. 'Look, Gus, I should really ring Philippa over at Owermoigne. I don't want her to hear about Redstart's murder and Sally finding the body over the radio or something, before I've told her.'

Gus waved his hand. 'Off you go then.'

Not only had Philippa not heard about the murder, but neither about Merinda and John-John's arrest. Appalled by both events, she said she very much wanted to see me, but could not leave the nursery until evening. Would Gus and I like to come over for a quick lunch? I hesitated before accepting because I didn't want to be away should Sally return.

She suggested I ring the police in Bournemouth and enquire the earliest we could expect Sally to be released, then phone her back. This I did, and was told that Sally was now with Digby Whetstone in his office and was expected to be there at least until some time in the afternoon.

So we set out for Philippa's, Gus driving me in his Popular. Was there to be no end to the shocks I would receive that day?

I sat back from the table. 'Thanks Philippa. It was good of you to go to the bother of lunch.'

She smiled and patted my hand. 'It was no bother. I give Tom Sweet something to eat most days he's here, and Molly too, when he brings her. So two more is no great effort.'

'The barn looks nice,' I observed. 'I saw it as I drove up. It looks nearly finished.'

'Yes, it is. Tom's done a marvellous job. And he hasn't had the best of weather for thatching, either. He reckons he will be finished by the end of the week, if it remains dry.' She looked at me. 'I was going to start hanging Merinda's pictures next week. I've got them stacked in the study at the moment. Really Peter, what can we do about her and John-John?'

I downed the last of my wine and Philippa pushed the bottle nearer me, bless her.

'They have to be innocent, don't they?' I said, replenishing my glass.

'They must be, otherwise, I'm no damned good at reading character.'

'Anyway,' I said encouragingly, 'from what I've read about those burglaries, they were pretty professional jobs. You know, burglar alarms and telephones disconnected; roofs scaled; dogs drugged; the kind of stuff you see in thrillers on television. I can't believe John-John or Merinda have that kind of expertise. John-John strikes me as – ' I stopped as I saw her expression. 'What's the matter, Philippa?'

She grimaced. 'There's a fly in your ointment.'

'What kind of fly?'

'John-John spent some time in the Forces when he left school. I guess it was a way of leaving his poverty behind. Tom Sweet did the same when he left school, he tells me.'

'So?' I said, but I knew what she meant

'John-John was in the Marines and I gather his special expertise was in electrical engineering.'

I looked at Gus.

'Get's better and better, doesn't it?' I said wearily. 'All we need to hear now is that Merinda's a dab hand at abseiling, is a qualified chemist and once worked for British Telecom.' I looked back at Philippa. 'Sorry, it's just that in the last forty-eight hours everything seems to have gone to hell in a hand-basket.'

'I know,' she smiled affectionately, looking at my face. 'And that's without your involuntary cosmetic surgery. Christ, Peter, I'm so sorry I've got you into all this mess.'

'Don't apologise. If I had made more headway on Gregory's disappearance at the start –'

'If,' Gus grunted. 'Don't hold with "ifs". Past is over and done with. Talk "whens", if you like.'

I looked at my watch. 'Gus is right. I shouldn't be here "iffing", but up off my jack, doing.' I rose to go and Gus followed suit, albeit more noisily.

Philippa took my arm. 'What do you plan to do, Peter? Don't take any more risks, for heaven's sake.'

I crossed my fingers and held them up to her.

'I'm going to wait for Sally to return first, hear what she has to say, then go over to Bournemouth and find out if they'll let me see Merinda or John-John or both. At least, I can find out about lawyers and –'

'I've done that already. I phoned my lawyer when you were on your way here. He will be over in Bournemouth by now, I would think.'

'Thanks,' I said. 'I'll keep you posted or phoned as to how things are going.'

She saw us to the door. As Gus and I were about to go out, someone bumped into me with a bang, coming in. I helped her back up on to her feet and picked up the empty plates she had obviously been bringing back.

'Hello, Molly. You're in a hurry.'

Her eyes lit up as she recognized me.

'Peter. Car.' she said, and mimed a winding action with her hand. I put the plates down.

'How's the car going, Molly?'

She thought for a moment and then took my hand.

'See car,' she said with a huge smile, and started to tug me up the drive towards the barn. I looked at Philippa and shrugged.

'You'll have to go along for a minute,' she smiled.

So I did, with Gus shuffling on behind.

As we approached the barn, Tom Sweet looked down from his great height on the ridge of the roof and waved a bent withy at us in what I took to be a greeting. I waved back. I noticed Gus didn't.

'Car, inside,' Molly smiled and tugged me even more energetically into the open side entrance of the building, which I saw was bordered by some neat stonework – no doubt John-John's handiwork.

Once inside, she pointed to some stone flags under a window. There reposed the Japanese toy car, seemingly in as mint condition as when I had given it to her. She mimed winding once more. I went over and picked it up and started to wind the key. To my delight, the clockwork mechanism was not broken and showed no signs of slip.

'Good, Molly. You've looked after it beautifully.'

'Good car,' she beamed.

I placed the toy back down on the flagstones and held out my hand.

'Still got the ball, Molly? Kept it safe like I told you?'

'Safe . . . safe . . . ball.' She took my hand and dragged me back outside, where her father's ladder leant against the wall. She climbed up the first few rungs until she could easily reach the overhanging thatch. Then, to my surprise, she plunged her hand up into the prickly straw until half her arm disappeared. When she withdrew her hand, it held a little white ball.

'Safe . . . safe,' she repeated and clambered back down the ladder. A moment later, and we were both in that innocent land where everything is possible and cars that keep balls in perpetual suspension are just par for the magical course.

I felt somewhat better on the way home, despite the slings and arrows of Gus's outrageous driving. The only explanation I could devise for the improvement in my mood were my ten or so minutes of childhood with Molly. Her happiness was so absolute, it was downright infectious.

Once back, Gus offered to stick around until we heard something from Sally, if I liked. I liked. Waiting is too lonely an experience. I gave him a couple of

Heinekens and he settled back in a chair. Soon Bing was on his lap, sniffing around his hairy sweater for the fish the odd odour promised.

I went into the shop to pick up my post and turn the 'Closed' sign to 'Open'. By the time I returned, Gus's eyes were closed, his mouth was open and the rafters rang with his snores.

I thanked him quietly for being such lively and distracting company, then, to fill in the anxious time, spent the next half-hour answering my mail – queries from toy collectors about their requirements (two I could satisfy, three I could not), two letters enclosing cheques for stock from my mailing list, (not big deals – one for fifteen pounds for a chipped Dinky Riley, the other for ten pounds for a plastic Minic Hillman Minx), and one letter from a local complaining that, recently, my shop seemed to be more shut than open. I had every sympathy with him.

My professional post dealt with (other than actually packing up the Riley and Minx), I felt in my pocket for the letter I'd been longing to read all day. I hadn't really got much past 'Darling Peter, it seems light years since . . .', when I realized that I wanted to hear Arabella's voice without it being accompanied by the massed bands of Gus's throat, so I went into the shop and spent my time with her quietly there.

This time there was much less in her letter about all the things she was doing in California and much more about what she would prefer to be doing in dear old Dorset. (One of the items, bless her, being yours truly.) She ended by saying that she had got the homesick bug in a big way and had already checked out with the *San Francisco Examiner* whether she could cut short her year's secondment should the bug prove overpowering. Apparently, their reaction was regretful but amenable. She asked me what I thought of the idea of her coming home early, because the last thing she wanted was to force me into anything that I did not, as yet, feel ready for. Then she rounded off by exhorting me to look after myself especially carefully and not to run risks of any sort in my amateur sleuthing. Thank goodness she couldn't see me then, bemused, battered and peg-legging about the place.

It was while I was still basking in the warmth of her letter, that the phone rang. I limped as fast as I could into the hall and answered it. But it wasn't Sally, it was Jimmy Richardson to say that he had now just about finished the restoration of my Carette and would I like to drop over some time to check it over. I said I would love to but it might have to wait a day or two – I didn't explain why. He sounded a trifle disappointed but said to give him a ring when I was free.

I was about to ring off, when he added, 'Remember our scare about my next-door neighbours the other night – the chap on the motor cycle?'

'Well, what's happened now?' I asked.

He laughed. 'We needn't have got so het up. It turned out to be rats disturbing the thatch. This afternoon the old couple had to have the council exterminator round, as they'd seen ruddy rats running all over their roof.'

'Has he got rid of them?'

'I hope so. I don't want them round me. When the guy ferreted round the eaves, he found a great hole deep in the thatch, like a warm little cave, my neighbours told me.'

'They should have kept their wire-netting in good order. After all, that's why netting is put over thatch, to keep birds and animals out.'

'I know. Anyway, it's just as well we didn't scare the living daylights out of them that night, by saying we had seen a burglar.'

I agreed and ended by saying I would be over to see the Carette soonest.

I had hardly put the phone down, when I heard a car draw up outside. I went into the shop and looked out the window. To my intense relief I saw it was Sally's

Mini, and a moment later she was in my arms and I was turning my 'Open' sign yet again back to 'Closed'.

It took two stiff Scotches to bring a dash of colour back into her cheeks and, even then, her hand still shook as she held her glass. Gus had woken up the instant she had come into the sitting-room, much to my relief. Not only did I not want snores punctuating Sally's story, but for Gus to hear it first hand saved me the bother of recounting it to him later second hand.

The great news was that Sally appeared to be no longer under suspicion for Redstart's murder, for though she had, as we'd surmised, been wearing gloves aboard the yacht and there were apparently no prints on the knife, the preliminary medical report on the body indicated death had taken place some hours before Sally's observed arrival. Luckily, a nosey-parking owner of one of the top flats overlooking the harbour had seen Sally both park her car and go on board and had, in his good citizen way, volunteered both bits of information to the police whilst they were still at the boat. I felt like awarding him a medal as I would have been of little use in providing Sally with an alibi; being in the land of Nod at the time, I had no idea when Sally had actually left my Toy Emporium.

'Oh, Peter, I thought Whetstone's questioning would never stop.' Sally shook her head. 'Even after he had got the preliminary medical report, he kept hammering on at me. But now about Gregory.'

'What about Gregory?' I asked.

'Can't you guess?'

'That you knew he was getting back-handers?' I ventured.

'No, he tried that one earlier. He was on about Greg, perhaps, still being alive. And that . . .'

She stopped and I finished her sentence for her.

'. . . he killed Redstart?'

She nodded. 'He said that Redstart and Greg might

211

have been hand in glove in some new racket or other, smuggling or the burglaries or whatever, and that Greg might have had to go to ground for some reason. He didn't elaborate why. Then he said that Greg might have been impatient to return to normal life and had a quarrel with Redstart over it, or they fell out over some other matter, like money. Or one might have been blackmailing the other and one of them grabs a knife and, hey presto, a second later, Redstart gets the worst of it.'

'I know it's a silly question to ask of anyone who has just found a dead body, but did you notice any signs of a struggle – broken or disarranged furniture, smashed fittings?'

'Not really. That was the horrid part. Everything looked so normal – except for the body . . . and the blood.'

'Was he lying on his back or his front?'

'On his front. A knife was on the floor to his right, and there was blood around the rent in the back of his jacket.' She downed a large slug of her Scotch, then looked at me. 'I don't want to talk about it any more, Peter. I just can't. It's been like a horrific nightmare all day. I should never have gone on my own.'

I sat down beside her on the settee and took her hand.

'Okay, it's over now. All over. You're back, Sally.'

She forced about an eighth of a smile. '*I'm* back,' she said pointedly, then lay her head on my shoulder.

I looked across at Gus who mouthed what I took to be 'Shall I go?'

I shook my head and mouthed back, 'Not unless you want to.'

He cupped his ear and smiled, the sod. He'd understood every word I'd not been saying.

After a moment, I whispered to Sally, 'Why don't you pop up to bed for a bit and try to get a little sleep? Meanwhile, Gus and I will rustle up something for us all to eat when you wake up.'

Sally looked at me and smirked. 'You and Gus?'

'Me and Gus.'

'Rustle up something to eat?'

'That's right.'

'For when I wake up?'

'For when you wake up.'

She stretched herself up from my shoulder.

'You know you have the nicest way of bribing someone to have a really long rest.'

I stood up with her and clasped her to me. 'Nice to have you back, Miss Newton.'

'Nice to be back, Mr Marklin.' She inclined her head to Gus. 'Mr Tribble.' She disentangled herself and with a last, slightly nervous glance, left for the stairs.

Gus looked across at me, when the footfalls had receded and observed, 'I hope it's not her boyfriend what did it. She's too nice a girl.'

'Yeah,' I said.

'What are you thinking of?' he frowned.

'Oh, why Redstart should be at his yacht so early on a cold winter's morning. And who he came there to meet. Presumably, the nosey-parker wasn't up at that hour, otherwise, he might have seen him, or her, too.'

'Must have been important, whatever it was,' Gus sniffed. 'Can't see that bugger getting up at sparrowfart for any old Tom, Dick or Harry.'

'That's what makes me feel it probably wasn't Abigail. He would have told her to ruddy well come and see him at a more civilized hour or forget it.'

'Unless she'd suddenly got the wind up over something or other and panicked, so he had to bloody see her early.'

I shrugged. 'I would imagine he knew whoever it was. You don't usually meet strangers at the crack of dawn, do you?'

'I don't,' Gus grinned. 'Not even women. I like to see them in the daylight first.'

'I dare say they feel the same about you and me, Gus.' I downed the last of my Scotch.

'Hell, I promised Philippa I'd let her know about Sally. Then I must ring and see if I can get to Merinda and John-John today. They'll have been charged by now.'

I got up and rang Owermoigne. Philippa was overjoyed to hear that Sally was back and reported that her lawyer had telephoned to say that Merinda and John-John had been charged and remanded in custody for a week pending further enquiries. She added that he was working on getting at least Merinda released on bail at the next hearing.

I then contacted the Bournemouth police, but was told that Digby Whetstone was out and only he could give permission for anybody to visit Merinda or John-John at this stage in their investigations. And surprise, surprise, they ventured no opinion as to when the Inspector could be contactable. 'Try again tomorrow,' was their only advice.

In my frustration, I tried one last fling at phoning. I dialled Abigail's number, which I'd got from the directory. I let it ring until I could hear the proverbial cowbells, but got no reply. I reckoned she was either with the police or, perhaps, hiding out somewhere until Redstart's murderer (or murderess) was caught – that is, if she wasn't the actual culprit herself.

Gus was in the kitchen by the time I slammed down the receiver. He had the local radio on full blast. I had to get him to turn it down so that I could bring him up to date with my lack of news.

'Well,' he muttered, 'things may not have been happening with you, old dear, but you ought to have heard the local news.'

'Thrill me,' I sighed and sat down at the table.

'Your friend Stringle seems to have been at it again, from all accounts.'

I perked up somewhat. 'Why, what's he done now?'

'Just given a warning, haven't they?' Gus continued in his typically oblique fashion. (If Gus reckons he's got someone's attention, he doesn't half milk it.)

'Warning about what, Gus? Get on with it.'

'Rabid dogs, old son, that's what. Some silly bugger like Stringle has gone and released some Alsatians that had been infected with rabies at those ruddy laboratories. Shouldn't be allowed that.'

'When did all this happen?'

'Last night, they said. They've kept it quiet up to now so as not to alarm everyone. Seems they interrupted the buggers in the act and they saw the dogs run off and hoped to recapture them quickly without any fuss.'

'How many dogs were there? Did they say?'

'Four, I think they said. So far, they've only got two of 'em back.'

I thought for a moment. 'Why on earth would so-called animal lovers release dogs infected with rabies?'

'They didn't know, old love. Seems the Alsatians had only just been moved to an area normally used for healthy animals. And the silly sods who broke in weren't up to date.'

'Have they apprehended anybody yet?'

'Got one chap, but the others got away in a van.'

'No mention of who the chap is? Or of Stringle?'

Gus shook his head. 'Nope. Ain't saying yet, I guess. But reckon it must be your Dobermann friend, don't you?'

'This time, having caught someone, I suppose the police have a chance of finding out.'

Gus opened the fridge door. 'Who knows, old son? But I'm more worried about the bleeding dogs than who sprung them. I'm sure as hell going to run a record flaming mile the next time I see an Alsatian until they're back where they come from.'

For once, I felt sorry for Digby Whetstone. He needed rabid dogs added to his problems like the *Titanic* needed a fresh delivery of ice. Suddenly, I came back to current domestic reality.

'Gus, what are you looking for in the fridge? The last pack of Heinekens is in that cupboard next to the cooker.'

'Not looking for 'Einekens, old love, am I?'

'Then what are you looking for?'

'Things to put in an omelette. You promised Sally you and me would . . .'

I was thunderstruck. Gus was a heater and eater, a dab hand at opening cans, not cookbooks. Even in his heyday as a fisherman, he's told me his piscatorial intake was mainly sardines and tuna out of tins.

'Gus, don't tell me you know how to make an omelette.'

He grinned round at me. 'Full of surprises, ain't I just? Got any better ideas than an omelette, then?'

I confessed I hadn't. My own culinary expertise was the equivalent, in educational terms, to a drop-out from a play-group.

'It's all right, Gus, you needn't go through every cupboard in the kitchen. I've got enough stuff for an omelette for when Sally comes down again.'

Eventually, I managed to persuade him to shuffle back into the sitting-room, where he plonked himself down in a chair and started to twiddle his great thumbs. I began wondering if I'd been wise in my decision to have him stick around. For a Gus with nothing to do (or drink) can be a very disconcerting animal – and that's when your mind isn't already in a turmoil.

I decided to humour him. 'All right, Gus, seeing that we can't really do anything else right this minute, take me through that list of yours. You know, the people who called in at Abigail's shop that day.'

He smiled with pleasure and ferreted in his back trouser pocket for his scruffy piece of paper. Three minutes into his hesitant recital, I sat up straight in my seat and was soon to curse my stupidity in not allowing

216

him to read out the full list in the wee small hours of Tuesday.

14

It was already too dark and too late that afternoon to carry out what I planned, following Gus's hint of a new lead. Besides, I wanted to be around when Sally at last surfaced for her surprisingly, er, interesting omelette.

Gus left that evening, his gnarled ears ringing with the praises for his unique choice of ingredients for the culinary delight, which included ancient curry powder inherited from my great-aunt. Soon after, Sally and I repaired upstairs to our still separate bedrooms. She did suggest we might try the one bed and not try anything else. But I reminded her of the old saying about flesh and blood – especially flesh.

Next morning, I was up with the lark, and had left the house before Sally appeared. My ankle, luckily, was now slightly more able to withstand a modicum of Marklin weight and thus allowed around half my gear changes in the Beetle to be achieved as Wolfsburg had intended.

It felt a trifle funny bumping up the track to the caravan, knowing that the van was now as empty as a snail's shell after a thrush, and I felt a little nervous as I got out of the car to have a ferret round. I certainly did not need to be 'Ercool Parrot to find from where the police had taken the loot. They had left the hole neatly roped off, like a miniature boxing-ring. I looked back at the caravan but it was just hidden by some bushes, proving what I had suspected – that the loot could have been planted there by someone at almost any time and they would not have been seen.

The grass almost crackled under my feet as I poked

218

around with a stick, so crisped was it by the heavy frost. Indeed, I rarely remembered such a raw day for November. I had no idea really what I was looking for; just something, I guess, to give the merest of backing to my wild hunch. But after ten bitter minutes or so, nothing seemed forthcoming, so I moved back to the van itself. Not having a key, I couldn't get in, so had to satisfy myself by peering in the windows from which I first had to scrape the frost.

The interior was hardly in the apple-pie order I had seen before in happier times, for the police had been patently more expert at disturbing and searching, then smoothing and replacing, I winced at the sight and longed to have a key to enable me to do a bit of tidying in case Merinda should be released on bail and find it like that. Even her wonderful pictures had been taken down from the cupboard doors and lay scattered over bunks and propped up against table-legs. Only the painting on the wardrobe seemed to be still in its original position and even this was hanging at a crazy angle.

I was about to turn away, when I felt a compulsion to look at the picture once more. It looked even more surrealistic than ever at its new angle; the crazy dog atop the thatch of the barn seemed to be in danger of sliding off. I suddenly realized why I had double-taken with the picture. The last time I'd noticed it I hadn't actually yet seen the building it was depicting. Now I had and Merinda's evocation of it was uncanny – only the bright new thatch had mellowed greyer since the time of its painting.

I looked at the dog again and shuddered. It reminded me of the rabid Alsatians that were now on the loose. Merinda's surrealism had been somewhat prophetic. I suddenly looked around me, almost expecting to see frothy fangs about to play snap. There were none, but for a cripple, I made surprisingly good time back to the safety of the Beetle.

I turned right at the end of the track, towards Corfe, not quite certain of how I was to carry out the next part of my still rather nebulous plan. But I had not proceeded more than a few hundred yards when I heard the unnerving sound of police sirens wailing up from behind. I slowed and two police Rovers roared past me, blue lights in a frenzy. Before they were totally out of sight, their brake lights added red to the blue, and they turned off to the left. There was only one place they could be going, so I decided to take advantage of their wake.

By the time I pulled into the rutted track that led up to the thatcher's, the police were already out of their cars and stood in groups around the now open boots. One constable looked around and cautioned me to stop. I did so and then saw, to my considerable consternation, what little goodies they were taking from their boots – high powered rifles of the gun-siege variety.

I immediately got out of the car, but my action prompted the constable to come running over to me, a rifle now in hand.

'What the hell are you lot going to do?' I asked fearfully. 'Don't you know there could be a child up there?'

He looked taken aback. 'Where?'

'I don't know,' I said. 'She could be in the cottage or the barn. Or anywhere.'

He hesitated, then said, 'I should get back in your car, if I were you, sir. The dogs could be anywhere too.'

'Dogs?' I said, now somewhat relieved.

'Yes. We got a report from a motorist that he'd seen some Alsatians on this bit of land. We have to check out every sighting, as you might imagine. These rabid dogs – '

I cut him short. 'Let me go up to the cottage and barn first. I know the girl a little and she will be scared out of her wits seeing all you lot bristling with bloody guns.'

He looked at me hard, then nodded. 'You had better come with me.'

We hurried over to the cars, where the others were now forming two sections, with a police officer gesticulating towards the frost-covered land like a Montgomery on D-Day.

'Gentleman here, sir,' the constable interrupted, 'is worried about a child who he believes might be roaming about.'

The officer sighed as he turned to me. 'What's your name, sir?'

'Marklin. Peter Marklin.'

'Know the owner of this land?'

'Yes, it's Tom Sweet. He's a thatcher. It's his daughter I'm worried about.'

'I'll send a constable up to his house to explain.' He pointed over the ridge. 'I take it, it's up past the barn there and down in the dip.'

I nodded. 'But Tom Sweet will be at work, I expect. He's thatching a barn of a friend of mine.'

'How old is this daughter of his then?'

'About sixteen, but she's really only five or six.'

'Oh come, Mr Marklin. She can't be both. Either she's six or sixteen.'

'Yes, she ruddy can!' I exploded. 'Do I have to spell it out for you? She's retarded.'

He was about to respond, but thought better of it. Instead, he turned and called to the constable.

'Constable Armstrong, would you accompany Mr . . . er . . . er'

'Marklin,' I said wearily, raising my eyebrows.

'. . . Mr Marklin to the barn and the cottage, so that he can find a young girl who might be frightened by all that's going on?' He turned back to me. 'Would you be willing, sir, to stay with the girl until we have either

221

tracked down the dogs or made certain they are no longer in the area?'

'Yes, of course,' I said.

'Well, off you go, constable. And when you find the girl, keep your gun as inconspicuous as possible, would you, in case she takes fright.

I didn't quite see how you keep a rifle with telescopic sights, powerful enough to blow a man away, inconspicuous, but there you are. Maybe policemen are built differently from us and have hiding places we never even suspected.

We tramped off together up the track and the first thing I did, of course, was skid onto my bottom on the ice-covered ground, which did my dignity and ankle a power of bad. The constable lived up to his name and helped me to my feet.

'Tricky stuff, ice, sir.'

I lifted my eyes up to the heavens. What else can you do after a remark like that?

To my surprise, Molly was not in the barn. Maybe the weather was just too cold, even for her. So I limped on up and then down to the cottage. She wasn't in the yard outside, so I went up to the front door.

'This thatcher fellow shouldn't really leave his daughter alone,' the constable muttered, 'considering – '

'Maybe,' I said. 'But he wasn't reckoning on rabid ruddy dogs, was he?'

His eyes went blank. Sorry, blanker.

I tried the handle of the door. It was locked. I knocked. In under half a minute, I heard a key turning, then the door opened a crack.

'Molly,' I whispered. 'Don't worry, it's only me. Peter. Remember, the Peter with the toys?'

'Toys . . . Peter . . .' she repeated and opened the door fully.

I indicated to Armstrong that he should keep back behind me.

222

'Can I come in?' I asked.

She shook her head gravely.

'Just for a minute?'

A second shake. 'Be cross,' she said.

'Your father would be cross if you let me in?'

She nodded.

'Then we'll talk here,' I said.

'Get the car?' she offered, her eyes widening.

'Not right now. In a minute. I want to tell you something first.'

She suddenly took fright at the apparition in blue and chrome behind me.

'P'liceman.'

'Nice policeman,' I encouraged. 'He's with me because there might be some dangerous dogs around here. Dogs that might bite.' I smiled. 'That's why I've come. To stay with you until the nasty dogs have gone.'

'Dogs . . . dogs not in house.'

'No, not in the house. Maybe in the fields.'

'Barn,' she smiled. 'Dogs go . . . to barn.'

'We'll stop them going to the barn, don't worry, Molly.'

She shook her head. 'Dogs go . . . on roof. Can't catch them.'

'Dogs on roof?' I queried and Merinda's painting suddenly came into sharp focus in my mind.

'Dogs like roof. Foxes too.'

'The roof of the barn?' I queried, but Molly's reply was stifled by the constable's interruption.

'I would suggest, sir, that instead of just chatting away, you, er, get her to let you inside, if that's possible. I should get back, you see, to the others, but I can't whilst you are still outside and she's unchaperoned, as you might say.'

'I wasn't "just chatting away", as you call it, constable. I was – '

He touched my shoulder. 'Well, try to get her to let

223

you in, sir and then you'll both be safe and can chat away to your heart's content.'

I could see I was trying to communicate with concrete, so I turned back to Molly.

'If you let me in, you can show me the car working, can't you? I hope you've still got the little ball.'

She nodded and beamed. 'Ball on chimney.'

I stood back and looked up at the chimney atop the thatch of the cottage. I felt a tug at my anorak.

'No, no,' she laughed. 'Chimney on car.'

'Ah, the one that blows the air that keeps the ball up.'

I could feel the constable fuming behind me and had a certain sympathy for him, for the present conversation must have seemed like the most irrelevant double Dutch in the UK.

'Daddy won't be cross,' I continued hopefully, 'if you and I just play cars. Anyway, he won't know, will he? He's at work at Lady Philippa's, remember?'

'Oh no, he isn't,' came a bellow from behind me. I turned my head slowly and looked up into the eyes of her father, Tom Sweet.

To say he looked none too pleased is a bit of an understatement and I could well understand his shock and wrath at finding his place not only swarming with me but also hordes of officers of the law.

'I'm sorry,' I stuttered. 'I didn't know you were around – '

He did not let me finish. 'Seems as how none of you lot did, by the looks of things.' He turned to Armstrong, who shuffled his boots. 'Get back where you belong with your guns and all and find those dogs you're supposed to be after.'

'I'm sorry, Mr Sweet, I – '

He extended a brawny arm back towards the fields.

'Go on. Off with you and stop frightening the daylights out of my kid.'

The constable seemed about to protest, but thought better of it. He looked across at me, rather despairingly, then started to walk back across the yard. I was about to follow the arm of the law, when Tom Sweet barred the way.

'Not you, yet, Mr Marklin. I want some words with you.'

'Words?' I queried, as innocently as I could.

'Yes. Words. And you'd better bloody well take note of them, too.'

'I've done nothing wrong. I was just trying to keep Molly in the house until the police had made certain that there were no rabid dogs around to harm her.'

'*I'm* around to see no 'arm comes to her, Mr Marklin, not you.'

'I didn't know that, did I? I thought you would be over at Lady Philippa's, finishing off the barn, seeing it's dry.'

'So I was. But my work's done there now. All I had to do this morning was cart all the old straw up the field and set light to it. Lady Philippa said she would look after the blaze for me so that I could come back to Molly.'

'Well – ' I began, but he cut me off.

'Well, it isn't.' He stared me in the eye. 'Ain't ruddy natural a grown man keep coming and bothering my Molly. I should have stopped it right at the start, only Molly so loved that there car of yours.'

It was my turn to get irate.

'No, come on. I'm not that kind of person and you know it. I think I know why you've taken such a dislike to me. You think I'm a wally, don't you? A grown man, for Christ's sake, who doesn't do a proper day's work. Just sits in a shop and plays with old toys all day – toys which kids could well enjoy but can't possibly afford at his prices.'

'No,' he said slowly. 'I don't think you're a wally, Mr Marklin.'

I didn't like the sound or the pace of that.

'Well, maybe I am,' I went on. 'But it's a living. And it's a living that doesn't hurt anybody.'

He strode around me, so that he was now between myself and Molly, who hadn't come out with as much as a peep since her father's arrival.

'I want you to leave now, Mr Marklin and I don't want to see you back here, ever. Understand?'

I looked at Molly. Her eyes said it all. I gave a slight wave with my hand. She was about to wave back, when her father pushed her further indoors.

'Now you hearken to what I say. If I ever catch you back here . . .'

I turned on my good heel and moved off down the courtyard. This was no time to argue with Tom Sweet. And I doubted, somehow, if there would ever be a good time now.

I was tempted to go right away to my next planned port of call, but was worried lest Sally would be awake and worrying about my whereabouts. The last thing I wanted just now was her wandering the Dorset countryside on the Marklin trail.

Two bear hugs and a considerable number of sloppy kisses confirmed her relief at seeing me return and still in recognizable form. I explained that I just wanted to go and check out the caravan site and I omitted all reference to Tom Sweet and the rabid dog episode. I felt her equilibrium might still be shaky after her terrible experience of the day before and I didn't want to rattle it further. She did, however, notice that I was putting less weight again on my ankle, which I explained was due to a slip on the ice as I was getting back into my Beetle at the caravan site. Immediately I was ordered to lie out on the settee and not move a muscle for the rest of the day. My protests resulted in an amendment to 'until after lunch', because I told her I wanted to pick up the Carette Jimmy Richardson had restored – which was, at least, partly true and was the port of call I had postponed.

Meanwhile, Sally, bless her, sat in the shop, waiting for the ding of customers. She had three, and disposed of a Schuco tinplate motor cycle for sixty pounds, a pre-war TM Nelson die-cast battleship for thirty-five pounds (one of a range of British warships made in a special factory in Wales that employed disabled miners), and an Italian Mercury Douglas Skyrocket aircraft for the same price. Her proud smiles when she came in to report each sale showed what splendid therapy old toy dealing can be, whatever one's problems.

Then just before we were going to close up shop for lunch (and indeed, for that day), Sally interrupted my settee ruminations by carrying in a large cardboard box that she said an elderly man had just brought into the shop and which turned out to contain a variety of toy farm animals, farm equipment and a compressed paper model country cottage, all exposed beams. And a wooden building I took to be a cowshed, with broom bristles arranged neatly and in depth across the roof and held by a wire, in a pretty fair imitation of thatch. Apparently, the old gentleman wanted a quote on the lot, as he wanted to sell.

Whilst Sally returned to him in the shop, I went through every item in the box, most of which turned out to be pre-war vintage Britains Ltd manufacture and quite delightful, as it always is. The cowshed I had never seen before and it wasn't listed in any of the old Britains toy catalogues I had collected. But it was cute and in scale with the many hollow cast Britains farm animals. I totted up on my calculator what I was willing to pay on each object and the total sum came to a surprising three hundred and five pounds.

I peg-legged into the shop, carrying the box and offered the gentleman two hundred and fifty pounds for the lot. It was lucky I had a counter for him to grasp onto, otherwise I think he would have had a nasty accident. When the colour at last returned to his cheeks, he asked me if he had heard right and the figure was in the hundreds, not the tens. I laughed and assured him it was. A moment later, I was writing him out a cheque, as I did not have that kind of cash spare in the till.

When he had gone, pleased as punch, I turned to Sally.

'You're bringing me luck.'

'About bloody time,' she grinned.

And we shut up shop and repaired to the sitting-room. After ten minutes or so, whilst I was lying back on the settee toying with the thatched cowshed in my hands (I tend to appraise toys I've never seen before in great detail – it's part of the pleasure of the business), Sally remarked, 'You've got some kind of plan on your mind, haven't you?'

'You can't keep anything from a woman.'

'What makes you think that?' I said, nonchalantly, running my fingers along the bristle of the cowshed roof.

'Elementary, my dear Holmes. It's because you haven't spoken a dicky-bird about what you're thinking of doing next.'

'Oh, don't mistake silence for thoughts. Silence more often means you haven't got a single idea in your head.'

'So you *have* got a plan,' she half smiled.

'Not really. I'm sort of just brewing on things, hoping a plan might emerge.'

She came and sat at the end of the settee, looking desirable enough to get even a bishop defrocked.

'You will tell me what your brewery produces, won't you?'

I took her hand. 'More than that. I'll tell the police too, and leave all the action to them.'

She kissed me on the forehead. 'There's a good boy,' she said and got up. 'Now I'm going to scrape some lunch together. That is, if you and Gus left anything *out* of the omelettes last night.'

It was soon after she had disappeared into the kitchen that I made the two discoveries. The first was a single Players cigarette card, 1938 vintage, depicting an Airspeed Envoy of the King's Flight. (Dinky, incidentally, made a very good model of this around the same period.) It had been totally hidden under the bristles on the roof of the cowshed.

The second stunningly significant discovery came a moment later, as I was turning the cowshed idly in my hands, viewing it from every angle. And angle is the right word. For suddenly, I felt I knew what Gregory's sole entry in his diary for the morning of his disappearance meant. If I was right, it had as much to do with art deco as nymphomaniacs with a nunnery.

Much to my irritation, for my original sketchy plan had me going alone, Sally insisted on chauffeuring me over to Jimmy Richardson's and, what's more, asked to come inside to see his workroom too. If it hadn't been for Jimmy's rotund and big-hearted wife eventually insisting that Sally went into the parlour to share a sherry with her, whilst 'us men' talked, I would probably have had to explain to her a little of what was in my mind. As it was, even Jimmy thought my request was somewhat crazy.

'I thought you had come over here to pick up your Carette, not go rat-hunting next door.'

'I have. I couldn't wait to see what a wonderful job you've done. It's really stunning. I'm half tempted to keep it for my own collection and not let that berk with the peerage have it at all.'

'But didn't he pay a deposit?'

'Deposits are returnable,' I said and I wasn't joking. The Carette was so unbelievable now in its restored condition that parting with it, I knew, would be painful.

'So what do you want to look at my neighbours' thatch for? You haven't got thatch at your place in Studland. And it can't be that you're interested in rats, surely?'

'Look, Jim, I'm just sort of intrigued as to what kind of nest they make, that's all. A friend of mine has got a barn with what seems like a similar hole. I wouldn't have bothered, but seeing as I was coming to pick up the Carette . . .'

He didn't believe me.

'All right,' he said, 'so you're not going to tell me what it's all about right now. Have it your own way. But you've got to promise to come clean sometime, otherwise I'll never touch another toy of yours.'

I put my hand on his shoulder. 'I promise.'

We went out the back door. The afternoon light was already poor and the cold wind pierced our clothes like they were new and belonged to a fairytale emperor.

'Looks as if you're in luck,' Jimmy breathed. 'No lights at the windows. They go to her sister's sometimes of a Thursday.'

I was more than relieved. My rat story was no more likely to convince the old couple than it had Jimmy.

'Now be careful. Don't go falling again,' he urged, for I had told him my bruises, abrasions and limp were due to falling off a ladder whilst fixing a slate.

I was glad there were no houses opposite, for nosey neighbours to marvel at my climbing up with a game ankle onto the water butt and then gingerly stepping up onto the ledge, so that I was able to inspect the eaves of the thatch in the fading light. The hole was quite conspicuous, the wire netting having rusted and rotted away from most of the eaves' length.

'They've rung the thatcher to tell him about it,' Jimmy shouted, 'but apparently he can't come to repair it for over a month.'

I plunged my arm up into the thatch. To my surprise,

230

the hole seemed endless and seemed to track upwards at the same angle as the roof.

'Nice and warm in there?' Jimmy observed, laughing. I took his hint. He was anxious to get back in the warm and I didn't blame him.

'It seems to go on for ever,' I said.

'Long rats,' he muttered.

I pushed up harder into the thatch, until the projecting straw around the entrance to the hole started to dig into my shoulder. Now my fingers were not able to make contact with anything – seemed to have reached some larger cavity or other. Push as I might, I could not discover its end or extent. Reluctantly, I removed my arm and Jimmy helped me down.

'Cor,' he chortled. 'Some people get their kicks a funny old way.' He looked at my hand. 'Lucky some rat didn't bite the end off it. You live dangerously, you know.'

I grinned to myself. He was more correct than he could possibly have imagined.

We were very glad to get back indoors to banish the blue from our complexions. When we eventually went into the parlour, Sally winked at me and asked how our 'man's talk' had gone. I replied, 'Fine', which wasn't entirely true – for I felt I might have achieved rather more, if God had made my arms twice the normal length.

Soon after we got back and my Carette was scintillating in the glass cabinet where I kept the most precious of my personal toy collection, the phone rang.

It was Digby Whetstone. And, surprisingly for him, in a conciliatory and communicative mood. His prime reason for phoning was to ask if he could come by my place at eleven the next morning to share notes on the Mann/Redstart case; and, at the same time perhaps, check on the odd detail or two with Sally Newton,

231

'should she be visiting you around that time', as he so tactfully put it.

Naturally, I had to agree and before he had a chance to ring off, asked him about PC Oliver Smart. He said he had been suspended from normal duties, pending further enquiries – these enquiries being currently rather hampered by the disappearance of a prime witness.

'Oh, who might that be?' I asked.

'Miss Abigail Gordon. Do you have any ideas as to where she might have gone?'

I said I couldn't imagine. Maybe she had gone to her parents or some relatives, while she got over the shock of Redstart's death.

He said they were currently checking all known relatives, but so far, none had confessed to having heard from her. And she hadn't taken her passport, so was unlikely to have left the country.

'Maybe she's gone because she thinks you suspect her of her boyfriend's murder,' I prodded. 'I take it you had a chance to interview her before she vamoosed.'

'Oh, yes,' Digby replied. 'She was brought to the station almost immediately Miss Newton left. I learnt quite a good deal from her. And one of the things I learnt was that she couldn't have committed the murder. She had spent the previous night and that morning with an antique dealer friend of hers over in Dorchester. We checked it out. It tallies.'

I was sort of glad my intuition had proved correct. That Abigail, with all her faults, was no murderess. The news somewhat backed up my new hunch.

'She didn't venture an opinion, by any chance, as to who might have killed him?'

'No. I asked her, of course. She didn't do much more than shrug. Still . . .'

'Still, you think she suspects more than she is letting on?'

He went all 'official' again.

'Look, Mr Marklin, we'll meet up at eleven in the morning at your place. Okay?'

'Okay.'

And click went the receiver. And that was that.

I was quite pleased with both the fact and the timing of the Inspector's visit on the morrow as, by then, if all went well, I might just have sufficient proof to back my present theories and thus be able to hand over all further action to the true professionals, as Digby loved to call his boys and girls. And for me, after the last ten days or so, the time could not be coming too soon. For Sally, however, I suspected no timing could be called convenient for what might be revealed.

The thought made me determined to make the evening as enjoyable as possible for her. So I asked her what she would like to do. To my surprise, she suggested it might be nice if we asked Gus up to join us and make a bit of a party of it, to thank him for all his help over the last few days.

I jumped at the thought, as I had been wracking my brains as to how to contact Gus that night without her knowing. So I suggested I hobble down to Gus's, whilst she popped out in her car to get some booze. We compromised. She dropped me down at Gus's, then went off to get the booze, which she said was a modest liquid reward for the Marklin sleuthing services.

I didn't waste any time at Gus's. I brought him up to date, then outlined my strategy before even telling him about Sally's party invitation. He was amazed at my theories and shook his head vigorously at my plans, but nodded vigorously at the invitation. He felt I should not take any further action myself at all, but just tell Digby in the morning what I suspected.

I countered by pointing out to him that I had not, as yet, got the slightest bit of proof for my theories, nor could I even plot any real motivation for the suspect or suggest what the missing links were in the whole confusing shebang. Therefore, dear old Digby would be likely to take me even less seriously than he had so far – and might even cap me with a piece of information he'd gleaned from his own enquiries that could well blow my theories sky high. So I repeated that I really had to have an iota of evidence before I met Digby in the morning.

Gus could see the logic, I think, but not the magic of my sticking my neck out. He looked at me hard.

'Are you sure, old lad, that you know what you're doing?'

'No. All I know is that I have to do it,' I grinned ruefully.

His sigh was as deep as the ocean, but more gurgly. 'Well then,' he grumbled. 'What time do I set me alarm?'

I put my arm almost round his shoulder. (Gus had Rambo-wide shoulders which, bulked out with his hairy sweaters, make a total embrace quite a feat – except for another Rambo.)

'Thanks Gus,' I said, 'but you don't have to, you know.'

'Don't I?' he grinned. 'That's what's so nice about this world, old son. You learn something new every day.' He side-stepped my punch, then added, 'So what would you like me to do then?'

So I told him. Then he and I strode and hobbled respectively back to the old Toy Emporium. As we were about to open my door, Gus suddenly looked at me in horror.

'You bastard,' he said.

Shocked at his outburst, I stuttered, 'What have I done now, Gus?'

'What have you done? You've bloody invited me to a booze-up, where I can't really booze-up, can I?'

I had to confess I saw his point. 'Not to the extent where we have to carry you home, no, Gus. Otherwise, you won't be much good to me in the wee small hours. But you can have have a few. But don't let Sally know

234

you're holding back a bit, will you? I'm going to pretend I'm drinking more than I am.'

'How on earth can I do that?' He looked stupefied. 'I've spent all my bloody life pretending I'm drinking *less* than I am.'

Before I could answer, Sally opened the door with a bottle of champagne in her hands. I saw Gus's eyes flutter at the glint of the gold foil and I prayed fervently that he wouldn't forget my attempt at advice.

15

I parked my Beetle up the caravan track and doused the lights. I picked up my big rubber-cased torch from the passenger seat and got out just as Gus pulled off the road and shuddered up to park behind me.

'Your lights,' I mouthed and pointed to the one and only lamp that was working. Needless to say, Gus had not taken his car to a professional garage for repair after his ditching, but had Heath-Robinsoned the damage himself. As a result, the broken headlight did not dangle any more, but it didn't work either. I had to mouth twice before he got the message and switched the other one off.

He got out unsteadily and stood by me, his breath in the bitter cold looking like an alcoholic smokescreen. My drinking advice had, unfortunately, mainly fallen on stony ground, but, at least, he was still capable of standing up.

'All right, old son,' he muttered. 'What now?'

He spoke as if I had never bothered to tell him the plan.

'Come on, Gus. Pull yourself together. You know what now. I'm going on ahead by myself. You come on in about ten minutes. Remember, look at your watch. Ten minutes, understand?'

He nodded, but in the dark I couldn't see if his eyes were registering anything but booze.

'You know where I'll be but keep well back down the track unless you hear me shout or scream, or you see anyone approaching, right?'

'Right.'

'Now, you haven't brought your old gun, have you?'

I frisked Gus, just in case he'd been fool enough to secrete the Colt he had bought for a fiver during the War. To my relief, he hadn't.

'Now, remember, don't move from here for ten minutes. When you do come up, keep quiet and out of sight. With any luck, I can be in and out of there in under a quarter of an hour. However, if you haven't heard anything or seen anything after twenty minutes, you had better pelt back to the car and call the police. Okay?'

'Okay,' he said. And I hoped it was. It was my sixth time of telling.

Crossing my fingers, I left him and started off up the narrow road, keeping as close to the hedges as I could, so as to merge with them in the dark. I looked at my watch. It was 2.17 – a little later than I had planned, but Sally seemed determined for the party to go on forever and I couldn't very well tell her to let us all go to bed because Gus and I had an early start in the morning – like just over an hour later. At least, she would sleep soundly, considering the number of bubbles that had tickled her nose, but even so, I had taken the precaution of pushing the Beetle out of my lean-to, instead of starting it up so near the house.

At last I reached a gate on my left, which I had noticed the previous morning and which I guessed led into a field that ran parallel to the property I was about to invade. I climbed over the five bars with not a little difficulty and then proceeded across the frost-crisp grass towards my objective. I hadn't gone far before the hoot of an owl almost gave me a heart attack, for not only predatory landowners but rabid dogs were very much on my mind – or rather, one rabid dog. The other, according to Gus, had apparently been recaptured earlier in the day.

I broke into a sloping run, as I felt very exposed in the open field and was glad to reach the comparative security of the hedge. I flicked my torch to check it was still in good order, then gingerly moved along the hedge to find some kind of opening large enough to crawl through. I found one within a hundred or so feet and at the expense of a scratch on my cheek and some pinpricks through my gloves from blackberry briars, I got through to the field, that I could now see did, indeed, slope down towards the barn.

Gripping my torch tightly, I took a deep breath, and crouching as low as was commensurate with running, I made for the menacing black shape of the building. The distance seemed endless, and I expected to hear a shout, a gunshot or a dog bark every second of the way. By the time I flattened myself up against one of the stone walls, I was distinctly as out of breath as I was of courage. And I wondered for a second what the hell I was doing, not being tucked up tight in bed.

I waited for about half a minute, eyes and ears straining, before I nervously edged my way round the side of the barn towards the door that Molly had shown me. It was shut and bolted, as I had expected but, praise be, not padlocked. I eased the bolts back as quietly as I could, but even the faint squeak of metal rubbing on rust seemed to me like a Butlins reveille. And the creaking of the door as I opened it like machine-gun fire. I listened intently and then went in.

To my regret, I needed some light instantly: it was dark as a tomb and twice as forbidding. I bumped into the ladder whilst I was still fiddling with the button of the torch. I held onto a rung for moral support, then quickly flashed the beam around. It all seemed so very different in the dark from what I had remembered – bigger and barer and I wished I hadn't come. Over to my right, I could see the old tractor that Gus had borrowed, to my left what looked like instruments remaindered from the Spanish Inquisition, but which were, in reality, odd rusting pieces of agricultural machinery and more lengths of chain than would adorn a masochists' convention.

I shivered and tried to get a grip on myself. I then took a risk and flashed the torch beam up the ladder to the roof. I moved it slightly to the right, trying to picture in my mind's eye exactly where the dog had been standing in Merinda's picture – the dog I had supposed all along had been just another of her surrealistic touches. I killed the beam and sighed. It had seemed much easier in theory, finding the spot about one third along the roof. But now I realized the scale of my problem and other doubts set in – like maybe, even if the dog had been real, Merinda might have exercised artistic licence as to where she placed him, or even on what building she placed him.

If I hadn't already gone so far, I think I could well have turned back. It was then that I heard a car in the distance, or thought I did. But then the sound seemed to die away into nothing and all I could hear was my breathing over the kettle-drum of my heartbeat. I flashed the torch onto my watch. With any luck, Gus should have been just about getting into his position towards the end of the track. I gave him another thirty seconds and then started to ascend the ladder.

I felt even more insecure up there. I flashed my torch around the floor to make certain I would not scare myself or others by treading on any of Molly's toys or model farm animals. But other than for a threadbare stuffed donkey over in the far corner, there was nothing.

I reached up high above my head and, as I had hoped, could easily touch the thatch. I flashed the torch over the area I felt was the most promising at which to start and noted that all the straw looked grey and ancient. This was no real surprise, as thatchers almost never remove all the laycrs of old thatch when they reroof, just those strata which age and weather have rotted away.

I started to pull at the straw above my head and was startled by how much noise I was making. I stopped and realized I needed something to stand on if I were to get both deep enough into the thatch and high enough into the ridge. Luckily, in the beam of my torch, I saw what looked like an old milking stool lying on its side by some tangles of rope. I went and disentangled it and brought it back under where I proposed to start probing, afraid that even my quiet shuffles were too conspicuous in the stillness.

At first, I worked by feel without the torch, but soon almost screamed aloud as my fingers closed around something soft and gooey. I dropped it like a hot coal and whatever it was hit the floor.

Trembling, I flashed the torch down at it. It was a half eaten, red and raw mouse. The corpse reminded me of the dead bird on Stringle's roof. I looked back at my hand. There was blood on it.

From then on, I just had to take the risk of working by torchlight. I reckoned beams were preferable to screams. Straw and dust sprinkled my shoulders and head and I had to stop frequently to rub my eyes free of what felt like rocks rather than particles. Piles of straw were forming on the floor and I suppose it was then that I really began questioning my whole plan. For if I found nothing, I would not only be done for trespassing, but worse, could rightly be sued for the cost of rethatching the roof, which could run into thousands of pounds. The thought made me hesitate, but only for a moment.

However, by the time I had stripped out an area approximately six feet by four, to the depth of some eight inches (I hesitated to go deeper in case my hand went right through to the night air), and had found sweet Fanny Adams that was untoward, I did, indeed, start losing what little confidence I had left and got down from the stool. Disappointed, I knew there was no way I could stay all night stripping the whole roof and I decided that one more section was all I should attempt. What's more, I was running out of the time I'd given Gus.

I moved the stool along the floor, now a little beyond the area where Merinda had depicted the dog, and remounted. As I did so, the stool wobbled and made a noise. I held my breath, as the noise had seemed rather strange, as if it were masking some other sound. After thirty seconds or so I decided I must have been imagining things and resumed my straw-plucking activities, but now even more carefully and quietly than before.

After around half a dozen more eye wipings, I had probed another four feet or so along the roof and found nothing. I crossed my fingers and with a heavy and despondent heart, started on the last few feet of the section I had designated.

Almost immediately, I heard a dog bark. Even though it obviously came from some distance away, it so shocked me I almost fell off the stool. In an attempt to maintain my balance, I grabbed upwards at the thatch, clawing to get a hand hold. As I did so, I felt my fingers close around something that had very definitely not grown in a wheat or reed field, but it was enough to prevent my falling off the stool. When I had succeeded in pushing my heart down from my mouth to my chest, I flashed the torch up to see what I was holding. It was then I literally almost died. For my right hand was gripping onto another right hand that now dangled, obscenely darkened and burnt, from the hole I had made.

As I recoiled in horror, the stool skidded away from under me and I landed on my back on the straw-strewn floor, the torch flying from my hand. A second later, an object fell from the roof across my body and I'm afraid I couldn't quite stifle a hundred per cent of my scream.

Almost instantly, the barn was flooded with light and I heard the voice I had been so dreading to hear.

'I had a feeling you'd come round again, Mr Marklin. That's why, this time, I'm all prepared for you.'

Trembling, I crawled painfully to the top of the ladder and peered down.

Below stood Tom Sweet, looking massive, even at this angle. In one hand he held a pointed iron bar, in the other what looked like a war-time Jeep's jerrycan. I did not need all my wits about me to guess what it contained – my death warrant.

'Aren't you going to come down, Mr Marklin?' he asked, his face seemed totally impassive in the eerie light shed by the low-powered bulbs in the barn.

I realized my only possible salvation was to try every kind of delaying tactic in the hope that Gus had not fallen asleep somewhere, but was keeping a wary eye on his watch.

'Why did you do it, Tom?' I asked quietly. 'It *is* Gregory Mann up there, isn't it?'

'Yes, Mr Marklin, but tell me something before I have to deal with you too. How did you work out it was me? The police haven't and never will, once my poor old barn and everything in it has gone up in smoke.'

'The lady you tried to frame painted a picture of your barn some time ago. Almost immediately after you had rethatched it. And she showed a dog standing on the roof. Dogs don't climb onto roofs unless something attracts them up there. They are not like cats.'

'I had a bit of trouble at the start.' He spoke softly, as if to himself. 'I thought when I burnt his body with all the old straw, there would be no flesh left to attract nobody. But I was wrong then. Still, now the dogs don't come. What's left of Gregory Mann's now dry as a bone.'

He suddenly came out of his reverie and looked back up at me. I hastily jumped in with another hopefully death-delaying question.

'Didn't Molly see you doing all this? How did you explain it to her?'

'She saw nothing,' he said emphatically. 'I hid the body under some straw, after I had struck him down. Ferreting around he was, under the eaves of the roof. Then I took Molly to her aunt's the very next morning; stayed overnight she did. I wasn't having my Molly seeing nothing . . . Just gave me time . . .'

'Why did you do it, Tom? Getting in with Redstart and the burglaries? Was it he who started you off?'

He put down the jerrycan, but retained the iron bar.

'No one can start Tom Sweet off, except Tom Sweet,' he declared firmly. 'I was the cause of it all. No one else. Would have gone well, too, if I'd never gone into that Abigail Gordon's shop to sell some pieces from my first job.'

'Let me guess. She recognized what you'd brought in was stolen and put you in touch with Redstart. And he promised, for a cut, that he could get rid of your loot for you – mainly abroad, I would imagine.'

'You're too clever for your own good, Mr Marklin.' He stooped down for the jerrycan.

My heart was pounding so prominently, I could hardly think, but to keep him talking was my only slender hope of survival and I kidded myself I could detect in him a need to share his guilt, albeit momentarily, with another.

'But *you* weren't clever to go with Redstart,' I said. 'After all, I would have thought you hardly needed him. Or had you run out of hiding places for your loot in other people's thatch? That was a very neat and original idea, Tom. You should have kept it to yourself.'

'Shows how little you know,' he glared up at me. 'Hiding places in thatch are as old as the hills. In that there Civil War time, they even made hiding room for the King's soldiers sometimes up in the straw. And only two year back, when stripping the roof off an old

243

cottage, I found a lead-lined container sunk deep in the straw and it still had old coins in it too.'

'Is that what gave you the idea?' He didn't answer and didn't need to. I quickly went on, 'But why, Tom? Why did you risk everything this way . . . Molly's future . . . ?'

I didn't get any further. To my horror, he started to clamber up the ladder, his eyes blazing with – I don't know what it was. Maybe a mixture of anger and pain.

'It's all very well for people like you. You don't know what bloody life's about, sitting in your toy shop, twiddling your ruddy thumbs.'

To my relief, he stopped in mid-ladder, the iron bar clasped across his chest, as if it weighed nothing.

'It was for Molly, I did it. To give her a future after I've gone. You don't imagine, do you, thatching makes me enough to leave Molly anything worth a monkey's, enough for her to live on for the rest of her life?'

'Maybe not, Tom. But surely, that's where the State – '

'State nothing,' he glared. 'The bloody State hospital killed Molly's mother in childbirth. I ain't having nothing to do with the State. Never have. Would you, if it had killed your wife? Molly's never going to go into no home, neither. She's going to have enough to have a nurse around all her life, more than enough, now.'

His voice started to crack and he stopped looking at me and descended the ladder.

As his hand reached for the jerrycan once more, I tried another. 'But Tom, you might well outlive Molly, be able to look after her yourself.'

Unfortunately, the comment was not of sufficient stopping quality. He picked up the can.

'What do you know about anything, Mr Marklin? I'll be bloody lucky if I live another year.'

'But – ' I stopped, as I realized now the full terrible extent of his motivation.

'That's why I started. I had to. Because I'm going to

join you and Mann and Redstart in no time at all, so
the quacks say. You've heard of cancer, no doubt, Mr
Marklin.'

I couldn't quite believe that this man, hewn as if out
of Purbeck stone, could be terminally ill.

'Well, your pain and death, unlike mine, will be
short-lived and quick, so I can't say I have much sorrow
in me.'

He took the cap off the can and started to sprinkle
petrol over some straw bales, stacked to the side of the
ladder.

'Tom, wait. Can't we do a deal?' I tried. 'Don't
murder again – for Molly's sake.'

He looked up at me and I could see the answer in his
eyes before he spoke. 'I've finished with deals, after
that bastard Redstart.'

'Why, what did he try to do to you?'

'He didn't keep his bloody word. He wanted me to
go on and on, you see, even after I had told him things
were getting too hot for me now, what with you snoop-
ing around and the police.'

'So you picked up a knife and killed him?'

'He was trying to blackmail me into going on. I had
to kill him. I threatened I would if he didn't stop, but
he didn't believe I had the guts.'

'Redstart didn't know that you killed Gregory Mann?'

'Why should he have? If he had known, that would
have been something else he'd ruddy well have black-
mailed me about.' He put down the can and started to
reach in his pocket. I tried one last throw.

'Why did you go to Abigail's shop on Monday?'

He looked up in surprise.

'How do you know I did?'

'A friend of mine was keeping watch and saw you
go in.'

'Well, clever dick, work it out for yourself.'

'All right. You tried to tell Redstart you were packing
it all in. He wouldn't listen, so you had a go via his

245

girlfriend. Maybe you thought you could frighten her enough – '

'Wrong, Mr Marklin.' His hand reappeared with a box of matches. 'I always played the humble thatcher with that Abigail Gordon. "Yes, Miss. No, Miss. Just as you say, Miss." I couldn't risk her splitting on me – had to keep her sweet, didn't I? Redstart was another kettle of fish. He'd got a lot at stake – too much to lose. She hasn't. I always thought she might be the cause of our being found out.' He smiled grimly. 'But I was wrong, wasn't I? It was to be the man with the toy car that keeps balls in the air.'

'You still haven't told me why you called on her,' I tried in desperation.

'Gave her a present, didn't I? A thousand pounds in notes to forget I ever existed. She promised she would and she'd try to get her bloody boyfriend to do the same.'

He struck a match on the side of the box, but it failed to ignite. He took out another and looked at me.

'But it didn't quite work out that way, Mr Marklin. Redstart went on despite my warnings. So he had to die. And now it's your turn.'

The second match flared and he stepped backwards towards the door.

'There's no escape, Mr Marklin. All the barn doors are locked and bolted and a bar is going right across this one here, the moment I'm out. So it's goodbye, this time for good.'

He doused the lights, then threw the match onto the bale and was gone.

There was a sickening whoosh that hurt the eyeballs and instantly I rolled away from the opening at the top of the ladder. But not fast enough not to feel the searing heat across my face. You didn't need a university degree to realize the only direction I could now take was upwards, and not just because of the flames. The smoke was already billowing up in choking clouds through the opening and seeping up through the gaps in the old floor boards. To survive, even momentarily, I knew I had to get into fresh air. I didn't really have time to think of what to do next, which was probably just as well, for once on the roof, the alternatives weren't exactly legion: I could stand on the ridge and ultimately be burned to death, or jump the considerable distance to the ground and probably have what was left of me beaten to death by the waiting thatcher.

However, in no time at all, I was back on the stool, scrabbling frantically at the thatch in the darkness, now no longer caring what bits of Gregory Mann I might be disturbing in the process. To the crackling cacophony of the flames was now added the unmistakable noise of a dog barking, and what's more, it sounded as near to the barn as the flames and heat would allow it.

I could feel my hands bleeding now, not so much scratched by the straw, as torn by the sharp ends of the withy ties that fixed the thatch down. The southern end of my body was starting to feel the intense heat coming up through the floor boards. I looked down and flames were licking up through the gaps, illuminating the attic with a ghostly, flickering light. I scrabbled on and after what seemed like an eternity, punched my way through to cold air.

Thank God, widening the opening did not take too long, for the flames were now not so much seeping through the floor boards, as consuming them, which my venturi tunnel of a hole in the thatch seemed only to encourage. I heard the sound of something collapsing below me and from the sparks issuing upwards through the hole in the floor, I knew it had to be the ladder.

Flames were now twining themselves around the legs of the stool and my own legs were burning hot. Choking with the smoke and lack of oxygen, I just managed to haul myself up from the stool, gripping onto one of the beams of the roof. But to my horror, I found it

247

totally impossible to squeeze up through the gap between the beams.

I held on painfully with one hand and tried to shrug my anorak off my shoulders and other arm, in the hope that, free of its bulk, I could manage to get through and on to the roof. But the jacket just wouldn't be shrugged, despite my frantic gyrations. There was nothing for it but to descend onto the now flaming stool once more and take the coat off with both hands free.

As I did so, there was a sudden horrific whooshing sound from below, which afterwards, I realized could have been the fuel in the old tractor going up, and flames leapt up through the ladder opening, high enough to lick the underside of the thatch in the roof. The straw ignited immediately and I knew I had only seconds, if I was to survive. I threw the anorak to the flaming floor, grasped the beam and tried again. At the third attempt, I just managed to squeeze between the beams, but I left a lot of Marklin skin behind to be roasted to a turn in the inferno.

The pitch of the roof had been deceptive, when viewed from the ground. Once I was out on its surface, its incline, in my panic, seemed to be at least one in one, and as I'd dislodged some of the netting, the shiny new straw of the thatch was slippery as hell. I needed all my strength and concentration just to cling on.

I inched my way slowly sideways, like a mountaineer on a ledge so as to be as far away as possible from the hole I had made in the thatch, for sparks were already issuing up from it like millions of angry fire-flies. I knew that any moment one of them could descend and set light to the thatch beside me. Fire up above, as well as fire down below, I needed like the proverbial hole in the cranium.

My first instinct was to crawl my way up so that I could sit astride the ridge, instead of clinging on by my finger-tips, but luckily, I saw the error of that thought in time. What I needed to be was down, not up – down at the base of the thatch, from where, maybe, I could drop to the ground before the whole roof was doing its imitation of the last minutes of the Crystal Palace.

The fact that I might be dropping out of the fire into a frying-pan held by Tom Sweet I just had to ignore, for I knew I would rather die like a baby seal at culling time, than like a male Joan of Arc.

As I let myself slide foot by foot down the slippery straw, I suddenly heard the sound of a car horn. It wasn't a modern twin-toner, but an old fashioned beep-beeper. I recognized it immediately. I looked down nervously. At first I could see nothing but the frosty glaze of the grass, reflecting orangey yellow in the light of the burning building. But as I was about to turn away, I saw the dim beam of a white light pierce the darkness beyond and a moment later, the dim shape of Gus's now so beautiful bone-shaker bounced into view.

I shouted down with all the lung power the smoke had left me, but against the noise of the flames and his blown exhaust, Gus obviously didn't hear me. The Popular disappeared from sight around the side of the building. It was then I saw the figure I had been dreading. He walked slowly up to the wall immediately below me. In his right hand, I could just see, he held an axe, its tip glinting in the glow.

I held on for dear life, but knew I could not stay hanging there for much longer. Flames had taken hold in several places on the thatch and the nearest were licking only some four feet or so from my white knuckles.

I began praying – not to God, but to Gus. If he came around again, he might be able to scare the thatcher away for the few seconds I needed to drop down and with luck then, providing any of my bones remained intact and/or connected, melt into the night, as they say.

Just as I had given up all hope and was about to deliver myself to mine executioner, I heard the revving of that old side-valve motor, shortly followed by the beam from the one remaining good headlight. Tom Sweet, illuminated by the light, stood his ground, axe at the ready. But Gus, driven on, no doubt, as much by Moët and Chandon as by his affection for his old mate, accelerated and, as the axe swung at the car, knocked the thatcher sideways with the Ford's blunt bonnet.

Gus instantly slowed to a stop below me and I could just hear him shout the one word – 'Jump'. I had no need of a second word. I looked down and aiming my body in direct line with the canvas middle of the Ford's otherwise steel roof, let go.

Gus said I screamed out as I fell. I can't remember anything myself, except the terrible pain in my bad ankle as my feet ripped through the old canvas, followed by the even more excruciating pain in my private parts as a roof support chose to break my fall between my legs. I doubled up in agony, my arms half obscuring Gus's vision through the windscreen.

As he shuddered away, I glanced back. In the flickering light from the conflagration and through the veil of tears in my eyes, I saw Tom Sweet attempting to rise from the ground. But now he was in a terrifying struggle of his own – to escape the fangs of the Alsatian that was savaging him. . . .

16

'How's it feel?'

I looked up at Sally as she came in.

'Heavy,' I replied and tapped the hard white plaster with my knuckle. 'But just about ready for your autograph.'

She sat down on the edge of my bed, her eyes now dry but still red-edged. I took her hand.

'How's it feel?' I asked back.

She pointed to my broken ankle. 'About as numb, I guess, as your cast.' She forced a glimmer of a smile. 'But I'll live.'

She lay her head down on my pillow. I made room for her.

'You almost didn't, Peter,' she said, quietly. 'I should never – '

I cut in, imitating Gus's voice. 'Don't hold with "should nevers", I don't. What's done is done. Never look back, look forward. S'what I say.' I sniffed like Gus. She squeezed my hand. I squeezed back.

Neither of us spoke then for a few minutes. We lay on the bed, the cold November sun just about blinking at us through the curtains. Still, even that sliver of brightness no doubt helped the therapy. After a while, I sat up.

'Well, this won't buy the baby a new spoon.'

Sally looked across at me. 'I didn't know we were expecting a baby or that he was short of cutlery.'

I leant down and kissed her lightly on the forehead. 'You're very brave,' I whispered.

'What, to make a joke like that?'

I gently wiped away a tear from the corner of her eye.

'I guess so,' I said and made a move to get out of bed.

She sat up instantly and gripped my arm like a vice.

'You're not getting up.'

'Oh yes, I am,' I persisted. 'I'm not seeing Digby Whetstone in my pyjamas.'

'He won't be coming in your pyjamas,' she half smiled. 'And you should be putting him off anyway. You haven't had more than two hours' sleep since they brought you back from hospital.'

'I want to hear his side of things, as well as him wanting to hear more of mine.'

'His side of things can wait.'

'And, knowing Gus, he'll be round at lunchtime, come what may. And I'm not seeing Gus in my pyjamas.'

I stemmed her next come-back with my forefinger across her lips and, praise be, she smiled again. She is quite a woman. Although she had really been expecting to hear that Gregory Mann was dead, the actual confirmation, I know, had come as a terrible shock and pierced her through and through. From the next bedroom, I had heard her muffled crying every time I had woken from my fitful and brief sleep.

This time, she reluctantly allowed me to slide to the edge of the bed and helped my heavier leg to meet the floor. Then she insisted she be my crutch (instead of the aluminium one the NHS had kindly provided), and we three-legged it to the bathroom.

It was the first time I had seen my image since all the horror, and I must say I looked about as appetizing as a punch-drunk boxer after a fifteen-round massacre. What was not bruised, abraded or scratched on my face, was either singed or burnt or covered with blobs of salve or plaster. I shuddered at the mirror. Behind me, Sally winced.

'How are your . . . ?' She pointed to my groin.

'Doctor says they should drop again before I'm sixty,' I grimaced, then added, 'Whether he meant off or just down, I'm not quite certain. By the way they feel, I think it must be the former.'

She came up behind me and put her arms around my neck.

'Would you like me to try to give you a shave?' she offered.

I smiled back at her in the mirror.

'Only on one condition.'

'What's that?'

'That it's not a close one. I've had enough of those to last me a lifetime.'

Digby made me go through my story yet again, but this time in meticulous detail, with a fresh faced, eager young constable sitting on the edge of his chair, taking down every single word. Only when he reckoned that he had squeezed every last drop out of the Marklin lemon did he allow me to quiz him. And he warned me before he started that he could not guarantee to answer every one of my questions.

'We have to keep some aspects of police operations under wraps, Mr Marklin, otherwise – '

'We could all do it and you wouldn't have a job?' I smiled, but he didn't smile back. I didn't really blame him. It was a cheap quip, but somehow I needed every quip I could lay my tongue on, to prevent me succumbing to the desperate sadness of my overnight discoveries.

It wasn't only the fact of Gregory Mann's death, it was the whole shebang and especially the terrifying need of a man doomed to die, to protect his daughter's future – a daughter who, through no fault of her own, had no way of protecting herself. A daughter who now would have to rely on the anonymous care of the State, the very circumstance her father had risked all to prevent. Somehow, the tragic flaw in Tom Sweet's concept seemed all the more tragic by its failure. And now he would probably succumb even sooner than the date decreed by his cancer – and die a death whose horrific nature can only be fully realized by those who have suffered the pain of seeing a rabies victim die.

'What do you want to know, Mr Marklin?' Digby rubbed his freckles together as if my central heating was not getting to him. Before I could reply, he continued, 'Perhaps I can forestall one of your questions by telling you that your friends from the caravan should be released this afternoon. Now don't look smug. We knew all along those two could not have been responsible for every burglary and break-in. But John-John, as I believe he calls himself, could certainly have been involved in at least two of them, and the girl, his willing accomplice. In addition, we thought that by their arrest we might be able to flush out or isolate the others in the operation – including Redstart.'

He smiled at my expression. 'Oh yes, we knew all along that Redstart was implicated in some way. And it didn't take a genius to guess what his role was. That is why we had the Customs boys go out to intercept his boat that night. But he blew it up before they could inspect what he was carrying. He was quite a clever customer, Mr Redstart. That's why I devised the little plan involving Constable Smart.'

I registered my surprise. 'So you asked him to play the bent policeman act? Why then did you suspend him from duty after I had told you about finding him round at Abigail Gordon's?'

'I'm afraid you will have to await the results of our official enquiry, Mr Marklin, for the answer to that one.'

'Let me guess, Inspector. He ended up being a double agent, right? Either because Redstart twigged him or bribed him. Or was it that he fell for dear Abigail's rather obvious charms?'

'Let's leave it this way, Mr Marklin. I perhaps should not have placed him in such a sophisticated situation at such an early stage in his career.'

As that little well had obviously dried up, I dug elsewhere.

'What puzzles me, Inspector, is why if you were keeping such tabs on Redstart, you didn't connect Tom Sweet with him. After all, they must have met reasonably often, I would have thought.'

'Obviously. But I suspect never at Redstart's house or Poole Harbour. You may now know that Tom Sweet has a boat. We got that out of him just before I left the hospital to come to see you. Only a small rowing boat, apparently. He kept it near Lulworth. It would follow that many of their meetings could have been offshore, boat-to-boat, so to speak. Certainly the stolen property could have been transferred that way. It was all smallish stuff, mainly jewellery and silver, that kind of thing.'

'Nothing so big, it couldn't be covered by thatch.'

'Exactly.'

'Have you found anything yet at Sweets place?'

'Mainly charred fragments, I'm afraid, but sufficient to prove he had secreted quite a bit of stuff up under the eaves of the thatch, as you'd suggested when I saw you at the hospital.'

'We should have guessed it all ages ago, Inspector, you and I.'

He looked offended.

'Why do you say that?'

'The doodle in Gregory Mann's diary, the only entry for the day he disappeared.'

He thought for a second. 'Are you referring to the figure four?'

I nodded. 'It wasn't a numeral at all. It was a sketch of Gregory's suspicion.'

Whetstone frowned. 'What do you mean?'

'I made the same mistake. So did Sally. Because it

looked like a four, we made the easiest assumption. But in reality, it was a thumbnail sketch of where he reckoned Tom Sweet might be staching the loot. If you could lend me something to write with, I'll show you.'

I picked up my morning newspaper, the *Independent*, and began sketching '4' with the Biro he had handed to me.

'The angle of what we took to be a four, was really the angle of the eaves of a building. The many thin lines forming the slant, which Sally and I took to be an attempt at a thirties style, represented, in reality, the thatch.'

He looked up from my scribble. 'But that doesn't explain the one thin cross line.'

'Yes, it does. That's, in effect, a pointer – a diagrammatic arrow pointing upwards into the eaves, to where Gregory Mann obviously suspected Tom Sweet was hiding his spoils.'

Digby Whetstone rested his considerable bulk back into his chair. 'All right, I suppose that's a possible explanation. But now, let me ask you a question.'

'Okay.'

'If Mann was being bribed by Redstart to keep his mouth shut, why would he have been probing around over at the thatcher's place?'

'That puzzled me too. But I have a feeling that we're looking at two different things. It seems likely that Mann was being bribed to keep his mouth shut about what he had discovered on his assignment from the insurance company. He probably had no idea that Redstart was up to anything else.'

'So why the thatcher?'

'Two possibilities. Perhaps Mann spotted the thatcher meeting Redstart somewhere and wanted to know why two such unlikely characters should have anything in common. Don't forget, Mann already knew of the thatcher because he was about to employ him to reroof the cottage he had just bought. Or he had come across

256

Sweet at some point stowing away or taking out his loot. Don't forget, I must have stumbled on him doing just that over at my friend Jimmy Richardson's neighbours' place. But with it being dark and he dressed in his motor cycle gear, I didn't recognise him.'

(When Tom Sweet finally confessed all, a few days before his terrible death, he said he thought it must have been something Molly had said to Mann on the day he had come unannounced to ask for an estimate for the rethatching of the cottage. Molly had, apparently, once caught her father stowing away some of the loot, which, I guess, went to explain why she kept the toy car's little ball up in the thatch to keep it safe.)

Whetstone sighed. 'Well, whatever the reason, it cost him his life. If it hadn't . . .'

He didn't finish his sentence; and I agreed with what he didn't say: it was far too high a price to pay – a life for the identity of a burglar.

The Inspector continued on a new tack. 'Sweet is one hell of a professional though. I suppose he must have learned all his tricks in his time in the army. I gather his records show he was a very able electrician, amongst other things.'

'He was a very able thatcher,' I said quietly. Then added, 'What will happen to Molly?'

'She's with the Social Services people at the moment. I guess they'll find a suitable place for her. Apparently, they have been concerned for years that her father should have let her go to a special home where she could have got much more help with her handicap than he could ever hope to give her.'

'Help is a different thing from love.'

Whetstone looked away. I think he was genuinely concerned too.

I suddenly had a thought.

'Tell me, Inspector, are there any rewards out for the discovery of any of the loot? As I remember – '

He looked somewhat surprised at my seemingly mercenary question.

'You remember rightly, Mr Marklin. But remember, we haven't recovered any "loot", as you put it, in a condition that merits any reward.'

'But you will do, Inspector, and you know it. All you've got to do is to investigate every building Tom Sweet has rethatched or patched in the last year. I prophesy that you will recover quite a haul.'

He looked coldly at me. 'So, do I take it, you are now putting in a premature bid for any rewards that might be going?'

'Yes.'

'You surprise me, Mr Marklin. To think of financial gain at such a painful time – '

'It's not for me, Inspector. I want to start some kind of fund for Molly, so that she can enjoy just a little of what her father planned for her.'

'But her father – ' he began but I cut him off.

'Her father's aims weren't criminal, just his means were. Now, please remember what I've said, because I think I qualify for some recompense for the recovery of the property, which otherwise could languish for centuries in the cosy nests he made for it.'

'All right, I'll let you know.'

(And he did. Some months later, some ten thousand pounds was added to what Tom Sweet had legitimately left Molly.)

It was at this point that Sally came into the sitting-room. I has asked her to give me an hour or so alone with Whetstone, just in case he might feel inhibited by the presence of the bereaved. Whetstone lugged his bulk out of the chair, expressed his deep regrets and announced, to the relief of both of us, that he would not be bothering her with further questions at such a delicate moment, but would soon contact her in due course.

She thanked him, then quickly changed the subject from herself to Abigail.

'Has Miss Gordon turned up anywhere yet?'

I wasn't surprised at her question. For, after all, Redstart's girlfriend had been her rival – thus her fate might well be of more than passing interest.

'Yes, she has,' Whetstone replied. 'We traced her to a hotel in Inverness. Apparently, she decided to hide away for a bit because she was scared that Redstart's killer might strike again.'

'Did she guess it was Tom Sweet?' I asked.

'Not as far as we know. She claims she had no idea who it was. And I tend to believe her.'

'It would seem dear Abigail knew very little really. I was barking up the wrong tree.'

'Except for the ten-grand sweetener,' Whetstone added. 'You're probably right. We'll know more, maybe, when we have her back down in Bournemouth again.' He looked round at his constable. 'Well, Rivers, we had better be going.'

Rivers pocketed his notebook without a word and followed Whetstone dutifully to the door. To my surprise, the Inspector turned back to me before he exited.

'Well, thanks, Mr Marklin,' he said, his eyelids fluttering his embarrassment. 'But next time, inform me before you take night-time prowls, will you?'

I smiled and waved. 'What makes you think there'll be a next time, Inspector?'

He shrugged. 'Oh, just call it the hunch of a professional.'

And Sally swears to this day that she saw him wink as he walked out.

True to prophecy and bang on time, Gus shuffled round. And true to character, started off with a Heineken and a grumble.

'Gor, you ought to see my bloody car this morning. Looks as if an elephant's gone through the ruddy roof and me grille looks as if some monster's taken a great bite out of it.'

'I'm sorry, Gus. But I guess eleven and a half stones of me and an axe weren't exactly allowed for when Ford drew up the original specification for that model.'

'Now don't sneer, old lad,' he went on righteously. 'Me car may be old but it saved your ruddy life. Now, if I'd had some new fangled machine or other with a solid steel roof, you'd as likely bounced off and landed on your goolies on that ruddy axe of his.'

He stopped, as Sally returned into the room, carrying a bottle of what had nearly been Gus's ruin the night before, but, curiously, my salvation – Moët and Chandon. (For if Gus had felt sober enough to walk up to Sweet's place as I had instructed him, and hadn't taken the car, then Tom Sweet would not have been bowled over and I would have had nothing to land on – but his axe, that is.)

'Talking about your marvellous car, Gus?' she smiled. 'It should be given a medal, that Ford Popular. So should you, for that matter.'

Gus's broken veins took on an even redder tinge.

'Oh, it's all in a night's work, my love.'

'A costly night's work, Gus. You must tell me how much it's going to take to get all the repairs done.' She looked round at me. 'Hey, why don't we ask your friend Jimmy Richardson if he can take it on? He'd make it like new. I reckon I can rustle up enough to cover his costs.'

'My Popular's not a ruddy toy,' Gus muttered into his beer, then looked up immediately and grinned. 'Don't want no gold leaf on it, mind.'

'No gold leaf,' Sally mimed taking a note in a diary. 'Just new roof, new grille, new lights, new chrome, new black paint . . .'

'. . . and a partridge in a pear tree,' I added.

Sally handed me the champagne to open and sat down beside me on the settee.

'It's Christmas soon, isn't it?' she said softly. I knew what she meant – she'd left out the word 'lonely'. I made a mental note to see that it wouldn't be.

'My cast might be off for Christmas,' I tried as a diversion and popped the cork from the bottle. Sally held a glass under its bubbly lip.

'Pity,' muttered Gus, as he exchanged the dregs of his beer for the champagne Sally now offered him.

'What on earth makes you say that?' Sally ventured, in her naïvety. She knows him better now.

'Well,' Gus continued, his eyebrows in the air, 'it's not everybody who gets a chance to be plastered over Christmas on the National 'Ealth.'

That's about it really. Sally left next morning and went back to her place in Sandbanks. I quite missed her. Her robust bounciness through everything, as well as livening up a rather empty house, had been an object lesson in how to deal with life's kidney punches. We still see quite a bit of each other, for she has restarted Ask Force on her own, Gregory Mann having made a will a year or so back in which he left everything to her. From time to time, she drops over and asks for my advice about one or other of her investigations and, from all accounts, seems to be making a great success of things and has more clients than she can shake a stick at. 'It's the tits that do it,' she explains modestly.

Of my other favourite female friend, Lady Philippa has now opened her craft centre and is already attracting quite a clientele, and Merinda and John-John, alas, have moved on. I quite frequently get postcards from the places where their caravan has rested.

Of local interest, the police did eventually catch up with Stringle of Urine Palace and he's now serving a term for a whole list of offences committed under the banner of his Animals Rights Action Group. The hairy headmaster of Ferndales and his matron resigned from the school, but no charges were ever brought against

261

them. The deputy headmaster was appointed in his place and the Ferndales regime, according to local gossip, is even more liberal than ever. As one local wit has it, the only thing obligatory now in the school's curriculum is breathing.

Oh, and Gregory Mann's big Honda bike? That was found, bit by bit, buried in the grounds of seven different houses that Tom Sweet had rethatched. Only the wheels have never been discovered, but I suspect, without their burnable tyres, they're very good at sinking into deep water.

There's only one other thing, I suppose, I should mention. Father Christmas was awfully kind to me that year and must have read the letter I had actually despatched to another destination. He brought me back Arabella. And I have to admit, of all the presents I received that Yuletide, it was her I most enjoyed unwrapping.